A Shadow's Kiss

By

Jennifer Teal

Copyrights

Dedication

Dedicated to her family and friends, who pushed her to take the leap to believe in herself enough to publish her work.

Contents

Chapter One

As the soft rhythmic patter of a cool summer's shower reverberated against the rooftops and gutters of the nearby homes, there was a calm in the streets of Southern British Columbia. People scurried about in attempts to flee from the unwanted weather. A shallow whisper from the evening breeze weaving through the pouring rain as the sun came to kiss the mountains at its setting state. Near silent and abandoned, it was in this cusp from day to night that these city streets were easily perceived as forgotten.

Fallyn watched them all run to their homes while he crouched upon a fire escape, the rain webbing down from his large-brimmed hat onto his black trench coat. He knew for what felt like forever that the world of humanity balanced on two axles, two realities conjoined so closely together that many times they were mistakenly believed to be one. Yet within his home, which was now the darkness, he saw countless times the slumber of man give rise to the dawn of demons in its stead.

He hunkered down like the predator watching its prey, concealed in the shadows that many would not see. Even the objects of nightmares that now rose didn't heed the danger that lurked nearby. The hum of the rain barely deafened the shrill of gateways that rattled open from the disregarded corners of the streets. Then, the groans and chattering of foreign languages materialized from the sudden smell of rot. And just as slowly as they lapsed into existence, so too did a blanket of fog.

A slight curl rose the corner of Fallyn's lips as a noise of bittersweet satisfaction mumbled out of his chest. Even though the fog concealed everything that was below him, Fallyn knew that someone was nearby. This didn't unnerve him. After unimaginable years, the sensation of cold death whisking his last breath was far too familiar to make him squeamish like an untrained soldier. Within seconds, Fallyn focused deep into the fog that swept the alleyway. His eyes peeled away into slivers of black, his iris a golden blaze of hollowness. With this revision, his perception planned finer than anything mortal, allowing him to see beyond the mirages that these evils disguised onto man to hide their intent.

It was two men who approached, speaking in tongues while they spat orders to other sluggish mutt-like beasts before they continued their way. Fallyn examined his next targets closely. Then, in an ever-slow motion that did not expose his position, Fallyn rose to his feet.

The patting sound of the evening shower didn't defile his reach for his long, slender katana that lay nestled upon his back, nor did the thick metal of the landing rattle as he propelled himself over the guard rail towards the ground below. With the drop of Fallyn's feet to the brick-laid road beneath him, only the roll of his first victim's head gave realization of the turn of tides.

His companion jumped out of the way instantly, confused yet aware of the imposing threat, with a hiss of surprise towards Fallyn. Fallyn's gaze remained averted as he returned to his feet towards the man once more; His blade's tip shrilled hauntingly upon the alleyway stone with every moment it dragged closer and closer to his opponent.

"Who the fuck are you?!" the man hissed with bared fangs.

Fallyn responded with silence, knowing there was no need to inform this devil what he already knew as his time had come. He loomed over the cursing vampire, his 6'4" size towering in comparison to the five-foot assailant. The vampire stumbled backward, falling against a sturdy wall he had come across.

"Get the fuck away from me!" he snarled again as he shambled through his pockets to find something to protect him. As jittery as he was, it wasn't long before a handgun took aim at Fallyn.

"Don't tempt me, you shit! I will pop you off!" But without time to weigh the response, the vampire pulled the trigger.

The speed of the bullet was of no competition to

Fallyn's uncanny reflexes as his katana intercepted it instead, sprawling it out in a different direction. The vampire cursed again as he tried frantically to cock the firearm again. He was a naive vampire who believed he needed a mortal weapon to survive. Not that he had any hope to, as it was. Fallyn was almost upon the vampire when he withdrew his second katana that remained nestled upon his back. This devil's fear was so thick Fallyn could taste it. *Delectably sinful.*

The vampire slid against the stone-worked wall, trying to evade the doom that was too close for comprehension. Their eyes connected with sparks, one with evil intent, the other with awareness. But, when a blood-curdling scream pierced the night sky, both were drawn to the woman who discovered them.

She stumbled upon her heels at the mouth of the alleyway, her hands covering her mouth as she saw with horror the headless body. The clouds suddenly thundered in aggression. Then, her eyes found them not even twenty meters away, and she paled ghostly white.

"Oh God," her voice broke, her heart hammering against her ribs.

The vampire took this hesitation as an opportunity, dashing out of Fallyn's reach towards her. Fallyn cursed; He knew what the outcome would be if the vampire reached her. Death of an innocent. And so, dropping his swords thoughtlessly, he instantly gave chase.

The woman couldn't think as she spun around to flee the aggressor, only following what her mind impulsively yelled. *'Run, run!'* She screamed out again in her own panic as she became too afraid to look. It was when she suddenly stumbled onto the pavement that her dread peaked beyond rational.

She tried to claw herself away from the danger she knew loomed behind her, but to no avail. The man's grip clamped onto her shoulder, pulling her weightlessly off the ground. But, as abruptly as his hand clenched onto her jacket, so did it also lose its hold. Her body flipped onto its back from the momentum to now stare in horror at the conflict in progress before her.

The two men struggled with might and fists. The strain of their raw power made it impossible for her to tear her eyes away. Yet, who was she supposed to be grateful to? It wasn't until the massively towering man flung the smaller one away that the answer became clear.

"Run away," he panted as his eyes darted toward her on the ground.

She stuttered and nodded, scrambling to her feet to do just that. Fallyn followed her retreat only enough to see her exit the alleyway before he returned to his original prey to dispose of him quickly.

When Fallyn glanced at the lifeless bodies upon the

ground thereafter, he stretched his senses outward to verify the perimeter was secure before returning his weaponry to their hilts with a sigh of relief. This was the repetitious cycle in which he lived in. Hunts and struggles and- in the end, victory.

But tonight was very much different than all the rest; he recognized as he glanced in the direction where the woman had been moments before. She defiled all the ignorance humanity was known for. She saw beyond the veils of lies and secrets. She saw... *them*. Something amidst the rubble suddenly grabbed his attention, and Fallyn stepped closer to examine it. It was a female's wallet; More appropriately, it was *the* female's wallet. With a flip of its lid, he found her driver's license.

Kathrin Rae Hanelon. The address wasn't far from his location, he pondered as he glanced at the photo on the card. The portrait was a pale comparison of her true visage. He was hardly prepared to come across this person he had. Hell, he was almost captivated by the woman who fell before him by chance. But after an eternity in this fate that was his own, Fallyn knew it couldn't be chance. For as he shooed her small curvaceous body away from the fight, looking into her alarmed turquoise eyes, Fallyn knew he must have seen a ghost, for the stunning woman was Tonia, a person who died long, long ago.

Chapter Two

"Please listen to me; I just witnessed a murder!"

The large, stout officer shook his head with exasperation after hearing the ridiculous story for the hundredth time. "I heard you, Miss. Hanelon. And tomorrow, I'm going to hear that the Easter Bunny robbed the bank on 59th Street."

With a look at her aghast expression, he then continued, "Even you must agree how implausible this sounds. A man beheaded by a sword, and- out of the two guys fighting- the one that gave chase to you had fangs like a vampire. But the one that assisted in your escape was the one that wielded the swords. Why would the killer be the one to help you and the victim be the one to attack you?"

Kathrin paused, frustrated with the question that she hadn't quite figured out herself. "I don't know, maybe he struggled the sword away, and that was when I walked around the corner."

"Really," the officer cooed sarcastically. Then he sighed, rubbing the back of his neck as he glanced towards Kathrin once more. "Have you had anything to drink tonight, Miss Hanelon?"

"What?" Kathrin gasped, appalled. "I'm not drunk! I told you I was walking home from work! Why would I be drinking at work?!"

"Look, lady, we've been over this story for nearly three hours. I've had officers check the scene, and there's nothing out of the ordinary. What kind of shifts do you do? Didn't you say you worked twelve hours tonight," he argued.

"That's not normal. Today was an exception cause a girl called in," she grumbled.

"Nevertheless, let's just say exhaustion got the best of you and call it a night."

Kathrin gawked for some time, astonished by the officer's ignorance, before she furiously grabbed her belongings to leave. "Screw this! I just hope that you *do* find the body cause then you'll have to grovel to me for a statement! How dare you insult me!"

Kathrin didn't wait for the Lieutenant to open the door for her as she departed on her own with a loud vibrating crash. He stared at the door for a long moment as he listened to the clicking of her heels on the tile fade into the distance before he picked up his phone to make a call. As he leaned back in his lounging chair and listened to the dial tone, he covered his brow with his hand. Then, someone finally answered, and the lieutenant blurted out only one simple line.

"Yeah, we may have a problem..."

Kathrin fumed as she stormed down the street to her condo, too enraged with the officer to be concerned about any other dangers within the night. *Arrogant bastard*, she seethed; *how dare he treat her like that*! But the lieutenant did raise more questions than she had before. For one thing, why would such a chaotic event even be happening in an alleyway? Secondly, why was she the only one who acknowledged witnessing it? And if what the officer said was true and there wasn't even a body, how was that possible? Even though her mind tried to rationalize the answers, Kathrin had this strange feeling that she had witnessed something more than common reality.

The man who chased her had fangs, *real* fangs, not like the silly caps some of the younger kids use nowadays to make a statement. He hissed and growled, utilizing them like a prey of instinct would depict. He was some sort of beast with a perverse, horrid nature. And even though she knew it sounded quite outrageous in comparison, she could only explain it as a vampire. Kathrin began to chuckle out her tension as she rattled open the lobby door of her condo. It *was* quite far-fetched. She chuckled after a moment while she headed up to her apartment. Reaching her place, she jiggled her keys into the lock and entered her home.

She needed to block out the craziness from her mind and attempt to unwind for the night. She dropped her belongings onto her entranceway floor, locked her door, and lazily headed to her room, flicking her heels off as her hips swayed enticingly with the motion. When Kathrin glanced quickly over at her answering machine, she noticed the light was flicking repeatedly. She didn't pay more heed than that, though. After all, all she wanted at this past midnight hour was the comfort of her nice, warm bed.

Kathrin was a small woman, barely reaching 5'5" on any given day. Yet, although she was rather petite in stature, with her wide hips, smaller waist, and chest, her body was well-formed to her size. Her chestnut locks were no different with their luscious body, the small wisps that hugged her temples only accentuating her long-lashed eyes. Kathrin slipped out of her clothing with a sigh and slipped into her bed.

'Run Away.'

The man's voice kept repeating in her mind, deep and roguish. Why did he pick her mind as he did? She was sure she knew him from somewhere, but where? And how could she ever forget someone as largely defined as him? But, as her body finally reached its slumber, those questions remained unanswered.

Kathrin furrowed at the paperwork that accrued on her desk overnight. What on earth happened in this God-forsaken place to make her have so much work within a few short hours? She swore they waited until she was gone to add such useless, petty nonsense to her desk that they could easily have done it themselves. She glanced around for her superior, praying that the papers left were just accidentally misplaced by him. That dream, though, was quite quickly squashed for a secretary in a law firm. *More like grunt*, she sneered. Discovering the note on top of the paperwork, she groaned aloud.

'Kate, this is the Tripnoff case. Please scan through and make copies where I say. Thanks.'

Kathrin slumped into her chair with a pout as she blew an exasperated sigh into her own face. Kathrin should have been used to this by now. She was always ditched with the most work because the other two secretaries were useless. The only reason they weren't canned was because they made it quite obvious how willing they were to do extracurricular events compared to what she was.

Kathrin spent a good portion of the day missing lunch and filing for her boss. It wasn't until she finished the last scrap of paperwork that she finally sighed aloud and collapsed her head into her arms upon the desk. She didn't know how long she spaced out there, too, gazing at her desk. Yet, it was with the sudden thud of an item dropped beside her that snapped her back to reality. Kathrin raised her head instinctively to examine it more closely. It was her wallet, open-faced to her driver's license. She frowned. *How, in God's name, did that get out of her purse?* Bewildered, she looked up to find the person who returned it to her. Her eyes widened in shock.

It was *him*. The tall, dark man from the night before. The mere presence of him threw chills down her spine. Why was he even here? Was he here to keep her quiet? Should she be afraid? Gazing up at his captivating eyes, he certainly didn't appear to be a threat to her. Yet, the sheer aura that poured off him definitely gave note to the power that lay dormant within. But even with this, he was still handsome and distinguished.

His rich copper eyes and thick brows complimented his square, chiseled jaw. She never knew of a man who was able to pull off long hair as well as he did, nor his auburn mane hugging his shoulders defiantly. His masculinity stirred the deepest core of her desire. His own eyes didn't falter as he returned her breathless gaze, examining her as equally as she was to him.

"You misplaced this last eve," he spoke up rather briskly.

Intimidated by the eyes that suddenly felt like they read her soul, Kathrin focused abruptly on her wallet. She fumbled through it rather clumsily in an attempt to distract herself, although it failed horribly. Was it because she could still see some of him in her peripheral view, or was it the rustic aroma that emanated from him? She groaned. After a third attempt to notice nothing was amiss, she stuttered, "Thank you so much. Here, you deserve something for your troubles."

She figured she should show some gratitude to the man who returned her belongings as she grabbed a ten-dollar bill from her wallet. But when she looked up to offer him the reward, she discovered he was already gone. Kathrin swiveled around slowly in her office chair. If she didn't know any better, she would've believed he was a mere figment of her imagination. Yet, she knew that wasn't true simply by the fact she now held her wallet in her hand. She just couldn't imagine *that*.

"Kate," a woman called instantly, breaking her concentration.

Startled, Kathrin glanced over at the woman and smiled puzzlingly, "Yes? What is it?"

"I was just coming to tell you that- because of your double shift last night- Dave is giving you the rest of the day off. Kinda like an early weekend." The small redheaded woman beamed sweetly as she held her bookwork close to her chest.

"Oh, thank you, Stephanie," Kathrin retorted softly

before she began to pack up for the day.

She wasn't about to argue with that after the last couple of hours she'd been going through. After all, even though she was all jumbled up by facing the man once again, she had almost convinced herself that it was nothing more than a bad dream before he showed up to prove it wrong.

Even during her stroll home, she couldn't shake her thoughts of him. What was his accent? Hungarian? Portuguese? Spanish? Well, whatever it was, it left her bumbling around like a naive idiot. It was when she was almost at her doorstep when Kathrin's cell phone suddenly rang in her purse. Kathrin jumped with surprise at the sound before she retrieved her phone.

"Hello?"

"Hey girlfriend, how've you been? I called last night, but I guess you were just too busy."

It was her friend, Nicole. Kathrin's shoulders slumped in relief to hear a friendly voice. "Ya, I worked a double. Natasha never showed."

Kathrin didn't think letting Nicole know about the rest of the night's events would've been any smarter. After all, she barely knew the details herself. If the police didn't believe her, why the hell should a close friend?

"And, let me guess, like normal, you were willing to pick up after her shit. You let them walk all over you, you know that?" Nicole sighed rather indignantly.

"Yeah, I know," was the only reply she could think of as she went through the same berating a thousand times before.

"She only gets away with it 'cause she blows him, you know. But nonetheless, I wasn't calling to shit on your job. I called to see if you wanted to come clubbing tonight. You know, a little fun in your life?"

Kathrin grinned at her friend's sarcasm as she entered her condo, dropping her bags on the ground like usual as she recalled the fluttery personality of her friend hitting on every guy they would meet. "You know, I don't really feel like it. I kinda had a rough couple of days, and I-"

"- Nope, I don't wanna' hear excuses. I'm coming to pick you up at 9 o'clock, so you better be ready."

"But Nicole," Kathrin argued quickly, but it was useless because her friend had already hung up the phone. She sighed as she hung up her cell phone and glanced at the clock on her wall. *5:23 pm.* Perhaps it would be a good idea to chill out with Nicole, Kathrin pondered after a while. It definitely would distract her from her crazy world for a *little* while. So, with that in mind, Kathrin headed for the shower to get ready for her night.

Chapter Three

"Damn, I can't get over how hot you look, Katie," her friend yelled over the thrum of the music, leaning in slightly to enunciate her compliment.

Kathrin rolled her eyes with a blush yet again. Nicole hadn't laid off the compliments since they met up, and although each time she did, it left Kathrin in a befuddled state, she was sure it was just her friend being nice. "Okay, I get it! Will you cut it out? You're embarrassing me!"

The tall, slender blond chuckled as she looked back into the crowd and took a swig of her drink, dancing in her seat. Kathrin knew Nicole's ulterior motive. She was looking for another victim for the night. With their long friendship, Kathrin understood Nicole's interest was for both women and men. She simply switched to her emotional needs when she deemed fit. It didn't bother Kathrin so much anymore as it used to in the beginning. But there was still a little awkwardness every time Nicole's flattery was aimed at her.

Kathrin didn't doubt that she was attractive tonight with her partial up-do, lavender shirt, and white floating skirt above her knees. Yet, as the night progressed closer and closer to the wee hours of the morning, she began to realize the reasoning for dressing up as lovely as she did was rather foolish. After all, did she honestly *want* to see that man again when she had absolutely no idea how dangerous he actually was? She sighed with disappointment; She knew he wasn't going to be there. So, sipping up the last of her cooler, she joined Nicole on the dance floor for another song.

It was after a couple more coolers and a lot more dances while they rested their feet that a young and somewhat striking-looking man approached them and nestled next to Nicole. He cocked a partial smirk, his eyes flaring with one intent as he began his introductions.

"Hey there ladies, why are a couple of hotties like you all by their lonesome?"

Nicole laughed out as she twined her arms around his, pressing in against his body invitingly, "Oh, well, we're not so alone *now,* are we, honey?"

His emerald eyes dilated as he grinned at the returned banter, leaning into Nicole to kiss her temple. Kathrin watched in horror the open displays of a more erotic dance but made no reply, attempting to smile to hide her shock. When the two of them finished playing their lustful game, the blond-haired man suddenly turned his attention to Kathrin. Then, almost slyly, he asked, "And what about you, sugar? You wanna' have a good time?"

Kathrin flushed thirty shades of red as she giggled nervously. How the hell did she get herself into this scenario anyhow?? Wait. She knew that answer. *Nicole.*

Awkwardly pinned into the situation, Kathrin couldn't draw her eyes away from his hand groping her friend's chest, "Oh, I don't think so."

"Aw, come on, Katie. We'll have lots of fun," Nicole whined, giving Kathrin the shocking realization of what they both had planned.

Kathrin looked back at the man whose eyes sparked electrically her way, a mischievous grin on his lips. She could see the fire flickering in his metallic blue gaze. Wait, weren't they green before?

'Come on, baby. I promise I'll only nibble."

But as her friend giggled towards the lustful promise, Kathrin instantly froze in fear as the sudden visions of what was to come flashed in her skull. She saw herself pinned between him and a wall, struggling frantically as he buried his teeth into her neck just like the man had from the night before. He was violent with his hungry whims. And beside her, in a bloody massacre of death, she saw her friend. There was no lust intended for tonight; She saw only a vow of death in his eyes.

Abruptly, Kathrin leaned back and frantically collected her purse. "No- I um- I mean, it's getting late. Nicole, we should go."

Then she grabbed her friend's hand impulsively, yanking her out of the stranger's grasp as she guided them through the crowd. But it was barely a minute before her friend jerked her hand out of Kathrin's. Kathrin spun around in surprise.

"What the hell's wrong with you?" Nicole snapped, disgruntled, her hands flaring in the air with frustration.

"Come on, Nicole, I don't trust him. Let's just go."

"I'm not going, Kate. I wanna' hang with him!"

Kathrin reached for her friend's arm once again. "Please, just trust me. He's no good."

"No! All he wants is what I'm looking for- a good fuck! Go home, but I'm staying here!"

Kathrin was appalled that her friend had such a one-track mind that she couldn't see the danger of the situation as she did. Wasn't trust in a friend more than a one-night stand? Obviously not. She knew her friend enough to know that it didn't matter what she said after that. It wouldn't change Nicole's mind. Kathrin shuddered, "Okay, okay, Nicole. But, please, *please* call me when you get home to tell me you're okay."

"Fine! I'll chat with you later," Nicole sighed, rolling her eyes as she twined back through the crowd to find her male companion.

Kathrin was beginning to think that she was going insane. Who the hell did she piss off now that everything in her world just didn't make sense? She exited the club hastily and waved down a taxi. Kathrin tried to shake off her nervousness with the rub of her arms until she arrived at her complex, but it was no use. So, when she arrived at her complex, she paid the taxi man, closed the door to the vehicle, and hurried to the lobby entrance.

Even so close to the place she could call haven, Kathrin glanced over her shoulder anxiously while she opened the lobby doors. Yet, when something instantly caught her eye on the rooftops across the way, she paused and blinked again. She could've sworn there was someone up there. But as quickly as she saw the shrouded figure, the person was gone. Man, she couldn't wait for the day when her world would return to normal.

Returning from his mission, the blond-haired man strode through the hallways of a large, age-worn mansion to meet up with his master. It was through his direction that he was to follow the young mortal named Kathrin Hanelon and make her "forget" she had ever witnessed their world. His intentions were to do just that, too, having the perfect opportunity to do so in the depths of a club. But, rather ironically, the woman didn't follow the cookie-cutter shape as traditional mortals did. She saw right through his mirage of passion. The friend, however, fell head-over-heels for him as she practically offered herself to him right in public. So, even though he was to silence Kathrin, he couldn't help but be tempted by the little sprite who lavished him with her body. It was a desire of the flesh he took all too willingly once Kathrin left their presence.

Kathrin's specialty would definitely be discussed with the leader of the vampire coven, Daimos. The mumbling of a crowd ahead slowly became louder. Then, the doors at the end of the hall swung open, and the myriads of other vampires turned their attention to him.

"What news do you bring me, Isaac?" A man at the center of the crowd bellowed, silencing the audience almost instantly.

Isaac sighed, a little perturbed as he retorted, "Less than favorable, I'm sure."

The man was none other than Daimos. Yet, even without knowing of his leadership, it wouldn't take more than a glance to know he was a powerful man. He stood above most of the crowd, his body sculpted from the hundreds of battles he fought before. His features were rigid and gauntly, and his shaggy jet-black hair cropped just below the ears. His pale blue eyes examined Isaac with skepticism. The color was the only tell of the age of a vampire above all else. The older the vampire, the brighter the blue in their eyes. Daimos was one of the oldest. Abruptly, he motioned Isaac to the conjoining quarters beside them. Isaac was more than pleased to follow.

It wasn't until the door closed behind them that

Daimos growled: "What happened?"

Isaac fanned his hand in his hair as he leaned against the wall, trying to keep composed. "The woman you asked me to follow, well, she is aware of our world, just like Trenton said."

"So, she's still alive?"

Isaac nodded. "I tried to sway her away from the public, even frickin' charmed her. Yet she resisted everything, panicked, and ran away. She saw right through it, Daimos. I swear she knew what I was."

Daimos lowered his head slightly, pondering the situation as he leaned upon the office desk with his arms perched upon his chest. "I've had others look into this, as well. Apparently, she is from a lineage of a former vampire. That's probably why she is so in tune with us; the call is in her blood."

Isaac arched his brow, correcting, "But vampires can't conceive."

Daimos assured: "You're right. But he turned after his wife was already with child, thus having the offspring, at least, aware of him. I was sure his line was wiped out, though."

Isaac cocked his head questioningly, "oh?"

"Let's just say it comes with the territory."

Then, Daimos lifted himself off the desk. "Get three of our best men to pay her a lovely visit. I wouldn't want her thinking she's *unimportant* to us."

Isaac nodded once again as Daimos left, knowing full well what his order entailed.

When Fallyn caught himself staring at Kathrin's condominium once again, he cursed aloud. What was wrong with him?! He had *never* been so aloof to the actions that drew him there as he had been for the past few days, nor why he kept returning in between raids thereafter. But he was nothing less than frustrated by it.

Yet, how could he truly avoid the lurch that came from his insides the moment he saw her? Was this some faint hope to reclaim a piece of his past that was long forgotten? Fallyn growled. There was *no way* some blind calling was going to interfere with his life-long mission! So, why was he at her steps once more?

She intrigued him. It was as simple as that.

Normally, a civilian would've never seen the body. She would've seen an illusion-any illusion-that would be the complete opposite of the truth. Not Kathrin, though. She saw it for exactly what it was; She even reported it to the authorities. But it was with that report that she also drew the attention of the vampires. He assumed that was the reason why he smelled them upon her earlier that week. It was because a scout was sent to investigate.

Fallyn lifting himself from the building he leaned

against with a groan. He wasted enough time tonight, he thought finally. Pathetically waiting. Yet, when his nose abruptly flared intuitively of danger yet to come, his eyes turned down the road, peeling into their bestial golden slits. The scent was moldy, demonic, and earthy; Vampire.

Hidden in the shadows, Fallyn waited for the devils he knew were approaching. It was only within a few minutes before the voices of four men came into range, disturbing the slumbering streets.

"So, why are we here anyhow? You're not serious about us taking out a mere mortal, are you?"

"If she's tasty, I don't give a shit who she is."

"Is it the covenant's request to let them decide?"

Three of the four men were large and husky, obvious that they had trained all their lives for the battlefield; yet, by their simple posture, Fallyn knew they were still amateurs. The fourth vampire was a much smaller built with sandy blond hair. It was obvious from the barking of his next orders that he was the leader of this charade. "This comes directly from our master. It doesn't matter what we do with her tonight if there's nothing left of her when we're through."

"Awesome. I love having a little S&M now and then. I miss the pleading for mercy."

With a round of chuckles from the other men, the blond-haired man concluded: "I'll await for your call."

They all nodded as they parted ways, the leader continuing down the street in the opposite direction from where he came. He knew they were after Kathrin; he was positive of it. Fallyn collected his Glock and took aim, the silencer hiding his assault as two bullets pegged the men in the rear. Then, in one smooth motion, he lunged out from the shadows towards his remaining target, trading his gun for his sword. It was when Fallyn ran to greet him that the last remaining vampire finally came to realize that they were under attack.

His eyes darted up with a curse as he saw Fallyn racing his way. Then, he dove through the lobby doors to gap the ever-closing distance, although Fallyn followed speedily behind. But, although the entranceway was accommodating, the elevator doors were not, closing too soon for Fallyn to be able to wedge through. Fallyn swore as he glanced up at the elevator dial to watch it rise slowly in numbers.

He was heading for her.

He wasn't thinking as he impulsively lunged towards the staircase, flying up the stairs as he raced towards the sixth floor that he knew Kathrin was on. Two, Three, Four. The numbers bled like wet paint as he spiraled further and further, a panic setting into his lungs like cold ice stabbing at each breath. *Five... come on,* he gritted, cursing that his untraceable speed still seemed too slow to get him where he needed to be in time.

Six.

Slamming the fire escape door with a thunderous boom, Fallyn scanned his surroundings quickly before he made his way toward the elevator. There was an auditory relief when he found that the elevator still hadn't arrived. So, blade in hand, Fallyn loomed over the elevator, ready to greet the demon with open arms. A soft chime rang through the hallway before the doors slid open, Fallyn instantly pinning the vampire against the farthest wall with his sword pressed tightly against his throat.

"Why are you here," Fallyn seethed through his teeth.

"Fuck you."

Fallyn didn't threaten or bargain with him for answers. Frankly, Fallyn didn't care. Yet, with a swift motion of his hand, the blade slid deep. Then, Fallyn released the body to the floor in a weighty thud. He watched the remains for minutes, breathing out the adrenaline that rang in his ears until the corpse finally began to dissipate out of reality. It was as he calmed himself, his own eyes reverting to their normalcy, that he pondered why he wasn't closed within the elevator after much time had passed. Yet when he glanced around in curiosity, his inquisitiveness was matched by the beauty who had begun this all.

Kathrin watched in dumbfounded awe to the body that dissipated by his feet before she glanced up at Fallyn for her own answers. How was it that she wasn't afraid of him anymore? Shouldn't she fear the danger that he possessed or- better yet- the impossibility he brought to light? Yet only her confusion mirrored his own gaze. For some ungodly reason, there was nothing but trust in her, and that left him speechless.

Fallyn lowered his gaze as he sheathed his blade, pushing past her to continue towards the stairway.

"Wait! *Please*, tell me what's going on!?"

Fallyn didn't answer her. Fallyn knew he couldn't if he wanted her to remain safe from the darkness no mortal deserved to face. But he knew being silent wouldn't keep her content for very long at all. When his hand reached for the handle of the stairwell door once again, he turned one final time back towards her. Her turquoise eyes were still upon him. And with that, he blurted thoughtlessly: "They will never harm you. I vow it."

The slam and latch of the door was the only noise that followed.

Chapter Four

"What!?!" Daimos thundered violently.

Isaac lowered his head, recalling how he witnessed Fallyn slay two of their brethren before he fled from the streets. Isaac knew returning with this less-than-fortunate news wasn't the smartest of choices. Yet, avoiding the return would be just as good as signing his own death warrant. So, although it was a tough choice with bleak odds either way, he knew he had to take his chances.

"I ask for the best warriors to be sent, and not even one of you could dispose of a measly little human?!" Daimos roared.

"It would've been fine if Fallyn didn't show up. It was like he was practically waiting for us," Isaac argued defensively.

With the reference to Fallyn, Daimos paused, turning his head towards Isaac. "Really?"

Isaac nodded with a nervous swallow. "Well, the report she gave to Trenton spoke of another man with a sword. I'm beginning to think it must have been Fallyn she was referring to. It would make sense why he was waiting for us at her building."

Daimos paused, contemplating the words until a snicker rose from his chest. It was far too perfect of a layout not to take advantage of. "To think I've tried to hunt him for centuries, and all I needed was a little mouse for bait."

Isaac raised his brow curiously, although it was short-lived.

"I'll have to cash in some bargains, but when I'm through, I'll see his head on a silver platter. As for you," Daimos growled as he adverted his stone-cold glare back towards Isaac, "I hope for your sake that I don't see you for a long time."

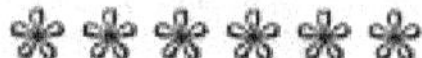

Trying to suppress the anxiety that held onto Kathrin's insides was like trying not to breathe. There was nothing she could do to shake it off, either. How could she when everything in her life spiraled into insanity in such a short time? And now, because of it, her work was suffering. She was filing things wrong, running on sleep deprivation, and could hardly eat an ounce. Add all up with her jittery nerves, and she might as well pack her bags for the six feet under. But none of her deteriorating behavior was ever spurned by the mysterious man who had proven his lethal capabilities. She couldn't explain exactly why, but she knew deep down that he meant her no harm. It was something else that had begun to plague the deep recesses of her mind.

At first, it began in the edges of her slumber, lurking in the depths of her nightmares that forced her awake. Yet, as days progressed further and further, it became more pronounced and sickening. It wasn't as simple as a boogie monster, either. *That* she could reason away. But how could he explain off the face of a man she'd never met before yet promised very keenly the horrors he had planned for her? Even now, she could recall his pale blue eyes and black shaggy hair as keenly as if he were a few feet away. He had consumed her thoughts so frequently that she couldn't even decipher the difference between night and day. She couldn't explain anything anymore, and that's what frightened her most.

Even as the afternoon sun cascaded into the bay windows of the law firm, Kathrin tried to brush off this high anxiety once more. Somehow, she pissed God off. That *had* to be what it was. She knew she couldn't turn to the police. After all, they hogwashed her story when she had gone to them in the first place. And the only other person she felt she could rely upon was a reclusive man who she had only seen around at the bleakest hour. She'd *never* get an answer at this rate from him either. So, really, all she knew she could really do was just focus. She'd be perfectly fine in the middle of the day at her work. That almost became a chant in the back of her mind, too.

No one's gonna' get you here. No one's gonna' get you here... No one's gonna' get you here....

It was as if fate wanted to answer her mantra of

security when, within seconds, all the hustle and bustle of the office came to a sudden end. And for once in an eerie long time, nothing was heard but utter silence.

No one's gonna' get you here.... No one's gonna get you here...

The hairs on Kathrin's neck prickled nervously with the rise of her head. It was like she was staring into a photograph as she observed every person in their motionless state throughout the room. They were joking. It was some sort of flash mob, right? Yet, as she tried to examine their many faces to discredit their little plan, absolutely nothing ever changed. It wasn't until she swiveled almost a full circle within her chair that her eyes connected with the man who stood out of the crowd. It wasn't exactly hard for him to. After all, *he* had been haunting her for quite some time. Was she holding her breath? Was she even awake right now? She stood up cautiously and stepped back.

He was exactly as he had been in her nightmares, his pale Norwegian complexion making his features dark and gauntly. Though his attire and looks were modern, she felt as if, no.... she *knew* he didn't belong in this time. Even his appearance was too rigid to be bred by this lifespan. And in the back part of her thoughts, the answer she'd been trying to deny chattered once again. *Vampire.*

"Nothing gets past the likes of you, does it?" he

chuckled slyly.

"P-pardon," Kathrin stuttered warily.

"Come now, you needn't be modest. You know there's something greater than you on the food chain, and it's getting more and more impossible to deny it."

She couldn't respond with her wide-eyed stare at the man of her nightmares. She was going crazy. Or it was her lack of sleep that was taking its toll. No. She just couldn't accept what even he was trying to make her believe. Yet, it was certainly getting harder and harder to ignore the events that had come to pass ever since. And if she did, what then? Everything she knew about her life would come crashing down. Was she even prepared for that?

"I'm sure you know, though, that your hide-and-seek game won't keep you safe for very long." His devilish eyes glimmered from under his brow, motioning to the sudden paralysis of the rest of her world as if to say even this couldn't stop him.

Kathrin choked on the dread lodged in her throat; She knew his words were true. Then, like a nail slamming into her skull, his face shot into her mind again. His blue eyes glowed silver as she faced his murderous stare, every brutal notion of feeding, rape, and death that he had planned for her forcing its way into her fragile mind. Yet, he delved her deeper into the realms of insanity with the blood that began to ooze from the corners of the room. It wasn't long before she was swimming within it, lost in a pool of red. And when she felt her lungs gargling on the blood of thousands, this man vowed: "I will see you very soon, little mouse."

In a flash, the vision ended in a wave of cold, the office springing to life once more as if nothing was out of the ordinary. Kathrin remained paralyzed on her feet, locked onto the place where he stood, but moments ago before, she welled up with tears. Was this feeling her sanity snapping like a fine twig? Was this even real? She didn't know how long she remained standing there before her boss arrived.

"What's the matter, Kathrin," Dave asked as he leaned casually to one leg, holding his paperwork with one hand while the other rested in his coat pocket.

"Didn't you see him?? The man standing over there!"

Dave glanced towards the direction she pointed to but saw nothing out of the ordinary. "I don't see anyone, Kate. Hey, are you feeling okay? I mean, it seems you've had a rough couple of weeks."

His concern was all it took to release what pent-up tears were within her. She *had* to be going mad. No one else saw the things she had, and she couldn't even explain them herself. Helplessly, Kathrin could only agree to the question Dave asked, helplessly rubbing her eyes with the back of her hand.

With a moment of observation, Dave concluded with the only thing he could think of. "You know, maybe you just need some time off work. You're a hard worker, and maybe it's gotten to you. Why don't you take some leave, okay? I'll set it all up for you. Just let me know when you're up for work again, okay? At least take a couple of weeks."

Kathrin looked at Dave, almost mortified. If she didn't have a place to hide from her god-forsaken nightmares, how would she possibly survive another night? "Oh, Dave, I'm okay. Please let me work!"

But Dave shook his head. "Don't worry, Kate, you're not getting fired. I'm just giving you some time off. Haven't you said you wanted to visit your mom in the States lately? Here, as a token of my appreciation, let me buy you a round-trip ticket. Go get some much-needed R & R and visit her. I'm sure it'll freshen you up, and you'll be as good as new."

Visit her mom? Kathrin hadn't thought about getting away from the troubles completely. Surely, removing herself from everything would make it all better, wouldn't it? A twinkle of hope shone in her eye. "That would be amazing, Dave."

Dave smiled at her lightened mood. "Think nothing of it. Just head home and pack your bags, and I'll have a flight ready for you in the morning. Just let me know where you're needing to go, and I'll give you a call when it's arranged."

"Sure, but can you call my cell? I think I'm going to hang out at a friend's house once I pack. My place has been a little creepy lately."

Chapter Five

It was almost a month later that Kathrin finally returned from her parent's home. It was such a wonderful place to find the rest and relaxation she greatly needed. And with her time away, Kathrin was more than convinced that everything that happened to her before was a result of lots of work and no play. Even her nightmares ceased the moment she got out of the city. When she returned to work the following day, it was like nothing was ever out of the ordinary. Her smile was vibrant, her complexion rosy with life, and even her co-workers could see the calmed persona about her.

"You look great, Kate!" was Dave's first reply to her. "Wasn't I right about the trip?"

"Oh, definitely!"

Kathrin couldn't stop thanking him for his kindness, even giving him an enormous hug of gratitude that had many workers ponder the relationship between the two of them. Kathrin didn't care, though. She was just so enthused to be back in such a stress-free environment. What made her time away even more enjoyable was how avidly Dave made it known how greatly she was missed.

But after another long shift, Kathrin returned to her home. The door to her apartment squeaked open as she instantly followed her engraved routine for the night.

Everything from locking the door, turning on the lights, and keys getting tossed onto a nearby end table to dropping her remaining belongings down with a plop. Once her dress shoes were kicked off in the corner, she started working on the pick that bound her hair.

"I have to get some better shoes," she muttered aloud before she headed into the kitchen.

Kathrin was far too hungry to want to spend even five minutes to warm something up. So, finding some cereal, she grabbed herself a bowl with milk. Then, finding a quick spot on the couch, she turned on the TV with the remote to watch the news.

Even now, as he watched Kathrin going about her evening by herself, Fallyn couldn't deny the inner sense of peace that overwhelmed his chest. After so many days of her home being lifeless, Fallyn quickly assumed she must have gone on a holiday-of-sorts. Frankly, he couldn't have agreed more with such an abrupt decision. He might not have known exactly everything that Kathrin was facing at the point she decided to leave, yet he knew it was becoming way too dangerous for her to stay without harm. Yet, even knowing that she was on an extended leave, he still found himself near her home at one point or another- just to be sure she was still away.

Why did that honestly matter? After all, he didn't owe

her anything, nor did she owe him. Saving people was his job. Plain and simple. So, then, why couldn't he explain the unremarkable drive to protect her *specifically* when she was no different than the thousands of innocents before her? She did need his protection- that much was clear by the last assault from the vampires alone. But so did everyone else that was surrounded by the immortals. She was nothing more than a civilian caught in the crossfire. So, he needed to treat her like one and move on. Yet, the moment that debate impeded his train of thought, Fallyn couldn't agree. He knew- from the bottom of his innards- that he was drawn to her for something much deeper.

It was *her*. The part of his past he prayed he could forget but, through her, the very reason that bred him into the warrior he was today. Even now, he tried to shake off her captivating face once more, but it was no use. As much as he wished he never recalled the darkest point in his life again, he knew doing so was as simple as ignoring his own reflection in a mirror; It was next to impossible.

As Fallyn began to delve into the memories of his past, he didn't sense the mist of darkness approaching. It was only through Kathrin's blood-curdling scream that he broke his concentration and snapped his gaze back to the balcony windows. Blackness. Fallyn instantly cursed aloud at his oversight as he shot to his feet. Yet, he was suddenly stilled by a dagger's tip pressed tauntingly into his back.

"This is a first for you, Fallyn," the voice muttered, a low gruff that had Fallyn clench.

Fallyn didn't answer the man's sarcastic tone. His eyes peeled yellow as he scanned his surroundings to see what challenges were waiting for him. Another inward curse. This was not a mere awakening of the night but a launch of battle.

"Why do you protect that mortal, Fallyn?" the man gritted through his fangs.

Nothing again. Fallyn remained deathly still, although every muscle in his body jolted with anticipation to change his odds. His silence only enraged the vampire further, having him press the dagger's tip even deeper.

"Answer me, you dumb fuck!"

Although everything about the predicament cried of his diminishing time to react, Fallyn closed his eyes as he welcomed the cool breath of fresh air. Then, he slowly exhaled the air through his nostrils, alleviating what nerves were beginning to consume him. And with Fallyn's collected composure, he finally answered the opponent he had behind him.

"Does it truly matter whom I watch when everyone's a victim?"

As the vampire hissed angrily, Fallyn couldn't ignore another scream that echoed from Kathrin's apartment.

"Then I guess it doesn't matter if she dies tonight…

just like you!"

The vampire thrust his dagger. Yet with a shift of Fallyn's torso, a snatch of the vampire's wrist with a spin by Fallyn, the dagger falling out of the vampire's grasp as now he dangled over the ledge of the building by the strength of Fallyn's one arm. Fallyn's golden eyes threw sparks of hate towards the unwelcomed vampire.

"You'll never save her; Daimos will make sure of it," the vampire grimaced, his hand clasping onto Fallyn's arm for some sense of security as he dangled over the stories below.

Daimos. Hearing the name of the vampire leader brought a chill to the tip of Fallyn's neck. He was all too aware of the massacre that the eternal demon was notorious for. For Daimos, mortals were mere cattle and were used as such before they were tossed aside like garbage. *Yet, for him to be involved in this onslaught,* Fallyn thought, *they'd planned on him being there.* Fallyn gritted his teeth.

"So you say...."

The monster wasn't aware until too late of the stake Fallyn retrieved from the trenches of his coat to impale into his heart before he hurled the vampire carelessly over the ledge. Then, Fallyn leaped into the air to cross the distance towards Kathrin's window. A bombardment of wicked, dog-like creatures that awaited on the streets below, called Digornath, suddenly sprung up into the heights to intercept him instead. Fallyn reacted with a swipe of his blade.

With their slick leather skin pressed tightly against their bony physique, the Digornath was a repulsive beast. It's broadness and height were familiar to a Dash Hound, although their muzzles were skinless, the sinew and bone vivid through the layers of their haggard face. And where their eyes should have been were sockets of nothingness. Sharpened bones protruded in place of their brows, spines, and nails. Mucus and oozing, it seemed like they themselves were birthed from the deaths of other husks. Perhaps that was why they had their own perverse version of life, although it was transparent to the world of man.

Three of the Digornaths fell dismembered. Unphased by this, another lunged out, his teeth gleaming. Reflexively, Fallyn deflected the attack with a boot towards his claws before launching away with a shove to its face. Then, he withdrew his Glock and sprayed a rain of bullets toward what Digornaths that littered the sky and streets remained. He was far too confident in his capability to need to verify if he subdued all his opposition with that act prior to his feet landing onto Kathrin's railing. Yet, he still glanced over the ledge to determine how much time he had before he would be faced with another wave. A few minutes at the most. With a kick of Fallyn's foot, the glass balcony door burst open in a shattering boom. He examined the darkened quarters for any signs of Kathrin.

Everything was destroyed in the living room. Her couch was overturned, end tables toppled, and books and lamps were strewn alike as he could almost visualize the scuffle firsthand as she attempted to flail out of her assailant's grasp. His amber eyes glowed brightly in their heightened form, surveying every speck he could for signs of her- or the threat he knew was there- when the sound of her faint breaths carried within the air from another room. He quickly replaced the empty magazine in his handgun before he stepped into the room.

"Where are you, Daimos," Fallyn called darkly. He knew the leader was here; He could smell him.

A loud thump instantly broke the unnerving silence from the other room before Kathrin let out another scream. "Help me, please!!!"

Fallyn dashed to the bedroom, his hand readied upon his katana. Yet the moment he saw the situation at the threshold of the room, Fallyn froze. She was pinned against Daimos' as his enlarged claws pressed sharply into her neck to keep her there while Daimos peered over her head.

"You're late, Fallyn. It's not proper to make your guests wait."

Fallyn glanced around, memorizing his

surroundings as he gritted out venomously: "Let her go."

Daimos chuckled sinfully, the humor from such a request almost unbearable. "I think not."

"What perversions do you seek, then?"

Kathrin whimpered frantically as her hands clenched onto Daimo's arms, her toes barely grazing the bourbon carpet. Daimos' eyes glowed with darkened satisfaction. "Well, beyond your head? I want to get rid of this little hiccup we happened across. It's not every day we have someone so eager to let our world be known, isn't that right? And look, she's begging for the salvation I can give her with her sweet death."

Kathrin's voice pitched in sudden hysterics. "No, please, please, no!"

Fallyn would have loved nothing more than to rip Daimo's skull apart, but with him at such a disadvantage, he knew there was nothing he could do without putting Kathrin in jeopardy. That was when four of the Digornath from the streets arrived through the broken balcony doors, as well. Fallyn's gaze shifted over his shoulders with his sudden awareness.

Daimos grinned with appeasement before he ordered towards the Digornath in the Lucian Tongue: "Kill him."

Simultaneously, all of the Digornath pounced towards Fallyn, and he was forced to divert his attention to them. He weaved his sword back and forth in a unique dance of blades as his motions drove both lethal and defensive attacks. And with each spin and dodge, Fallyn disposed of one of the beasts, only to then advert his strength to another.

Daimos smirked with gratification as he looked on, Kathrin struggling and shrieking with horror. Yet, when the smell of the freshly spilled blood began to flare Daimos' nostrils, the dull ache of hunger grew within his jaw. His eyes dilated with primitive instincts as he glanced down at the mortal female within his arms. Her neck was so inviting and fragile, and he was too for the taking. So, without a moment's hesitation, he opened his mouth large and buried his fangs into her flesh.

Kathrin gasped, unaware of what it was that exactly happened. But, before she could find an answer to it, her pain swam into desire. All her senses faded into a mush of fervent delight, which quickly cast aside any will to fight with it. He was far from gentle, too. He clamped down aggressively onto her with both snarls and pain, bruising her neck with his feeding. Yet, none of that mattered to Kathrin.

It was beyond Kathrin's euphoria. Her body darkened involuntarily with want, although she knew what gravely delicious level of danger was involved with such desires. Through this demonic kiss, she understood her body was nothing more than a mere trinket for his desires, and- when that was done- he would toss her aside just as carelessly. And, for some *ungodly* reason, she liked it. To feel used, to feel tempted by the fates of hell, it felt wonderful.

It was the unnatural silence that had Fallyn's attention dart over towards Kathrin after the last Digornath fell. But when he noticed Kathrin in the bond of Daimo's vampiric embrace, Fallyn stepped forward, stunned by the feeling of defeat that washed over him.

"NO!!!"

She was bitten, and not by some newborn offspring of the last few decades. She was bitten by the very devil's grandson, a second-generation vampire. Such a meaning was fatal, and the hidden curse behind it was deadly. Through his sudden distraction, Fallyn didn't notice one of the Digornath rises to its feet once more. It hunkered down and sprung onto Fallyn's shoulder, imbedding his teeth into Fallyn's blade. Fallyn made a faint growl of agony before he snatched the mucus scruff of the beast and flung him over head like a paper doll. Fallyn's sword intercepted the monster enough times to leave only remnants upon the already-stained carpet.

Daimos gleamed with sinful satisfaction as he rose from Kathrin's neck, her blood oozing from the corners of his lips. The look between the two men was brief. Fallyn vowed to Daimos with his hateful glare that he would meet destruction by his very hands while Daimos taunted him with mockery to test that theory.

"Help her o' savior," Daimos jeered. Then, without a chance for Fallyn to ponder the meaning, Daimos hurdled Kathrin out of her bedroom window in a shattering explosion of glass.

Fallyn shot towards the window, unconcerned with Daimos as he dissipated away in a cloud of smoke while he chuckled at Fallyn's plight. Adrenaline pumped through Fallyn's ears, a ring of dread overtaking his senses as he dove through the jagged opening and used the tip of the window's ledge to propel himself toward Kathrin. *'I must save her, I must...'*

Falling into a dazed state of oblivion, Kathrin didn't know that her life was almost at the end of its thread. Even when her hair whipped into her sealed eyes, stinging them groggily open to look upon the ground ever approaching, she didn't scream. Nothing connected to her consciousness nor bled open her fears like they should've. She simply felt tranquility.

Fallyn extended his hand, desperate to reach the tip of her heel as the distance between them closed. His fingertips brushed the soft skin of her foot, flicking the flesh earnestly in an attempt to grab hold. But try as he might, he just wasn't close enough. The ground grew closer and closer, his longing for this one task running thick in his veins. The street came even closer. *'So close, so close,'* he groaned. The time he needed was almost gone.

"KATHRIN!!" Fallyn bellowed thunderously, using a panicked last command to reach out to her dazed mind.

Kathrin stiffened her legs at the sound of her name, elongating enough for Fallyn to snatch hold of her foot. In one swift heave, he yanked her sagging body to his side and wrapped his arms around her legs and back as he twisted their feet to the pavement below.

Fallyn rebounded like a coiled spring into velocities unknown to man, his coat billowing like a devil's shroud as they twined through the streets of BC. He jumped over cars, mailboxes, and any other obstacle in his way to get away from what remained of the Digornaths. Even though the Digornath breezed through the streets, slamming and pushing down people and things alike, not one person shrieked in fear, ran in horror, or fainted from the shock. If they fell onto their knees from being shoved, they simply rose to dust themselves, assuming they only stumbled and continued their way. This was what they were to the world: Ghosts that phased from a reality unknown to earth.

Fallyn didn't think twice about it, though. For he knew even if he did refuse to believe the inner workings of the shadows, it didn't prevent their opportunity to tear him asunder any less.

Fallyn needed Kathrin to be in a better position to defend them from these ever-nearing hounds. But Kathrin was still too dazed from the effects of the feeding, and the fiends were too close to pause.

Fallyn had noticed with his years of hunting that each victim would respond differently from a vampire's bite. Some would feel only a little ill, while others could swim in obliviousness for hours on end. He assumed by her current repose that Kathrin would be the later. That was until a scream of terror shrilled out, darting his gaze in front of him to see that another Digornath had emerged to intercept them.

"Hold my neck tightly!" Fallyn bellowed, giving her only seconds to comply before he spun her over his shoulder to straddle his back.

Kathrin closed her eyes in alarm towards the act that happened so hastily that the next moment she knew, her nose slammed into the center of his back as his hands grabbed hold of her thighs. Fallyn leaped up, then off of the Digornath's skull in an attempt to widen the distance between them. Then, Fallyn retrieved his Glock, took aim, and fired at the five hellish beasts. The demons fell to the ground with the spray of bullets, alleviating the immediate threat to them both. It wasn't much further when Fallyn found his Kawasaki bike. He placed Kathrin upon the rear seat and, with the quick assurance that Kathrin was secure, straddled his bike, as well, and drove off into the night.

The highway lights flickered as Fallyn swerved in and out of traffic far beyond the designated speed limit. It was a short while longer before Kathrin was fully aware of where she found herself and the blood upon her neck and chest. She dabbed her fingertips into its slickness with confusion. Why couldn't she recall anything before them fleeing from some monstrous dogs? *What the hell happened?* Yet, here she was, with the very man that started it all. And, better yet, he saved her once more. Who's to say she wasn't in danger with him, as well? Kathrin knew the damage he was capable of. Even now, she was sure she could feel the weaponry concealed underneath the thickness of his coat. But, within her heart, she knew such was not the case. Hesitantly, Kathrin looked at the mysterious man.

His auburn fair flickered out of the clasp that bound it, his black cabana hat mysteriously staying on the crown of his head, although the speeds they faced logically said otherwise. His broad shoulders concealed any part of the road ahead for her to see.

"Who- are you?" Kathrin felt rather awkward to begin the introductions they had never officially had.

"Fallyn."

Kathrin was silent for a moment. "What happened?

What's going on?"

"You have stumbled into an immortal warfare that has been held to secrecy for as long as there has been man. Your bite upon your neck will give witness to that." He answered as his eyes never strayed from the road ahead.

"A- bite?" Kathrin gasped in shock, "But I … was in that man's arms. He bit me?"

Without a response from Fallyn, the answer came to her like running into a freight train. The same answer she had been trying to deny since everything normal in her life came crashing down. "This is... a *vampire* bite?!"

Fallyn didn't reply as he veered around another vehicle, knowing all too well that she knew the answer herself.

"But- it can't be! Vampires are fictional- demons are fictional!" Kathrin rebuked instantly.

"Then I pray God may wake you from this cursed nightmare."

She was rather stunned at the sincerity she found in Fallyn's voice. He seemed so connected to this peculiar story that had quickly involved her life. It all seemed second nature to him. But, at the same token, she was sure she could hear that he would've given it all up if he could.

"But why me? I'm a nobody. I can't do anything to *them*."

"You spoke of what you saw."

"You mean the report I gave to the cops?"

Fallyn nodded. "If people discovered that everything in their lives was not what they perceived, it would create a manhunt and a slaughter."

Kathrin pondered how such events would come into play if humanity did become aware. Unfortunately, she could only visualize the annihilation that she knew would be so easy for them to do. How ironic that such a pinnacle moment like an apocalypse could begin with a few simple words.

"So, what do I do now? I'm guessing they're not going to go away if I just keep quiet, right?"

Fallyn shook his head in doubt as they passed the final streetlight of the highway with the exit out of the city. Then, taking a turn off into a rarely used dirt logging road, he answered her.

"We mend your injuries. The rest will be discussed in a safe haven."

Chapter Six

Kathrin examined the extraordinary quarters she found herself in, slightly surprised, while Fallyn attended to her injuries. Everything about the stone-worked cavern looked as if it came out of a history book. Either that, or that he was a collector of many, many props from a studio. If it wasn't for them entering his abode from an abandoned mine shaft, she would've even guessed that she found herself in a castle-of-sorts. Yet, after everything else she had happened across tonight alone, she decided it was much safer to assume there would always be more things to rattle her mind on than this.

During her investigation of the place she assumed was his home, Fallyn made sure to tend to the puncture wounds on her neck first. But, although he was satisfied with his handiwork and continued on the next, the continual thrum of her heartbeat constantly pounded against the now tender skin. She watched him as he meticulously worked upon her legs, barely giving a nod of satisfaction before he averted his attention to another. And, unfortunately for him, there were a lot of them.

Even now, with the time that passed, Kathrin still couldn't recall what had happened during the moment her mind began to blur. She had learned through Fallyn, though, that the mucused beasts that were chasing them were called Digornath. He also told her she had been tossed through a window. It seemed rather far-fetched for Kathrin to believe, although she couldn't blatantly argue with Fallyn. How the heck could he have saved her from something like that and live to tell the tale? Not bloody likely. Yet, if someone would've told her two months ago she would've been dealing with vampires now, she would've chalked that up to idiocy, as well. So, as skeptical as she felt towards what he informed her, she swallowed the extravagant story as a possibility.

That was when her eyes fell onto Fallyn once more, trying to ponder the many questions that surrounded him. He had always piqued her curiosity, even since their first meeting. Now, though, all her anxiousness that she thought was fear was gone. It also surprised her that the inexplicable itch that she couldn't shake for over a month was missing, as well.

It wasn't that Fallyn had dampened at all in the roguishly handsome department. Far be it. Even as she observed the attention he gave to his work, a few unruly locks fell onto his face. She exhaled. What was he doing that night? Hell, each night, she saw him dispersing the men she now knew as vampires. And why was he always there to save her when she was in trouble? He didn't know her any more than she knew him, did he?

"What troubles you so, Kathrin?"

Kathrin stuttered quickly, baffled by his insight, "I'm sorry, was I staring? I was just trying to figure things out..."

"Which is why I asked such a question." he returned simply, although she was sure she heard a slight level of amusement in his voice.

"I- well- I-," Kathrin stammered, feeling rather awkward. Yet, with a slow inhale, she began again. "What do you do, exactly? Do you just hunt vampires? Or is this just like a side job?"

Fallyn's concentration didn't falter for a moment as he intently removed a piece of glass from her leg. The thick silence had Kathrin concerned she was prying where she shouldn't be as she began to trial: "I suppose it's none of my business. After all, I don't know what, the hell, happens when I'm not looking-"

"I am a demon hunter. A mercenary-of-sorts to what has been considered a dying cause."

When Fallyn put the piece of glass collected from her leg onto the tray beside them, he continued. "My title is referred to as an Infernal Hunter."

Kathrin watched him as he focused on her wounds. "How's it 'a dying cause'? Aren't there more people like you, more hunters?"

Fallyn nodded slightly. "There are. Yet, within the years, our numbers have dwindled substantially. What were once our allies have now become tainted by the evils of the abyss, and fewer join our cause each day."

"Well, who do you have to help you?" she queried, thinking it wasn't an illogical question until his lips pressed firmly together.

"I work *alone*. Too many of my comrades have fallen to the cause to wish to see another."

"I'm sorry I asked."

Fallyn shook his head against the apology. "It is not the question that I find frustrating, Kathrin."

Yet, still concerned with his agitation, Kathrin tried to change the topic quickly. " What exactly does an 'Infernal Hunter' fight?"

His lips curled a little as he answered rather curtly, "It is not limited to vampires, although they are the most prominent out of the species. Most are creatures that are believed to be nothing more than folklore. Spirits, ghouls, devils, and demons are some names that humanity has given them under abbreviation."

"Devils and Ghouls?" Kathrin asked sarcastically, feeling rather foolish to be even considering it. "So, you're trying to tell me there are werewolves too?"

Fallyn's eyes continued to examine her leg as he muttered rather slowly, "There are."

"Then why has humanity been so completely ignorant of this? I mean, enough people should've known to have an outcry or something."

Fallyn applied another bandage upon her leg. "There are far more than one would hope. Few of these people have a strong enough will to become part of our cause. Yet, there are many within our society who will discredit the findings and observations of others who are mentally weak. Most commonly, mortal minds are lifted of this burden by forgetting it had happened."

"So, you make them feel like their loony. I must admit, I'm glad to know what I witnessed actually happened than for me to think I lost my mind. I'm sure it wouldn't have been long before I would've been in an asylum if I had to believe it was all my imagination," Kathrin huffed.

"No," Fallyn assured quickly, glancing up at her for the first time in their conversation. "Your mind would have been eased of such torment before then. Only a few trickle past our grasp."

His gaze seemed far too wise for his age, although Kathrin would've guessed that he was no more than thirty-six. That didn't prevent her from being irritated at his carefree response of mind-erasing, though. "Then why can't I have that satisfaction? Huh?? Why don't you just go ahead and wipe my mind up to the point of seeing you!"

She knew how deep the words stung the moment they escaped her lips and cursed inwardly. He adverted his gaze back towards her leg, a look that seemed close to hurt appearing before it suddenly washed over with an emotionless glance.

There was a silence that arose between them for some time before Fallyn finally answered her sarcastic tone. "The pleasure you crave is a gift I can no longer offer. Now that you have been kissed by the realms of the dark, you have been awakened. Nothing I nor anyone else does now will change that."

Kathrin was left speechless. Nothing could change it. She bumbled over her panicked thoughts as quickly as they entered. "Why not? How is that possible? What am I supposed to do now, then? And what about my family?"

Fallyn shook his head slowly as his words remained calm, almost monotone towards her fears, "You must view everything from your life as lost. For, if you stay connected to those comforts, they too will surely meet their demise."

"I can never talk to them again?" Kathrin was mortified at such a request and wanted to believe she heard him correctly.

"It is unwise. Learning to love the heart's treasures from afar secures that they continue to live unharmed."

She felt like she was completely numb. How could she just abandon everything in her life?? She couldn't talk to them *ever* again?! Even though Kathrin wished there was another option, Kathrin dreadfully comprehended why Fallyn was right. Her tears fell. She never felt as helpless as she did then.

"I'm sorry. I just... I feel so lost! I have no idea what I've stumbled into!" Kathrin cried aloud.

Fallyn was moved by the emotion he knew all too well, for he even felt the sudden shock of becoming an outcast in the life he once cherished. And he knew there should've been many places that she could've stayed, too. Within the Infernal, there were factions where mortals who had been aroused to the dark could hide and learn about their own fate. But as Fallyn looked at the bandage that nestled Kathrin's neck, he knew it couldn't be the same for her.

She had been bitten, tainted. If it had been anyone else from his association who had saved her from the clutches of Daimos, she would have met the blade by now. Or better yet, she wouldn't have even been rescued from her fall. The reasoning for this was that the Infernals viewed vampires as the greatest threat of all. Too many allies had been turned into horrid, vicious monsters when they were once kind and caring comrades before. It is the hunger and bloodlust that drive them to become far more important than a cause, a friend, or even a lover could signify. So, with that violence, there were laws that were passed to forbid an early generation's victim to live past the initial bite. Fallyn glanced at her small figure and furrowed his brows.

He should have let her fall to the streets below like the laws demanded. But as he watched her fly out of the window to meet that fate, he couldn't control the torrent of energy that pulled him out to save her. He went against all his reason and inbred distaste for vampires to save the woman from his past. Now, here she was, mended by his hand and troubled by what *she* was to do.

No, there was no place within his guild for her, but Fallyn couldn't fathom disposing of her himself. Fallyn pondered how the chances of her survival were slim as it was as she sobbed her woes. Not every soul bitten would attain the fate of a vampire. Many of them die, and the potency of the vampire pathogen is too great for the human body to accept. Most commonly, only one person out of fifty would turn vampire. This was the reason why the Infernal had no hesitation in dispersing them so quickly. If they didn't transform, they would meet their death.

The actions he had already taken with Kathrin could have had him questioned by his order to see if he was betraying them. At that point, Fallyn didn't know how to answer that possibility. Never had a person stilled his hand before.

"You needn't fret over where you shall stay, Kathrin. For this will become your new home while you discover where you lie in the world you've only just discovered. As for what you shall do from this point forth, I see nothing better than to bestow upon you the insight I have learned throughout my years. If you deem it fit, I can even give you the tools to defend against it."

"You? You would teach me?" she whimpered, astonished.

Fallyn could only nod, knowing in the back of his mind the deceit he was announcing by it. But he just couldn't follow the decree he was supposed to for her when he knew full well something otherworldly drew them together in the first place.

"Time, Kathrin, is something you will have plenty of. It only seems proper that you learn the ways of the abyss like so many others. But I must conclude; you are surely exhausted. Let me show you to your quarters." Then, he stood up with a formal gesture towards her.

Kathrin noticed it quickly, the slight bow as he offered his hand to her for support. It was far too formal for anything she had ever witnessed in her lifetime. Yet, he displayed it beautifully. It was almost autocratic. How had such a civil gesture become lost in their modern society? It was through this act that Kathrin suddenly connected everything about him and her surroundings together. Even the clarity behind his words was nothing from the likes of this era. Had he even used one slang term at *any time* that he spoke to her? And how could someone have been raised so far under a rock that they were *this* formal? Well, his place alone matched his behavior.

She meekly followed Fallyn as he drew her down another tier of doors, centered by a lounging area further in the depths of the mountain. His hand offered another courteous motion as they came upon a room, and Kathrin entered the chamber to glance around. *Rather barren*, she thought to herself, as only an end table, lantern, and bed filled the room.

"The privy is across the way, the door upon the right. If you are in need of me, please simply call. I assure you I will hear it. Good night, Kathrin. I will retrieve you in the morn' for a hearty meal." Then, he bowed his head slightly as he departed.

Kathrin watched him as he left. His coat flowed behind him from the swift pace of his footsteps as he walked away.

"Fallyn, wait!"

Fallyn instantly paused down the corridor and turned his head slightly.

Why did her throat become so dry, suddenly? "W-When we first met in the alley, it seemed as if you knew me from somewhere. But I can't- for the life of me- place where. Is this just me? Or have we really met before?"

Fallyn turned his head away, his long auburn mane

and the level tone of his voice becoming the only means that she could read him by as he assured her, "We have never crossed paths before that night."

Yet, that didn't feel good enough. God, why was she even considering making herself into a heel by saying this? "But then why does it feel like... God, I don't know how to say it!"

Kathrin looked back at his rigid shoulders. How could she explain the calming effect he had on her like nothing before? And if they had never met each other before, why did she feel like she knew he was here all along and she was simply trying to find him?

"It is late, Kathrin," Fallyn spoke up with a pause.

"No. Well, I know it is, but I gotta' say this! Doesn't it feel like... in some part.... like we've finally found each other? God, I can't say it without it sounding pathetic!" she sighed, exasperated.

Fallyn began to walk away again. This time, the curtness in his voice was even more vivid. "Good *night*, Kathrin."

Chapter Seven

With only a few hours before dawn, Fallyn screeched his motorcycle to a halt as he glanced up at Kathrin's complex. Fallyn waited until he was sure Kathrin was asleep before returning to her place, commonly staying up past the rising sun to satiate his ever-going thirst for retribution. But, although he figured he had about settled his hunger for death that night, his perplexed thoughts from the conversation he had with Kathrin kept him dreadfully awake.

Fallyn tried to deny the connection he had felt with her, blindly convincing himself that it was merely a lost hope that had swayed his actions in the first place. Yet, the moment she explained that very connection he attempted to ignore, it flamed his desire to twine her deep into his arms all the more. Fallyn couldn't honestly say it was simply the irony of Kathrin's looks that drew him to her. It was much, much more. But every time his thoughts trailed to the possibility, Fallyn would growl at his distraction and continue on, more aggravated than before.

Now, his anger had settled in, edgy and tempting, as he slammed open the plexiglass doors of the lobby. Fallyn wanted a fight. He was practically praying to see another damn monster lurking in the corridors so he could ease his rage.

He stormed up the stairs towards Kathrin's condo. Fallyn wasn't surprised that the police hadn't shown up yet. It was all too common that the magic workings of the night made everyone oblivious to the cries for help until they were far too late. Her door was also still unlatched. He remained at the ready as he used his preferred weapon of choice, his M1911A1 gun, and pushed open the door. Everything was destroyed but barren; no one else was there. Fallyn cursed at his disappointment and grumbled as he stepped over the disarranged belongings. Then, he quickly found a sports bag in all the mess and began to travel from room to room to collect her belongings.

Clothes, pictures, wallet, and anything else he knew that could be used while she stayed with him. But, Fallyn wasn't dainty or even careful with her possessions as he slammed them into the bag, being too disgruntled to care about anything. Yet, he was sure not to take too many belongings from her home. If he did, his attempt to bring closure to her life would fail.

When the sack was full, he tossed it onto his back and headed for the phone sprawled across the floor. He returned it to its mount before he picked it up once more to dial out.

" 9.1.1. Do you need police, fire department, or ambulance assistance?"

"There has been a murder."

Kathrin rose drowsily from the mattress as her eyes focused on her surroundings. It took a moment to recall exactly what had happened that had brought her to Fallyn's guest room. Yet, her thoughts were cut short with a beating pulse on the side of her neck. Kathrin sighed as she raised her hand to her throat. Tracing the bandage in hopes of easing its ache as she spun her feet off the side of the bed. Kathrin wondered what she was going to do with herself now. True, Fallyn told her that she could stay with him. But in some ways, she felt like she abandoned everything she was and needed to return to it. Even now, she looked at the clothes she was wearing from the night before, dismayed that there was nothing she could change into.

"Fallyn?" Kathrin called out, hoping it wouldn't be such an unreasonable request to ask to return to her home.

Kathrin called again, peering out the bedroom doorway. That was when she heard the roar of an engine blaring into the silence, which drew her down the path she vaguely remembered to find who she sought.

Fallyn dismounted his motorcycle, the sack on his shoulder falling slumped upon the floor as Kathrin entered the room. He was fully aware of her presence the second she entered, raising his head with a brief nod of acknowledgment. Then, with a drop of his hat on a nearby workstation he had for all of his belongings, he began to unload his weaponry. Kathrin broke the silence.

"How- how long did I sleep for?" She rubbed her arms nervously. Then, she noticed the artillery he unloaded and swallowed.

"It is noon'. You have slept soundly nine hours, Kathrin." Although his voice was harsh and sharp, his face was far from it. He was merely concerned with the lightening of his load.

"Where'd you go? I didn't hear you leave," Kathrin pondered.

"There were affairs that needed tending to. It matters not where I have been."

"Okay," Kathrin groaned, although her eyes strayed towards her only means of freedom. "Do you think I could head to my condo? I mean- I don't have any of my belongings, and I feel rather awkward in these same clothes."

"You cannot return, Kathrin. The investigation has begun," Fallyn retorted with a quick glance her way. Kathrin frowned. Why did he look like he was hiding something?

"What? Oh, you mean beings that it's all messed up. All the more reason to return. I wouldn't want anyone to think something was wrong or get my wallet stolen or other important stuff-"

That was when he handed her the sports bag, and Kathrin instantly recognized it as her own. She looked at him skeptically for a moment before she began to rummage in the bag. Much to her surprise, it *was* all her belongings, finding even her wallet that she had mentioned there.

"You- you went and got my stuff?" she asked defensively.

"It had to be retrieved before any law enforcement arrived. Your accounts have been cleansed of their funds, as well," Fallyn shrugged.

"But, how could you- never mind that- why does it matter if the police are there or not?" She growled. It was irritating how he evaded her questions.

"Kathrin-," he started in a coaxing voice that made Kathrin's hair bristle. She knew he was going to 'lighten' the response.

"No," she cut in. "Please don't give me some puppy-kissed answer and tell me why, the hell, I can't go to my house?!"

Fallyn eyed her frustration through her puffed-up features before he retorted, "In society, you are undoubtedly believed dead. By now, your family has been informed of the news, and your home is under investigation to find any evidence of your murderer."

Kathrin stumbled back from his cold-sounding response. "What? They think I'm dead? But... how can they think that? There's not even a body...."

"Such details are trivial."

"Trivial?! A body is the center of all investigations. If there is nobody, then I'm simply a missing person."

"That will not be the case, Kathrin."

"Why, the hell, not?!" But, as she asked, his own surety made everything clear. She glared at him with hurt. "You set this up?"

When his expression went blank, she cried out in rage. "I couldn't say a proper goodbye! You took it away from me! I wanna' go home! How dare you take that away from me!"

Fallyn didn't move as she stormed past him toward the cavern exit. He knew it was hardly the time to try to reason with her. Yet, in one vain attempt, Fallyn called her name once more.

"No! I'm not staying here for another second! I'm going home!" Then, she left the mouth of the mine-like exit.

What she wasn't prepared for was the wave of rushing liquid that slammed into her like a belly flop into a pool. In that instant, she felt light on her feet, tangled in a mass of webs while she floated aimlessly within an opened pit. She would've done anything to avoid the sensation that sent shivers down her spine. *I wanna' go home!*

The next moment, the noon sun pierced through her limbo abyss, which caused an exhale in relief to find some way out of that god-forsaken place. But, just as quickly as her hope settled in, Kathrin's bite mark upon her neck pulsed with a pain that brought her to her knees. She grimaced towards the stabs she couldn't control, grasping at the ground beneath her to balance her from this frightful nightmare.

Yet powerful arms came out from the darkness and pulled her back into the cavern's safety. It took a while for Kathrin to ease the pain of her neck, and she focused solely on her deep, even breaths to calmly collect the senses that seemed to be taken from her. Yet, how calm could she be when everything suddenly felt like she was beyond drunk and high? She could only guess where she was. She didn't *actually* know. Kathrin attempted to open her eyes to shake off the dizziness but was met with blinding stabs that shot at her temples.

She was almost beyond the point of helplessness when the agony instantly stopped. Even her mind grounded out of whatever psychedelic roller coaster it decided to go on. Wait. Was there a hand overlapping hers as she held her neck?

Kathrin looked up groggily to find Fallyn beside her, examining her for any signs of improvement.

"Wh-what happened?" she groaned; all of her previous frustration washed away with the sudden fear this situation brought forth.

"Undoubtedly a result of your bite. Are you still ill?"

Kathrin shook her head, although her hand remained pressed against her neck, almost afraid that it would start all over again if she moved it.

"I am truly sorry, Kathrin, for what I have done. Yet, my intentions were truly for your safety. If you continued to remain among mortal society, it would be slowly taken from you and more violently at that."

And as saddening as it may have been, Kathrin agreed. "It's just hard to think it's the end of everything I know."

Fallyn nodded with comprehension. "As cruel as it may sound, the best thing for you would be to become acquainted with your new home. Here. How about you put your belongings away and freshen up while I gather us a bite to eat?"

Yet, he was gone before she even could give him an answer, having Kathrin ponder how she'd ever feel at home if the only companion she had kept up with was his 'running' personality. She contemplated the question while she returned her possessions to her room.

Chapter Eight

After a full day of having Kathrin around everywhere he went, Fallyn couldn't wait another moment to get away from his home to return to his nightly excursions. He wasn't used to the companionship of another. But the fact it was her that was near him shouldn't have shaken him like it did, neither. She was possessing his mind in a way that drove him nearly mad. All he could imagine was her in his arms, his lips upon her breasts as he filled her deeply. And it was with these thoughts and the response they had upon him that he knew full well he had to leave before he'd regret what happened next.

Through the means of his haven's gateway, Fallyn now sped down the streets of New York. It was actually possible to travel to any location by it; all a person had to do was think of their destination to appear there. Yet, the reason he chose New York City was because it was the darkest and most criminally laced city in the world. He could smell the scent of hell even now as he sped into the city, and his lips curled with knowing contentment. There was no doubt about what he was going to do tonight. And he wasn't going to return home until he shook off the mind-hypnotizing thoughts of her.

Fallyn felt a sudden pinch on his shoulder where the Digornath had bit him. *It must have been deep.* But beyond the initial recognition of discomfort, he didn't give it a second thought as he squealed his tires around a corner. He knew it would be only a matter of time before he would be as good as new. Then, once Fallyn parked his bike in an alley, he took off immediately to track his first victim of the night.

Hate, anger, and revenge washed over him with each dispersal of the monsters. He hated them all; He despised them as the aberrations they were. They didn't deserve life as much as a convict would. But what spilled over his rage even more was that- when it came right down to technically- he was one of them, too.

Just like all of them he faced, he was twisted by the nightmares of the dark. It was a fate he would've changed in a heartbeat if he was given the opportunity, though. But that, too, was a punishment for his curse. For him to die would have to come by the hands of another. The only ones strong enough to do that were the demons he hunted. And like hell, he'd be defeated by their hands without a fight.

The death smells good.

Fallyn shook away the thought that suddenly hummed in his mind, recognizing it as none other than his own demon. He raced to another beast, this time a vampire, his favored kind of prey.

You hunt without mercy, such as I-

Fallyn growled at the voice as his twin Katanas sliced the vampire in two. But Fallyn couldn't wait for the body to dissipate as he tracked another, his nostrils flaring from the death of another ill-fated beast.

How many have you killed tonight?

Twenty? Fifty? Frankly, Fallyn didn't care. His chest tightened at a rage he couldn't disperse quickly enough. His eyes dilated involuntarily as he became more and more the primal monster he was cursed as. He wanted to kill them. He wanted to kill them all.

I'm sure nothing could sway your hand tonight, could it?

Kathrin. Her name spiked into his thoughts instantly by the demon's taunting, and his rage washed away. Her petite, supple face, her calm yet high-spirited presence. Everything about her was a balm to his burn. And somehow, just by the thought of her, it loosened the claws that his demon had hold of him by. He knew she was the only one who could sway his hand because she'd done so already. Yet, no one ever came close to that before, be it the opposite sex or not.

Opening his sight beyond the red haze of his fury, Fallyn looked around at the morning sun cresting over the peaks of the buildings. *How long had he been slaughtering the devils for?*

It's only suiting that she will meet your blades one day.

Never, Fallyn vowed as he bathed his face in the sun, his own eyes closing at the warmth. *I could never hold her life in my hand.*

The reeling of Fallyn's motorcycle engine woke Kathrin with a start as she glanced towards her bedroom doorway. It had been quite a solemn evening prior to his leaving the night before, saying that he had to continue with his hunting like she had witnessed before. Yet, being trapped alone in his castle-like home brought on an anxiousness she couldn't get rid of. She needed companionship; She practically craved it. True, Fallyn was around most of the time. But it had become apparent very quickly that he was a man of habit, and his habit was to be left alone. So, the moment she heard his return after the torturous night of occupying herself, Kathrin grabbed her silk housecoat and covered her body to search for him. It was almost making her feel like she was nothing more than a displaced house pet running to the skirts of its master. But, what more could she do, she thought disheartened. She was completely out of her element, and everything she knew about now came directly from him. Yet, Kathrin didn't make it to the entranceway before Fallyn rounded the corner.

The smell of bloodied smoke permeated the hallway as he entered the narrow quarters, looking like he's been through an all-out war. He was worn and exhausted. Stolidly, Fallyn took each step as if weighted by anvils, yet Fallyn didn't pause. The moment he reached her, he simply tried to squeeze past her. Yet it was only through that moment when she could see under the rim of Fallyn's hat that she gasped in horror.

"Fallyn… you look awful. Are you okay?"

He instantly bowed his head in an attempt to shield his snarlish features from her. "Never better, Kathrin. I have merely been following my duty as a Demon Hunter."

The croaked voice that came from him barely sounded like Fallyn. He sounded like he'd been punched repeatedly in the chest. But what she saw was vicious and chaotic, like whatever deed he had done was at the price of his humanity. That was when she noticed the blood on his jacket.

"Are you hurt? Can I help you??"

"No!" Fallyn barked suddenly, his thunderous voice having her jump in her skin as he spun around to face her.

His body towered over her as she shrank away from the sudden growl. It looked as if his body contorted into the Devil himself. Kathrin stumbled back from his venomous glare in terror as he stepped closer. Only at the moment, she believed she had no other choice but to face the threat she brought on with a close of her eyes was when Fallyn instantly reverted away towards the direction he was heading.

"It is nothing a soft bed could not mend, Kathrin. Make yourself at home."

Then, he departed. She opened her eyes in confusion as she heard the strain in his voice to soften its harshness. How did he instantly look so... so evil?? Did he really wager his life every time he followed this 'hunting'? If he did, he certainly had to get a wakeup call. That concern made her follow him at a safe distance. He staggered to his room heavily, almost oblivious of her proximity at all. When he entered his quarters, Fallyn barely put out the effort to peel off his jacket and shirt. Each of them fell to the floor with a heavy thud before his hat followed close behind. Fallyn barely made it to his mattress before he collapsed in exhaustion. Then, it was utterly silent.

"Fallyn?"

But he was already out cold.

❋ ❋ ❋ ❋ ❋ ❋

Fallyn woke up after a long, much-needed sleep. He barely recalled returning home, the chattering of his demon failing to cease even after his hunt. *Did he walk here himself? When did he arrive home? What time was it even now?* He did vaguely recall speaking with Kathrin.

What happened?

He leaned up onto his arm to regain his sense of placement when he noticed his boots neatly placed on the floor at the foot of his bed. *Odd*, he pondered. He didn't recall taking them off and most certainly didn't give them the time to be neatly placed. When he glanced around some and found that his coat and hat were not even in his room, his brow furrowed curiously. *Where did they go? Had Kathrin taken them?*

That curiosity rose him from his bed and rushed him through his morning routine. The fact he couldn't remember anything unnerved him. It is hardly ever wise to be in that state. After he was freshened, Fallyn began his exploration. Within only a few minutes, he discovered that Kathrin had been cleaning. None of his trinkets and nick-nacks were the way they were, having more of a 'woman's touch' than they ever saw in their life. Actually, many of his rooms were quite spotless.

Why didn't any of her workings rise me?

Fallyn knew the answer to that. It was because of his curse. Whenever it came close to his time- when he couldn't keep his demon at bay- the voice would become more and more pronounced. Contemplating from what had happened the night before, Fallyn assumed it was only a matter of days before that time would come once more.

At present, though, he was only focused on finding Kathrin, even if to thank her for the chores she had done. Fallyn found her in the last place he thought to search;] washing dishes within the kitchen. She was sporting a black satin-like skirt and a milky-colored sweater, her wavy chestnut hair hugging her temples and shoulders while she worked. Then, he listened in to the beautiful tune she was humming.

Fallyn leaned against the door's frame in silence as he listened to the lovely sound, folding his arms across his chest with a grin that curved his lips. She was oblivious to anything but the chores she designated for herself. Yet, Fallyn instantly recognized the tune as she purred the hypnotic song. The variance of octaves showed how remarkable her voice was. *Funny*, he thought, *that Kathrin would know that particular hymn*. It was a song created in his own era before he became immortal. *Exquisite* was the only word he could think of when his eyes locked onto her face.

Kathrin jumped with a start when she finally noticed Fallyn, giggling her shock away with her rambling, "Oh, Fallyn! You scared me half to death! Did I wake you? I thought it would be nice if I tidied up a bit."

"That tune, where did you learn it from?" His gaze rose to meet her own.

When his gaze held hers firm, Kathrin's face

instantly heated. Oh, how he pulled the butterflies from her stomach!

"-Oh, that? I um-it was something my mom used to sing to me when I was little. She said there were words to it, too. But she couldn't remember them," she stuttered.

Fallyn nodded, his eyes still fixed on her. "It is quite an old tune."

"Oh, you know it?" Kathrin asked with surprise in an attempt to further the conversation, as well, but he simply continued to watch her. It unraveled her nerves. "I- um- I took the liberty to clean up the place. I hope I wasn't intruding or anything by doing so."

Only with the mention of her chores did Fallyn's eyes part from hers: "I am grateful, Kathrin."

"-Oh, and I washed your hat and coat. I have to say, this place is rather curious," she blundered as she tried to evade what he did to her, although his eyes practically burned her with his examination. She looked up at the kitchen walls as she explained what she meant.

"I mean, this kitchen is better than mine, yet the only means there was to wash clothes was an old fashion washer pail."

When she glanced back at Fallyn, her voice became caught in her throat. He was only inches away instead of at the doorway where he once was. His passionate gaze was unreadable, yet it consumed everything about her. Kathrin swallowed hard as she was grateful for the countertop's support. He definitely was handsome, with his damp hair clinging to his rugged features. Hell, she could barely recall the ferocity they had just a few hours prior. Perhaps it really was his exhaustion taking its toll. But now that she stared into his eyes, they spoke quite clearly a different message than she got before. There were many, *many* immoral things he wanted to do to her. Kathrin's knees began to buckle.

Somehow, she had to find a way out because she knew her willpower was diminishing by the instant. She probably wouldn't be able to if she didn't back away soon. Her legs couldn't move. *Shit, Too late.* She watched him with wide eyes, stuttering to find the words that his presence whisked away. He came even closer; his eyes dropped to her quivering lips. She could almost read the very questions he pondered at that exact moment. *How would they taste? Would they mold to my own?* She felt like a ball of fire.

Please kiss me, Fallyn.

His lips feathered across hers, following his primal desire before he suddenly stopped.

"Do I frighten you, Kathrin?"

She opened her eyes that instinctively closed and looked up at him. Frightened? Was she frightened?? She definitely couldn't speak, that was for sure. Yet, she didn't think anything her body was responding to was a result of fear.

"-Kathrin," he soothed instantly. "When did I give you such reasons to be afraid?"

How *did* he know she was even the slightest bit wary of him? She didn't think she'd find her voice as she replied, "Umm, no. Just, umm- there is a side of you... that is different than what you are now... When you yelled this morning, it was unnerving. But I assumed it was nothing more than a rough night. It really wasn't-"

"Please forgive me, Kathrin. It was never my intention, but you are correct with your insight. It was a 'rough night,' but not by your doing." His voice was a mere whisper but sincere, earnest, and seductive. Yet, even with his averted conversation, Kathrin shamelessly wondered how his arms would feel around her.

To Kathrin's disappointment, Fallyn backed away thereafter, blatantly avoiding the electrifying chemistry fizzling between them. "You have toiled enough, Kathrin. Here, let me serve us some refreshments."

He gestured her politely towards a kitchen chair.

Still, as a trembling ball of nerves, Kathrin could only nod and follow his direction. He assisted her into a chair before going about his task. Then, the silence ensured. That same silence clawed at her loneliness. Kathrin was instantly shoved into a desperation to be out of the scenario.

"Are- you sure you don't want me to help?" Kathrin asked as she rubbed her arms with an exhale.

A small grin cornered his lips. She really loved it when he smiled. "Have you not enough blisters upon those hands?"

He didn't look over at her with his retort, but- if he did- he would have seen her blushing profusely. Kathrin wasn't used to the attentiveness. Hell, she never even had a friend serve her as a host in her life.

"Would you enjoy a meal that starts off the day or, for it is now after noon, a feast designated for such?"

"What?" she stared at him quizzically. She'd definitely have to get used to the way he spoke. It was so beyond normalcy; it was practically like a math equation on its own. Yet, when she finally realized what he meant, she exclaimed, "Oh, you mean breakfast or lunch? Whichever you like, I haven't eaten today either."

"'Breakfast' or 'lunch'?" Fallyn questioned in return with an arch of his brow. Boy, he really must have lived under some rock if he didn't understand that terminology.

"Umm, yea. Breakfast is the meal you start the day off with. Lunch is what you eat at noon time."

He looked back at the countertop where some vegetables were already pulled out from the refrigerator. "I see. So, it matters not what to eat?"

"No," Kathrin shook her head. "Make whatever you like."

He accepted the answer as he removed a frying pan that hung from the kitchen wall and began his creation. Kathrin watched him, somewhat amazed at his culinary handy work. Everything about him and his place seemed like a walking ball of irony. How could someone have a place like this and the weapons he had yet know *nothing* of modern slang? She shook her head. Perhaps one day, she'd understand how everything came to be with him. But, in the meantime, she'd study the man who was the most peculiar person she knew. His culinary skill presented an omelet filled with many vegetables and meats served to her within a short time.

"Thank you. This looks delicious," Kathrin awed as he sat in the chair beside her with his own plate.

Yet, the appearance of the meal was a trivial representation of its flavor. "Oh my God, are you kidding me? This is amazing! I've never tasted something so exquisite in my life!"

"Then I shall pleasantly take that as a compliment. It has been many-a-year since I've learned the ways of a chef," he smiled as he witnessed her devour her food.

After a few moments of them enjoying their meals, Kathrin struck up a conversation again. "So, how long have you lived in this place? The paintings you have in some of these rooms are spectacular."

Fallyn shrugged casually as he swallowed a part of his omelet, "At least a few decades."

"Decades," she asked, rather puzzled. "Then those masterpieces are family heirlooms?"

Another bite was consumed. "I suppose they could be given that title."

Obviously, he would've preferred to avoid the topic she had decided to draw forth, so she let it drop. "Well then, what were you hunting last night? Going after that vampire guy from a couple of nights ago? I think you called him Daniel?"

Fallyn shifted in his seat uncomfortably. "Daimos. No, he is a trying vampire, indeed."

Kathrin sat her cutlery on her plate in dismay at his sour retort. "I'm sorry. I'm trying really hard to strike up a conversation without offending you at all. I just figured- because you knew his name- that he might be on your list."

Fallyn whisked her plate away the moment he finished his omelet and returned them to the sink. "He is on a-many-of-lists. Yet, it is not through that that I know his name. He is the leader of the region you resided in."

"The leader?" Kathrin frowned suddenly. "So, there's a hierarchy with vampires? I kinda thought it's every-man-for-himself out there...."

"There must be order, Kathrin. Could you imagine the mortal world if there was no governing body? Such is the same for them. Yet, leadership is earned through might."

Comparing what he said with their government, she slowly began to pale. Fallyn simply continued to tidy.

"Why would some vampire king get involved over me, then?"

"Because of what you saw was the initial reason. You threatened their existence. Yet, when he discovered how I had come to your aid thereafter, it was a weapon to use against me. So, in the end, you merely became bait for Daimos. Our feud has been around for such a long time; We are blood-driven rivals."

"Well, even as bait, I'm lucky you arrived when you did. Otherwise, I'm sure I would've been dead."

His expression altered as he finished cleaning the last of the dishes. He knew Kathrin wouldn't have felt that way if she truly knew what was going to happen to her. Either she would die or turn; There was no in-between when it came to elder vampire bites. Even now, he saw her symptoms of this. Her body cringed from the sun's rays, the bite's pulse continually bothering her, even when she didn't think he noticed it. It was only a matter of time before that fateful day would be upon them, and he would have no other choice but to follow the Infernal law and destroy her. When a mortal turned into a vampire, it never held the traits of who they once were. No, he was sure Kathrin would've begged for her death if she truly knew what was in store for her.

"Did I say something wrong," Kathrin questioned rather meekly when his silence ensued much longer than comfortable.

Yet, Fallyn tried to shrug it off. "All is well, Kathrin. My thoughts have been troubled of late. Come; Let me show you to my study. I believe it is as good of a time as any to begin your understanding of the abyss."

Chapter Nine

Fallyn glanced up at the tangled web of branches on the large pine tree and noticed the colors of crimson and bronze beginning to paint the tips of its thistles. He was unable to count the time he traveled this path, engraving its familiarity into his mind whenever he needed guidance in his life's current endeavors. With Kathrin becoming a problem of its own, this time was no different. He made sure he left well after Kathrin had fallen asleep, wanting to avoid any worrying on her part because of his departure.

Through the magic that was imbued in his home, nothing from the abyss could penetrate his abode. Yet, he knew that would be difficult to explain to Kathrin. Why wouldn't it, though? And how could he fault her for being nervous about things that she had only discovered under a month prior?

"Let me pass, Hakeem," he called out to the presence of the tree, breaking his train of thought.

The tree instantly shifted and moaned, using its roots like spiny legs to move its heavy trunk away from a hidden entrance beneath it. Fallyn crouched into the opening before the tree settled back into the soil once more.

Peeling his sight into their heightened form, a sudden glow took shape to show him the way.

Fallyn knew he had already become too close to Kathrin, *far* too close for all his knowledge, skills, and defenses to save him. But she was exotic. As soon as he saw her from the kitchen threshold, he wanted to kiss her, and it was overwhelming. The fact that she sang the song he had written to his beloved, Tonia, didn't make things any better. But Kathrin didn't know about the tune or the effect she had on him. Fallyn couldn't blame her for that. But, with each moment he saw her, he felt more and more drugged by her presence. How many times had he imagined her lips melding against his own? And he knew she wanted it too; Her scent was deep with desire. If it wasn't for her reference to the night before, he probably would've acted on his impulse. Thank heavens. The last thing he needed was to have this woman blind him from his tasks.

A haggard voice called out from the depths of the tunnels.

"Ah, the killer of demons. How I've missed you so."

Fallyn continued down in silence, refusing to stop until he came upon the mouth of the open cave where the creature resided.

The tentacled monstrosity reminded Fallyn of the very roots of the tree that sealed it. Spiny and knotted with hundreds of arms, Hakeem was the most unique earth elemental to exist. His body was round, smooth like a toad's belly, with a hide back covered with stones and slabs of rock like a turtle shell. Thousands of green eyes glowed gauntly over his face, which hardly separated from his inflated torso. His mouth was no better, it being a tentacled mess that barely had enough space to fit a tractor into it. Although the light was dim, Fallyn knew his color was variable, from the blackened moss of the earth to the vibrant greens of a field. His size, though, although he was relaxed in his domain, was at least 100 feet tall, making Fallyn look like a measly insect in his presence. But it didn't seem to bother Fallyn.

"What brings you here, Fallyn? I was sure I made your haven adequate for you."

Fallyn shook his head towards the comment as he settled down onto a nearby rock. "No, the haven is fine."

"I've also overheard that any foe that you come up against easily meets your blade. So much so that none of them wish to cross paths with you. Does your visit mean there is a new devil on the rise?" Hakeem queried.

Fallyn shook his head again as he stared at the floor. This brought a chuckle to Hakeem. "Then, whatever brings you to see me this time?"

Silently, Fallyn drew out his dagger nestled beneath his pant leg, lifted the sleeve of his trench coat, and slashed the skin on his forearm. Hakeem merely watched in curiosity. Yet, when the blood rose to the surface for

Hakeem to see, it was hard for him to hide his longing for the warm liquid of life. The moment Fallyn outstretched his arm toward Hakeem, his tentacles lashed out towards Fallyn's arm to lavish in its delights. Fallyn corrected his sleeve after a few seconds more.

"Most desirable, Fallyn. But I sense there is more to this gift than a mere kind gesture," Hakeem grinned as he cleaned the saliva from his malformed face.

"I need all that you know about a woman I harbor."

The demon laughed. "I should have known a female would've concerned you most."

Though Fallyn was unimpressed, he refused to defend himself.

"Why does this woman bother you so? You've never been interested in any before. Are you hunting her?"

Fallyn glared at Hakeem as he demanded rather curtly, "I need you to foresee of what lineage she comes from and what is to become of her."

"Do you figure she is a person from your past?"

"Stop wasting my time and do as I say!" Fallyn barked harshly in return.

Hakeem didn't pay any heed to Fallyn's outburst as he retorted: "Very well, Fallyn."

That was when his eyes turned gray like they had died within his forehead as he hummed within the rattling of time. This was the monster's specialty. He could witness the flow of past, present, and future on whomever and whatever it chose. Yet, his only downfall was his prison beneath the soil.

Centuries ago, his life was not so barred from creation, though. Many of the dark rulers used to barter with him for guidance into their own plights. It was a time when man was believed to be near extinction. Death and disease, famine, and hatred were running so rampant across the land that even siblings would kill each other. All the history books lace this era with far lighter events than they truly were; Hakeem made sure of it. He believed if a man was aware of all the haunting that shaped the reality of the demise they almost faced, indeed the realm of the dark would also be much different.

But one day, neither mortal nor dark lord came to greet him. A man shrouded like a devil's avatar came to Hakeem to bring about his fall. He growled how Hakeem's aide to the demons was undoubtedly what would destroy humanity, which was what was meant to survive through all of the ages. It was believed at that point, Hakeem was slain. To this day, this myth is still believed. This was a crucial blow for the dark lords as their plans plummeted to an end. Both Fallyn and Hakeem much preferred it that way, too.

It was some time before Hakeem's eyes returned to their livened self, a smirk rising widely on his twisted face.

"In all the years I've known you, I never would've never guessed you would receive such a pinnacle fate."

"I did not come here for your mockery," Fallyn snarled.

But Hakeem only chuckled. "Your life's a real mess, isn't it?"

"Hakeem," Fallyn warned again. "Tell me of her ancestry."

Then, Hakeem leaned back on his frog-like legs and began. "Well, your instincts are correct. She is from the Larnwick legacy."

"How is that possible, though? They were annihilated all in one night. Was it a distant cousin or bastard child fathered by the Duke himself?"

"Neither. She is directly related to Tonia."

Fallyn was instantly numb. *How could that be? I never touched her....* Thrown back by the announcement, he instantly refused it. "It cannot be, Hakeem."

"I don't know how else to break it to you, Fallyn, but Tonia conceived before her death. Her parents gave the offspring to relatives who were barren to save face," Hakeem muttered.

It wasn't long before Fallyn's confusion turned to unbridled rage. This little tidbit of information really screwed up everything he thought he knew about his past.

Everything he felt was based on *lies*. No, it wasn't the child that spurred this anger. It was entirely Tonia's deception. If he had known of her treachery then, perhaps he never would've become the monster he is today.

"Was that all you wanted to know? Surely there must be more to this than Kathrin's lineage," Hakeem sighed.

With the reference to Kathrin's name, all of Fallyn's irritation washed away. Although what he learned was disturbing news, the events of the Larnwick clan meant nothing to what Fallyn faced now. He couldn't avoid his thoughts that only focused on her. And even though Fallyn never spoke about his turmoil to anyone, it was like the ties that bound his emotions in check had loosened to spill forth his uncertainty.

"It was her similarity to Tonia that enticed me to her, like a haunting recollection of my past that I hoped to redeem. But the sense of pull that I have towards her now is beyond anything before. I feel amiss when she is gone, and the calm I have when she is there is like I've been waiting for her all along, although I knew nothing about her. Am I losing my mind? Or is there truly something I have forgotten?"

Hakeem couldn't help the smile that turned the corner of his horrific face, seeing all too well the factors of life he never guessed even the hunter of demons would discover. "No, Fallyn, you are well. You've only stumbled upon what many search for. You have found your *amante interno.*"

Hearing the words didn't ease Fallyn; it actually made it a hundred times worse. Yet, he rose and left the underground chamber without saying another word.

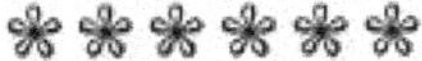

Kathrin woke up with a howl of agony and clawed at the pounding of her neck. The pulse was becoming more and more prominent even though the bite had long since healed over. Her fingers were icy cold, her lips blue as she panted desperately to fill her lungs. It was like something was trying to kill her. She was sure some frozen claw was clenching onto each of her organs to shut them down. She glanced around the room.

There was nothing unusual.

A sting pierced her stomach. Kathrin yelped as her arms pressed to hold the torrent at bay. Cold. Everything was cold, each pound jabbing violently at her stomach. What was wrong with her? Was this the virus Fallyn mentioned?

So very cold...

Quivering with barely enough strength to move, Kathrin reached for the duvet at the foot of her bed and covered her body. The blanket didn't help. It was like a wind was cutting right through to her bones. Her limbs ached, her stomach hammered, and her jaw throbbed.

Was there even pain in her teeth? *Nonsense,* she cried to herself; *it was only her mind playing tricks on her.* Kathrin cried out once more at another pummel of agony.

Oh, someone help me….

With a rage that surfaced from his prior conversation, Fallyn didn't bother to head into the city for further hunting. He truly believed that Tonia loved him; She was everything he ever wanted. But with his sudden realization about a pregnancy he knew nothing about, he was so enraged he could barely speak.

Fallyn knew it wasn't his, for he was the honorable man who believed in the traditions of saving it for their wedding night. How wrong was he to believe Tonia felt the same way? Deceit, he fumed inwardly. It was all deceit. If Fallyn had even remotely caught wind of this, he never would've been there when her family met its demise. But out of every morsel of knowledge he discovered, the tidbit that ate him apart from the inside out while he sped back to his haven was that it was a lie of a female that cursed him to his fate.

Yet through the lie came something else, something he couldn't bring himself to say was a mistake at all. Kathrin.

No, Fallyn rationalized. *How could me having to wager her life in my hands be any better than her ever being born?*

Hakeem's words flooded his mind, which made Fallyn's brow furrow. *Amante Interno.* Those words, in many languages, were identical in syllables and meaning. They were even rooted in the language of the demons, although very rarely used in that manner. *Amante Interno*, roughly translated into English, meant 'inner lover' or as Hakeem referred, 'soul mate'.

Hakeem is a fool, Fallyn argued. She wasn't his soul mate. She wasn't even *his.* And he would make sure it stayed that way. He'd never allow his emotions to blur his sight again. *Never again.* For- aside from Tonia's deception- if it wasn't for his irrational behavior because of them, she never would've died. That was the option he wasn't about to take again.

Upon his arrival into his cavern, Fallyn sensed something was wrong within seconds. It just lingered in the air, pungent and raw. *Darkness.*

"Kathrin?" Fallyn called as he dismounted from his motorcycle, looking towards the hallway for signs of her.

He was greeted with silence. Fallyn didn't wait for a response as he hurried to her room. Yet, he was only a few meters from the doorway when a tearing cry shrilled through the light-less hallways. Fallyn's skin instantly crawled as he rushed to her room.

He found Kathrin buried beneath her blankets.

Hesitantly, he closed the distance between them and knelt beside the bed. He prayed that she was simply in the grasp of a nightmare- or even a fever. Yet, what he saw when he rose the covers from her body drained all thought.

Vampire. Kathrin was twisted into the maddened monster of her curse-to-be. Her glowing silver eyes barely offset the primeval features of her face, her skin already the palest of blue. He observed how she scrunched her knees against her stomach, too; it didn't take a genius to see that she was in horrible agony. What worried him more was what else jutted forth from her mouth. Fangs.

That was when she finally noticed him, her tears streaming down her face with pleading mercy. "Fallyn, the pain... it hurts all over..."

He wasn't sure he wanted to respond to the vampire she was becoming. *I need to kill her- right now- before the beast takes over.* Yet, although his thoughts screamed his duty, they repulsed him.

I- I cannot.

He looked into her eyes that flickered between their turquoise sea and the silvered beams to find his answer. Something in them had to force him into his obligation. All he saw, though, was her fear of what she didn't understand. There was nothing of a devil he hoped she'd be to sway his hand.

"Focus on the touch of my palm, Kathrin. Understood?"

Her teeth clamped tight, her own fangs piercing her lower lips as she nodded. But, when his hand brushed the tender flesh of her neck to absorb her suffering, he cursed aloud at the ice of her skin. Fallyn had never witnessed the beginnings of a vampire turning before, but he never assumed it would've been so horribly violent, either. It was no wonder only a fraction of mortals survived if this was how it was for all turnings.

"Tell me what visions plague you, Kathrin?" Fallyn questioned sympathetically.

The blood from the twin punctures on her lip began to ooze as she snuggled into the warmth of his hand. "A void... death...."

Fallyn began the transference, noting the call of darkness all too well from his own welcoming from it. But why did he feel so inclined to take all her pain away? Was it simply because he was witnessing her within the clutches of her awakening? Why else would he make her suffering easier?

Her death is a good way.

Silence, he growled to himself as he concentrated harder on Kathrin.

But you can imagine how delicious she would

taste.

He could. Her sweet smell of lilacs, the honey-laced aroma. He could well imagine how her skin would tang his tongue. When Fallyn realized what his demon was trying to do, Fallyn snarled: *Enough! I will not be swayed by you this night!*

Ah, but the time is coming when you'll not have a choice.

Fallyn knew he was right. The tightening in his chest was increasing as each day drew near. Even though him trying to ignore it, he knew his time was running out. Shaking his thoughts away, Fallyn remained firm on his current resolve to relieve Kathrin's pain.

"How fair you?" Fallyn coaxed softly.

"Okay...," Kathrin croaked, a small level of color already returning to her complexion.

"When did this begin?"

"I...don't know... I woke up from it... am I dying," she groaned, the tremulous pitch caught in her throat.

Yes. Fallyn knew he should tell her the truth. He would want nothing less if their roles were reversed. But the quivering gaze that barely held tears at bay while they begged him for some sort of consolation deterred him from saying anything at all.

"No, Kathrin. It is your body fighting the virus. Give it time. You will feel better soon." What was wrong with him? He never had lied so much in his life! Who was he trying to kid?

She nodded and swallowed the thick lump in her throat. Her appearance softened, the fangs receding back into what they should be. But, as he absorbed the dark ooze of the abyss, Fallyn could feel it snake through his fingers. Cold and thick. It would be his price to pay for giving aid to another. If it was fated to be, someone had to suffer, no matter who absorbed it. Fallyn's body tightened. He knew he could withstand far more than Kathrin could, although he knew tonight would be hell. He wouldn't be surprised if a migraine broke before day-brake. Yet, for some reason, that knowledge didn't bother him.

Her head slumped onto the pillow when the last ounce of her discomfort washed away. Fallyn exhaled in relief. He highly doubted she'd rise again before morning. Then, his muscles stiffened. More specifically, his shoulder. Innately, he stretched his arms back, although he practically knew the motion was pointless. It was getting rather peculiar that his shoulder hadn't stopped stinging since that battle for Kathrin many nights before.

Chapter Ten

"Kathrin, there is something I must ask of you."

Startled, Kathrin jumped at the broken silence and glanced up at Fallyn. It was practically second nature for them to be disassociated amongst themselves. She understood from the beginning that Fallyn was a man of many secrets and fewer words. It was one of the things that added to her loneliness. He barely even glanced at her as he went about his business!

The event in her room was over a week ago, although the chill beneath her skin never went away. And beyond the initial inquiry of her well-being, Fallyn had since ignored the incident altogether, hardly explaining why it had happened. She didn't fathom why conversing about it mattered either way.

"What is it," Kathrin asked, brushing away a few tendrils of her hair as she lifted her nose out of a novel she was reading at Fallyn's request.

As he stood towering beside her, his fingertips rested precariously on the side of the wooden table that Kathrin sat beside. She couldn't read his expression from under the veils of his black cabana hat, which gave her the shrinking sensation of a schoolgirl about to be scolded by her teacher. When the silence ensued longer than anticipated, she shied a quilt onto her shoulders for warmth. *Hell, it was cold*, she muttered to herself.

"I hope by now you are aware that for each demon to be able to roam the land that, there is a price to pay for that privilege?"

Confused by the question, Kathrin nodded slightly, "I think so.."

Fallyn exhaled in an attempt to ease what tension he had. "A vampire is graced with strength and lifeless immortality but is cursed to hide from the sunlight's rays as they drink the blood of life from god's creatures. A Digornath is graced with a transparent reality, using this world as a playground for their malcontent but always being the servant to another as their fleeting lives diminish in a mere year. Everything in the realm of dark works on this 'level of equality.'"

Kathrin listened keenly as she tried to determine where this conversation was heading.

"Someday, you, too, will discover how this 'level of equality' affects you. For, every creature touched by the fires of hell becomes part of this ritualistic law and must live forever with the curse they are forced to follow."

With the end of his sentence Kathrin noticed the fingers that were balanced on top of the table had balled into a fist, his hat lowering towards the floor. He seemed tortured by something; she could almost see it festering painfully deep. *Why didn't he just get it off his chest?*

"Just as I am…." he muttered suddenly to Kathrin's bewilderment.

He was cursed, too? But, before she could answer her own question, his fist tapped lightly against the table repeatedly until he sank onto his haunches. At her eye level now, his frustration was all too vivid. A wave of urgency instantly flooded her. He glared into her eyes, somehow knowing that whatever he was about to say was as important as her next breath.

"There are things you must never see, Kathrin. Devils drift across this land to absorb anything innocent it can. It would be no different for you, which is why I have you here. These toils would become more persistent with each day that passes; You'd have no place to run now that you have been awakened." That was when Fallyn touched the tendermost part of her neck and caressed the old scar that flawed her skin, showing her what he referred to. Heat pooled in her belly as her mind tried to remain focused on what he was telling her. But his mention wasn't far off from the truth already. Aside from always being cold, she hadn't slept comfortably for days.

"But there are times when even I am haunted by my curse…." Fallyn grimaced as he avoided her gaze. She frowned, sympathetic to the feeling of helplessness she felt from him as his hand lowered to his leg.

"You're… one of them?" She was sure her question

would remain unanswered, and she was right about that.

His hands instantly clenched onto her arms as he emphasized the importance of his words. "When this happens, I cannot protect you. Do you understand? Even if your life depended on it, could I avert what will become of me? I could even be the one that holds you in that peril."

Kathrin gasped as she involuntarily shied away. She knew Fallyn would never have confided such knowledge unless he had no other choice. But the idea that even her savior-of-peril thus far would become what she most feared disconcerted her. It took a few moments for Kathrin to swallow her anxiety. His look was so pleading, so perplexed. She had to be strong for him. With a cracked voice, Kathrin questioned, "This time…. when does it happen, and what should I do?"

He rose once more and stepped away, his hand diving into his trench coat. She watched inquisitively while he muttered almost bitterly, "There is nothing you can do. It is just how things must be. Yet, I can tell you when it is upon me."

That was when he found what it sought from his coat's inner pocket and placed the item on the oak table. Kathrin leaned down to inspect the object of curiosity.

It was an orb of sorts resting in the palm of a wicker-worked claw, a smoldering tint of gray etched into every bark-like crevice. Though the item itself was very intricate in its design, it was what floated inside the translucent substance of the orb that caught her attention: a crimson-blue teardrop crystal.

She leaned in further. She was sure it was changing color, wasn't it? When the crystal suddenly flipped upside-down, Kathrin jumped back in astonishment.

"This is called a Whispering Orb. When someone attunes themselves to its magic, it will emanate that person's psyche, such as you relate to a 'mood ring' only this will morph and glimmer colors that represent their consciousness."

Confused with the item, Kathrin glanced back at Fallyn.

"Do you see what color it is now?" Fallyn questioned, gazing back towards Kathrin's puzzled expression as he waited for her to reply.

"It is almost a deep mauve," she retorted plainly with a quick glance back at the item.

Fallyn nodded in approval. "This will tell you when the time of my curse is upon me. If at any point I am nowhere to be found and this orb boils with the most vibrant of red, I am under the clutches of my damnation."

"Okay," Kathrin stuttered, unable to think of anything else to say as she returned her attention back toward Fallyn. It was his look of apprehension, though, that caught her off guard. In that simple gaze, Kathrin felt nothing else in the world except for him.

"Please, Kathrin. I must have you promise me one request," he almost groaned. His hand reached for hers upon the table, drawing it eye-level between them.

His distress charged through her as he clenched her fingers within his palm. He must have been positive this was what her life depended on. "What is it?"

"Stay in the safety of my domain, Kathrin. Promise to never depart without me by your side. To leave from this haven while I am possessed by Hades' wrath out there....it would be fatal."

His words were weighty. Kathrin lowered her head as her skin crawled, pained by a dread his demand created. She knew she would be helpless against any evils she only just discovered. That was clearly proven the night Fallyn rushed into her apartment and rescued her. But, to hear that she would be left by herself had her tears trickling down her cheeks.

Fallyn was aware of them, the terror and longing in her eyes that this must be a joke. But there was no other way, and the Almighty knew how badly he'd sever this curse if he could. But, even now, he could feel the ties of his humanity slipping. Deep within, a looming predator was longing to get out.

"How long would it last for?" she spoke to his surprise, her voice deceiving her valiance.

"A day, and once it is over, it would be as if nothing ever happened."

A silence passed before she finally whispered in agreement. "I-I promise, Fallyn."

Instantly, his features softened, and a smile curved his lips. It was the first she had seen since their meal together almost a month ago.

He went to exit the library, merely gesturing before his departure, "I must take my leave, Kathrin. I have many things I must tend to before evening rises. I shall see you in the morn."

He didn't wait for a reply as he left, leaving the overwhelming knowledge lodged in the air like an anvil waiting to fall.

Chapter Eleven

Kathrin sprung up from her mattress to the sound of china crashing somewhere in Fallyn's abode in the late hours of the evening. She scanned the room with the light cascading from the fireplace. Nothing seemed out of the ordinary. But when a thud came from outside of her room, an overwhelming sense of dread filled her veins. Something sounded wrong, but what? *Was it Fallyn?* Another crash of glass fell onto the floor, followed by a loud groan of pain. Kathrin slid herself off the side of the bed, and her curiosity picked up. It was difficult strides to reach the threshold of her room.

"Fallyn?"

Fallyn was doubled over. His arm pressed firmly against his abdomen as he clenched onto the table's edge for support. He twisted, curled, bowed, and arched. His agony was beyond all description. Mortified, Kathrin could think of nothing else but taking a step forward.

"Go....to your room, Kathrin," Fallyn croaked with barely enough strength to speak.

More concerned with his well-being, Kathrin whimpered, "What's happening?"

Fallyn shook his head slowly as he quivered to stay balanced on his feet to continue towards the exit. His body contorted once more, a wet snap echoing within the cavern. Fallyn bellowed in agony as he crumpled onto his knees.

It was too much for Kathrin to bear. As it drew tears to her eyes and a step closer, Fallyn's glare darted fiercely over towards her.

"*Stay back*," he hissed with a voice of uncontrollable torment, snarling with something much darker out from his chest.

His eyes glowed with golden fire; She never knew such unnatural eyes could be so hypnotic. Somewhere in the back of her thoughts, she knew she was screaming. But his stare wove like a drug into her mind, showing Kathrin quite clearly all the evils he could conjure as they glowed out from under the shadow of his mane. Fallyn instantly looked away when he realized the dominion they held, leaving Kathrin in the cold wake of the aftermath.

Kathrin rubbed her arms as tears streamed down her face. Was she witnessing the death of her savior? "What's happening?!"

His brows furrowed as the constant throb etched his features. It was only a mere whisper when he spoke. "This is my damnation, Kathrin."

His words brought back their prior conversation. Kathrin had no idea it would be such an unspeakable rending of the body. She struggled between compassion and fear, yet she didn't run away. She couldn't turn a blind eye to his suffering, the only one that was her pillar of strength.

"Tell me, what can I do?"

Her yearning to help him was like a burning sugar in Fallyn's nose, weaving into his twisting mind like erotic fingers. It stirred the beast even more, battling the ties of his psyche as it tried to claw free from its confines even more violently. Another bone snapped to its new intended home, the wet crunch echoing within the room. He even pondered how delicious her flesh would taste.

"No," he scowled hoarsely. Fallyn would never hurt her. Yet, his control was whisking away like water trickling through a sieve.

"What?"

It took all his strength to fight the urge to let his primal demon tear her apart. As he rose onto his weary feet, he used his last pull of humanity to lung toward the entrance of the cavern. But, before he did, he growled almost incoherently: "Do not follow, Kathrin."

That was when he raced away, traveling like a storm through the countryside with uncanny speeds. Even the fabric of Kathrin's nightgown whipped about as she covered her face from the lashings of her hair. Then, she ran towards the cavern's exit. But when she reached it, he was already gone, flung through the blackness that devoured the night.

Kathrin's fingers twined nervously as she waited for Fallyn from the comforts of a lounge chair. She knew many hours had passed since his departure. With the way he was rendered before he left, she couldn't avoid the gut-wrenching feeling that she needed to know if he was fine. Unfortunately, the only thing she had for comfort was the Whispering Orb he had given her earlier. Kathrin glanced at it now as her stomach flipped in anxiousness. It bubbled red, just as Fallyn explained it would. It almost seemed as if the rippled orb could barely contain it.

Looking toward the grandfather clock he had in the living room, she saw that it was almost dawn. Kathrin had already tidied the disarray from earlier while she waited for him. Even as her eye lids heaved for slumber, she anxiously waited for the moment he walked through the door.

A dull pain stabbed her chest, and her fingers rubbed obliviously over the area. Again, she felt cold. Would there ever be a point where she *wouldn't* feel that ache? After so long enduring it, she hardly thought so. Yet right through it all, her mind still lingered on Fallyn. She never could place a finger on it, but it seemed like something was picking at her memory. It was something about Fallyn. Why was she so sure she knew him from before? It was like the memory was on the tip of her tongue but she couldn't swallow. His rich copper eyes had always looked at her like there was so much more between them, although he never admitted anything to her. Was it something so horrible that he was just trying to avoid it? Or was her mind really playing tricks on her? No... she was positive she knew him from before.

Kathrin closed her weighty eyelids as she pondered her connection with Fallyn. Then, exhaled a calming breath and snuggled into a heavy, down blanket. A soothing cloud layered her mind, lifting her away from her concerns as it gently averted her attention to something much deeper. Darkness passed in silence for a few moments until Kathrin could hear laughter. It was a pleasant sound, sweet and intoxicating. It even brought a curl to Kathrin's lips. Then, a face erupted from the fog. It was Fallyn's, albeit a much younger face.

She was on the shores somewhere, with the summer skies setting in hues of crimson while Fallyn relaxed beside her. His eyes shone with vivid admiration and love. Like, amongst the sounds of the sailors setting sail or the fishermen dragging in their catch for the evening, she was the only person he wanted to be with. His arms rested on his knees as the shade of a spruce tree dampened the warm breeze. His eyes focused on her again. Then, she said something.

She wasn't sure what she said before Fallyn gleamed

with a chuckle. He shook his head and averted his gaze toward the sunset in an attempt to calm himself, but in the end, he was helpless to it. He lowered his head in a chest-reverberating laugh. It made Kathrin want to laugh as well. His hearty chuckle was so irresistible to deny such fun herself. *So very handsome.* She loved his smile, and though she never heard him laugh like this, Kathrin knew it was the sweetest noise she could have known.

His eyes were soft when they finally turned to hers in a single sentence, changing the topic to one more serious. "Let us sail from our birthrights. I cannot bear the thought of life without you."

Her skin flushed, her innards bounding for joy at what she knew she had begged for many nights already. She answered him, something she wished she could've heard for the life of her although it only came out as a muffled sound. Yet, his obvious beam with pride made apparent what decision she made.

"You honor me so. I vow that you'll never regret your choice."

When was this?

Kathrin jumped awake in her seat with the sudden boots slamming upon the stone-worked floor. It took her a moment to re-orient herself back into Fallyn's domain. Yet, when she finally recognized where she was with a sigh, Kathrin dropped her head back in her seat. *I must have fallen asleep.*

Kathrin glanced over at the Whispering Orb perched on the end table beside her to see how Fallyn was fairing. She blinked once before she noticed that it had transformed into a blackened diamond. His damnation must be over. *Was he already back?* Kathrin prepared to rise from her seat in search of Fallyn when she suddenly noticed him at the mouth of the living room, leaning against the wall with his arms crossed. He was far from impressed.

Paralyzed from his gaze, she remained half poised in the air, trying to understand his expression that she just couldn't read. Was Fallyn angry with her? Was he curious? She swallowed down the lump in her throat and examined him for injury. He was clothed from the waist down, his black slacks hanging from his hips. Her core warmed. No scars, no cuts. He was completely normal. Were the popping and cracking of bone nothing but a doubtful memory? His arms were still broad, his chest wide, the pelvic bone in his hips still lucid to her eyes. She observed him head to toe, then back before finally settling on Fallyn's face. His gaze was still fixed on her every move.

Kathrin blushed when she realized he had witnessed her skepticism, especially considering what had happened the night before. Time passed in an awkward silence with Fallyn reading her now like a book for his own curiosity.

" Why do you wait for me, Kathrin?" Fallyn asked gruffly.

"I - well- I needed to know you were okay. What happened… well, it frightened me." She stammered.

Fallyn's eyes flashed with emotion, although too quickly for Kathrin to notice, before he growled, "Usually, such horrors would make a person hide from the source. Yet here you are. So, again, I ask why?"

It was very clear by his stern, matter-of-fact voice that he wasn't messing around.

"I was worried for you, Fallyn," Kathrin began, feeling her helplessness weld up into her throat. "I don't know anything about anything here, and all I can do is sit around and wait for your return to help me figure it out. I'm completely out of my element here."

When his eyes didn't falter, and the silence pursued, she added, "God, don't you see how helpless I am here? I only know what you've told me. All I've learned within the last few weeks, for sure, is that you will help me out with the answers I need. Then- all in one day- I'm told that the *only* person I can depend on will ditch me to fend for myself."

He remained fixed on her, his stare unsettling as they flecked into gold. Kathrin stood up from her seat, emphasizing her frustration with her arms.

"Damn it! I used to know where I was going with my life! That I was going to be one of the ones swept under the carpet like all the other worthless people in society. But now-!"

She stopped; the answer caught in her throat. She looked back towards Fallyn, who had haunted her since their first meeting. *Now it was all screwed up*. Nothing made sense at all. A small sting vibrated from her chest and Kathrin wondered if maybe this secret was trying to get out all along.

"Now?" Fallyn insisted from his place at the door.

"Now..." she paused. She simply couldn't hold it back anymore. "Now... I wait here and worry over someone that I supposedly never met before. I'm wondering if the visions I've been having are my own or not. I'm recalling things in my mind that never happened between us. Yet, in each and every one of them, all I see is you! All you give me for an answer, though, is that I'm completely loony after all!"

His lips pressed into a fine line, like he did know what she referred to but wasn't about to acknowledge it. Her skin began to chill.

"See?! You *do* know what I'm talking about, but you choose to shove me away just like you always do! Enough is enough! Where do I know you from?!" Kathrin stormed, her ineptness bothering her to no end.

A tightness grew in her lungs as she waited for his answer. Her chest heaved in attempts to fill her lungs; it took real effort as she focused on Fallyn. He watched her struggle and gasp for air.

"Fallyn! Tell me how I know you!"

"Kathrin...perhaps you should sit down," Fallyn finally replied. Yet, the reason for his retort became clear not even a second later.

Instantly, a violent stab pierced her chest. The force wrenched an involuntary yelp of pain from Kathrin as she clenched her bosom. Her mind buzzed, her skin turned to ice, and- before she knew it- her knees had given way beneath her.

Chapter Twelve

Although Fallyn was more than insistent on getting an answer from Kathrin, he couldn't ignore the illness that suddenly paled her to a deathly white. Even her eyes flickered from turquoise to silver as she yelled her frustration at him. Yet, when she collapsed to the floor only seconds after he suggested for her to relax, he knew this was more than a mortal ailment.

Her body quivered in convulsions while he carried her to her quarters. This was far different from the incident before. True, he could feel the darkness creeping into her even now. But something about this moment, the discoloration of her skin and the state she was left in now, told him that deep down, this was permanent.

He softly laid her on her bed and covered her. Then, with a placement of his fingers against the artery on her neck, he attempted to ease her suffering.

She screamed out. Tears poured down her face while he tried to weave spells within her; it assisted rather dimly. That was when he understood that her pain was meant for her and her alone, and he couldn't share it. Reversing the spell, Fallyn infused his own strength into her instead. Her body relaxed within minutes, the severity dampening to a dull ache. Her dreary eyes turned toward Fallyn's like she already knew what this all meant. So did he. She was going to die here tonight.

"I'm…sorry…I'm such a hassle," she moaned, tears still covering her face.

Fallyn shook his head as he cooed softly, "Never have your trials been a hassle for me, Kathrin."

Kathrin half-smiled, her doubting expression ever present before she squinted at a much milder jab of pain. Her eyes were filled with so many questions like they always were, which brought forth her demands ever clearly to his mind once more. Fallyn lowered his head. How could anyone pass in peace if they had as many unanswered questions as she? Then, he sighed, glancing into the eyes of the only person who would ever hear his secret.

"There was a time before I was punished to my demonic fate that I lived as any mortal would. I was born of nobility but with only minor wealth and land to my family's name. I was gifted with an aristocratic education and, such like any other man with titled birthright, was destined to wed another woman of similar stature."

"A noble's birth'? Fallyn… how old are you?"

A faint smile curved his lips as he returned her gaze once again, "The year of my birth was 1051 A.D.

Her eyes widened with shock. He nodded in acknowledgment before he continued.

"My arranged marriage was of no argument to me

in my childhood, for that was how things were in any household of hierarchy. I was accepting- that is- until the year before the wedding was to take place. It was then I met my Aphrodite, the lady-of-my-heart at a ball celebrating the harvest moon. I was quickly informed that she was a Duke's daughter, but my heart was captivated. I snuck out into the moonlight to greet her and found out it was more than I who felt the same."

Kathrin couldn't understand why this seemed so familiar. Was it because of the visions she had of Fallyn? Were some of these what he was explaining? With the conclusion of his sentence, his brow furrowed, and his lips thinned to a grim line. He wasn't happy recalling what he went through. But, even with the unpleasantness he continued on.

"I found out only recently that what I had believed was a lie, but I was smitten none the less. I slipped into her home any moment I could spare, and after months of courting her in secret, I asked her to abandon her birthright and sail away with me to wed."

The dream she just had was of him speaking to his love. Yet, why did it feel so much closer than that?

"She accepted, and we chose to meet at the harbor by sunset the following day. But... that day never came..." Fallyn trailed, coming to a halt as his face chilled even darker.

Kathrin wondered how hard it must have been for him to live what he had, seeing the wounds were still too fresh to heal even though over nine hundred years had passed since then.

"Kathrin… the night you happened upon me in the alleyway was as if a reflection from my past came to haunt me. Your eyes, hair, and features were just like the woman I loved centuries ago. I believed you were Tonia."

Tonia. Kathrin's eyes widened in horror as the visions of Lady Tonia poured forth into her mind. It was then Kathrin understood why their link was so strong. It was because she *was* Tonia. As the key opened the chest that lay dormant within her, more memories spilled forth like ooze bubbling from a boiling pot. Their courting, their agreement, her death. Fallyn was cursed because of her! Her eyes blurred with guilt. Yet, before she could say anything at all, her body shuddered as the vile fingers of death began to pull her into darkness.

"No," she moaned regretfully. Her stomach was pitted with both her knowledge and her doom.

A heavy slumber flowed over her as her hand clenched for Fallyn's. Their eyes connected at that moment, as he could feel her slipping away.

"Fallyn, I'm sorry… I didn't know… I never wanted you to meet… this curse, "she whispered hoarsely, wishing she had just a little while longer.

"Kathrin," Fallyn called. His heart lodged in his throat to the words he didn't understand.

Yet then she fell limp, her last breath escaping her lips. Fallyn cursed aloud as he now knew his duty would come into play whether he wished it or not. If only she could've been like she was only a few days before. But now that her time of transformation was upon her, he feared it. Fallyn grimaced. What was she trying to tell him? She seemed so full of guilt. *Why did she feel that way?*

"That was very kind of you to let her live out her last moments of humanity," a shrouded man spoke up from the corner of the room.

Fallyn jumped away as he instinctively prepared for battle. *How on earth didn't he hear him enter?* "How are you here?"

The man's smile could barely be seen under the shadows of his hood as he replied, "Not everything in creation is beholden to the laws of demons, Fallyn."

Fallyn could feel a cold sensation run through his body. This man concealed in white garb and silver trimmings knew who he was?? How was that possible?

"Who are you?"

A noise of bittersweet amusement escaped the man's lips as he retorted, "Simply a messenger."

Fallyn's eyes narrowed as he approached the bed where Kathrin lay.

"It's only a pity that my message couldn't be a more pleasant one."

"Explain yourself."

The man looked over towards Fallyn and nodded slightly. "I believe you deserve as much."

When the concealed man leaned over Kathrin, Fallyn fought to stay where he stood. "Stay away from her!"

"A lifeless husk? Come now. Surely, I don't need to explain this out to you. Why do you think you've had such a bond with Kathrin?"

"'Twas simple irony is all," Fallyn grumbled towards the insensitivity of the words.

"Really? ... Funny. I've seen many ironic things in my days, yet none of them had me leaping out of windows."

Fallyn's neck prickled. How did he *know* that?

"You've must have felt something more than that, Fallyn. You've even awoken Kathrin of it before her passing."

"She was hardly making any sense," Fallyn muttered back.

"Oh, I'm sure she was. Are you sure you were really listening?" the man queried, lowering the duvet from Kathrin's chest. Fallyn's hands balled into fists as he restrained from decking the stranger. "Well, I guess it really doesn't matter now. After all, I'm sure you know the answer already. Kathrin was begging for your forgiveness over what happened to you."

"Do not speak in her stead!" Fallyn growled, watching the man as he began to wave his hands in a peculiar manner over her chest.

The man chuckled with a shake of his head, "How can you seriously claim there's nothing between you two when you're defending her, even in death? Alright, enough joking around. Tell me who she is."

"Kathrin," Fallyn snorted.

"Obviously, you haven't looked close enough. So, come here and tell me again who she is."

Fallyn sneered at the man's sarcasm as he looked over at Kathrin again, merely to please whatever insanity the man was trying to accomplish. For several minutes, he investigated her face as symbols that were once hidden beneath her skin now appeared in an illuminated glow— Fallyn's face blanched white.

"Tonia?!"

"Now you got it. Kathrin was Tonia all along."

Fallyn denied the words with a shake of his head as he stumbled back. "It cannot be! I witnessed her death- she died ages before!"

"You certainly did, Fallyn. Yet, I'm sure- by now- you've figured out that you've also become a pawn in something far greater by rescuing her that fateful night.

But I assure you, Kathrin *is* Tonia."

Fallyn was speechless while the man explained the bigger scheme in play. "Fallyn, you know that the battle for Earth has existed since the beginning. The heavens and hell have been trying to gain worshipers from the mortal playground to continue their growth. After a few thousand years of witnessing this, the creators deemed Earth a planet to destroy because man seemed inevitably incapable of anything but evil. But, because they wanted proof of this madness, they gave the world three chances to prove it should be saved instead. The first one was whom many praised as the son of God, Jesus. He was the avatar of purity. The second was Lady Tonia, who never awoke into her awareness before her demise."

"- She had *no* purity." Fallyn snarled bitterly. "She bore a child out of wedlock."

"Which was completely by the creator's doing. They impregnated her before she even met you, then wiped from her mind. So, she never deceived you because she never knew it happened."

"Then why do such an act?"

"When they foresaw that humanity's second chance would be cut short, they believed breeding an angelic line would be the only positive outcome. So, Tonia's offspring was given to a barren family to guard it. Then, her life continued as if nothing happened."

The markings were now deeply impressed into Kathrin's bluish skin. Fallyn's curiosity couldn't be ignored any longer. "What are you doing?"

"I'm calling forth the Arch Angel of Judgment. The time of your end is upon you."

"What?!?"

The man nodded as Kathrin's hair began to turn crimson, "Kathrin was the final chance for humanity to save themselves. There is no more."

"Cease your actions!" Fallyn panicked, lunging at the man to thrust him aside.

Fallyn's hands began to burn, the tips of his fingers melting away even before they touched the fringes of the man's attire, although he was still capable of following through with the act.

Cursing as he regained his balance, the man bellowed, "You cannot change it now! This is what has been decided!"

"Man must be given more of a chance than the simple affliction of pain. What of the men who fight for justice?!"

"Fallyn... we know of your deeds- which was why we brought Tonia back to meet you. We had hoped you would've protected her as you have. It was only unfortunate that she was bitten. But now, it's too late."

"Wait! I beg of you! If humanity cannot redeem itself,

then at least give me a chance to prove its worth," Fallyn pleaded with the only thing he could think of.

The man looked at Fallyn, his expression- which was hidden under the veils of the cloak- full of contemplation. "You would prove man's worth even though you, too, were punished by the hells?"

Fallyn swallowed, looking over at Kathrin with longing, "Man is not to blame for my punishment, and I would do anything to spare them."

"How curious. I could have sworn your thoughts had blamed everyone else before, even Tonia."

Fallyn's head bowed at his shortcoming. "I passed judgment without knowing all sides of the debate. Would you not be doing the same thing if you do not allow humanity to fight for itself?"

"Time had surely made you wise, Fallyn."

Fallyn grunted. "Please, give us time to show the testimony of our convictions. Then, if I fall before there is enough cause for retribution, you may continue with your punishment."

The man pondered the plea for a moment, unbeknownst to Fallyn, debating with the gods silently before he announced: "You shall have your time, Fallyn. The world shall be spared if you can prove man's worth before you die."

The man returned to Kathrin and began to lift her

from her bed when Fallyn argued, "No! I want her by my side. Do not take her."

"You wish Tonia to stay with you? A woman who is so overwhelmed with remorse that she will undoubtedly shy away from you in guilt? When I spoke of her awakening, this was what I meant. It won't be the Kathrin you once knew if I let her live from this point."

The man's words were weighty on Fallyn's mind as he looked towards Kathrin.

"Let Kathrin's fate be as it would've been had you not intervened. Then, cleanse her mind of the conversation I had with her just as you had with Tonia's birthing of her sired child."

"You would chance Kathrin remaining dead?" Fallyn never ceased to amaze the man.

Fallyn cringed, knowing even if she survived, he might still need to remove her himself. "Yes."

The shrouded figure nodded, waving a hand around Kathrin to remove the incantations upon her body. Her skin fleshed color once more. Her hair returned to its chestnut self as the transparent markings receded into her skin. Then, Kathrin appeared as if nothing had ever happened.

"It is done. May fate rest in your favor, Fallyn," the man finally stated before disappearing in the blink of an eye.

Fallyn glanced around the room, pondering if he had dreamt the whole thing before sitting on the bed beside Kathrin. Then, he reached for a dagger hidden in the bedside drawer. Oh, how he prayed to see some sign of her again.

Seconds. Minutes. The time spanned for what seemed like forever as Fallyn gripped to some perverse level of hope. But when the time spanned for an abnormally long amount, Fallyn eventually sighed in defeat. *She is gone*, he moaned. It almost felt like a hole had grown in his chest. *Never shall I see the sparkle in her eyes again.* He placed the dagger back into the drawer.

"Rest well, Kathrin. Rest well."

He lifted to depart from the room to collect things for her burial when, unexpectedly, Kathrin lunged up from the mattress. She wheezed for air like a person drowning. Coughing and choking, her own lungs were barely able to fill enough of the air she needed. And, as she stared at the mattress, her hand grasped onto her throat impulsively.

"Kathrin?" Fallyn moaned, wary of moving any more than he already had.

Kathrin glanced up at him in despair as she croaked, "Dry...I can't breathe....Thirsty..."

She had turned.

Fallyn found himself giving a silent prayer, pleading to absolutely anything that could hear him for her to remain whole.

"Fallyn... I'm scared... what...do I do?"

A question for guidance. Vampires were blinded by instinct and bonded by violence. If she was even remotely evil as her brethren past, she wouldn't have needed to ask nor care for his guidance. Her fangs protruded from her mouth as sweat beaded her face. So impulsively, Fallyn returned to her side on the bed and offered his wrist.

"Here, Kathrin. Feed quickly."

She glanced at him in horror before the sheer thirst had her faint. Fallyn braced her shoulders as she fell back and shoved his wrist against the sharpened two-pronged fangs himself. He could feel his blood flow into her mouth. After only a minute, her lips impulsively suckled his life essence into her.

He knew he was disregarding so many rules- so many pacts- by feeding her from his vein, but it didn't matter. It was simply the two of them. And, although he wished he could deny it with every fiber of his being, he knew he cared for her too much to do anything else but help. He felt like he would give it all if it meant her survival, and that- in itself- perturbed him.

Fallyn watched Kathrin feed in oblivion while his mind reeled on the information he had learned. Kathrin was Tonia and Tonia hadn't deceived him after all. But even though this had comforted him, it didn't change his feelings towards Kathrin. They were both the same, but his care and connection were much stronger with her now than it ever was with Tonia. To Fallyn, Tonia was dead and there is where she would remain.

Kathrin fell back asleep after her thirst was quenched like a newborn infant would. Fallyn lowered her back onto the softened mattress. He hoped his mind wasn't misled as he returned the blankets to her. Yet, with his contemplation of the conversation and event thus far, Fallyn could do nothing but leave the room.

Chapter Thirteen

Disoriented, Kathrin opened her lids and looked around the room. She was surprised to be seen again. *Didn't I die?* She glanced around. Everything seemed okay. But then, as logic settled in, she pondered how it was possible to see her room in such pristine detail. There were no lights on and no candles flickering from the living room next to hers. But everything was so sharp it was like she was holding them in her own palm. Kathrin rubbed her head, baffled. Her last memories were a haze. The only thing she could vaguely recall were splotchy pictures of her in her death bed with Fallyn by her side before she passed, only to be driven out of the comforts of her bed with a thirst unlike anything she had ever felt before. Yet, she couldn't recall if even that was resolved. She raised herself from the bed, still feeling a little beside herself.

Actually, she never felt better than she did at that moment. She felt renewed, warm, and aware of everything around her. Could she even hear a mouse skittering across the floor in the quarters next to hers? Why did suddenly her home smell so different?

She had to search for Fallyn. Surely, he'd be able to tell her what happened. Was it all just a bad dream? She went into the shower and wash for the day. That was when she discovered that her skin was extremely sensitive, as well. Even the faintest touch of the breeze was like fingertips on her flesh. The water was like silk, each strand weaving an erotic dress of sensation around her figure. And the sound…it was both deafening and a mere whisper in the lobe of her ear. Kathrin wondered if she was listening to even more than the spray of the water upon her body, but she argued it off with improbability, although everything still remained so clear. She could see more acutely than she ever imagined was capable with the human eye.

After being cleansed and dressed in a baby blue spaghetti-strapped sun dress, Kathrin headed to the kitchen for her morning routine. Taking the first step into the room was like entering a food market as her nose flared with hundreds of different scents, none of which seemed appealing at all. Nonetheless, she made herself a cup of fruit and some tea just to be sure something was in her stomach while she waited for Fallyn to arrive.

She searched everywhere she could think of. She would've thought he was just gone for the night, yet his motorcycle was still parked in the entranceway. Was he deliberately hiding away from her? If he was, he was doing a damn good job at it.

Kathrin sat down at the table and eyed her fruit cup, unimpressed. She usually loved fruit. But the mere sight of it repulsed her, almost to the point of her stomach curdling. She tried to shrug it off and took a bite. She was barely able to chew the gritty contents enough to swallow, only to have to, a second later, spit it into a napkin with a gag.

"God... this is awful," she moaned aloud after emptying her mouth.

Kathrin took a sip of her tea to rinse her mouth of the chalky flavor, but even it tasted bitter, almost making her spit it up.

"I must have thrown my taste buds out of whack or something," she muttered as she shoved the meal aside.

Then, she glanced around the kitchen with a renewed perspective. Why hadn't she noticed the spider's nest in the corner of the room or the leaking faucet before? And why did everything finally smell damp like a watered cavern would? Lost in her thoughts, Kathrin scooped herself another bite of her meal to only choke and spit it out with a curse. Then, like a breeze of warning in the wind, a distinct odor filled the room.

"You cannot enjoy the luxuries once gifted to you, Kathrin," Fallyn spoke up by the edge of the doorway.

She looked over at him with confusion. "I really must have gotten a cold or something for, my God, these taste horrible! What happened last night? I had a really horrible dream."

Fallyn was dumbfounded by the question and even

more unsure how to answer it after the explosion of knowledge that he had learned and requested her to forget.

"What dream burdened you?"

Her eyes returned to the tea again with distaste, and she pushed it further away before she answered. "Well, I was dying- I knew that much- and you remained at my bedside till my passing. You were just assuring me that things would be okay. Then I slipped away. But I remember a thirst lunged me from the bed before I passed out once more."

"Kathrin," Fallyn acknowledged tactfully after a minute of thought. "What you recalled was no dream. It has been a few nights since that event took place."

She definitely wasn't prepared to hear that. "I died?"

Fallyn nodded slowly as he approached the table and sat beside her. He even seemed bewildered by this situation, although he composed himself quite well.

"Then...the thirst?" she moaned, knowing what it meant, although she prayed he'd say it was something else. Anything else.

"Kathrin, you have turned. You are now brethren to the vampires."

She was dazed by the answer for the longest time. She wanted to believe that even this was a nightmare, that she would wake up in a minute, and that it would all be over. But it didn't. Her daze turned into panic, "No...no...it was just a bad dream! I've gotten a cold, and that's why I can't eat the fruit. I-"

"Kathrin," Fallyn called, reaching over to place his hand on her arm for comfort. "I speak nothing but truth."

She looked at him with fear of what it meant. From what Fallyn had told her, vampires were mindless, heartless monsters who wanted nothing more than to kill anything they could. She didn't want to become such a thing! The thought frightened her.

"I am sorry, Kathrin. The Almighty above knows of the guilt that courses heavily through my veins, but the deed is irreversible."

Her horror reminded Fallyn so much of himself when he had been cursed. The shock, the loneliness, the fear of being a predator now hunted. He could more than empathize with her. Yet, she wasn't what he ever dealt with before. She didn't even understand what happened until she was informed of it. What kind of vampire does that?

Her tears fell as she bit her lip to hide her anguish. So, this was what Fallyn meant when he said one day, she would know what rules she would be held to. Even though his hand laid upon her arm for support, she felt completely alone. This was her pain, her problem, and she had to learn to deal with it herself.

"So...I will never see the sun again?" she quivered.

Fallyn wished he could have wrapped her up in his arms and told her it would work out in the end. But frankly, he didn't know if it would. "It would be fatal, Kathrin."

She nodded again, using the palm of her hand to wipe away her tears before she quickly left the table to dispose of her breakfast. Then, she began washing dishes in the sink. Fallyn watched her from his seat as her anguish bled off her aura. At that moment, she firmed his resolve about her. Although she had become immortal, her heart was human. Fallyn rose from his seat, skipping the wooden legs against the marble floor. The only acknowledgment of his approach was when he came up behind her.

Kathrin blurted out to the response of his nearness to keep her sorrow hidden, " It's okay, Fallyn. I'll deal with it. I'm really okay-"

Fallyn spun her around and pressed her deep into the comforts of his chest. His arms twined around her body; his hands held her head and torso close. She needed him and his strength. When Kathrin felt the warmth of his embrace, her pent-up tears poured out by the handfuls.

Kathrin shuddered against him, somehow knowing that, no matter what would come, Fallyn would always be there.

"I don't want to be a vampire… I don't want to hurt anyone…"

Fallyn simply held her close. No words, no judgment, just the simple need to take all her pain away.

"Kathrin," he started but stopped before his words left his mouth. By the Gods, he wanted to claim her for his own. Why was he being so irrational?

You must not lose yourself.

She lifted her eyes to meet his. They were hurt and pleading; Her beauty was angelic. The vampiric blood within her had enhanced her features. There was a miraculous difference to what it once was. Her eyes were brighter, her lips fuller, and her hair voluminous. She looked like she was plucked from the stars. Even now, her hair played tantalizingly with her shoulders.

"Forgive my errors," he stammered thoughtlessly as his heart spilled faster than his guard could sustain. "For I have stained you unjustly by not preventing the actions that have turned you that night."

His fingers rose from her back to caress her neck. How he wished he could muster the spell that would be able to remove the bite and its curse.

Kathrin shook her head, "I've never blamed you. I will never blame you."

Her eyes, now that they were fused with vampiric cells, were hazed to metallic. Even her canines seemed to protrude a little. But she was radiant. All of her.

His head leaned down, nearing his lips to hers.

Somewhere in the back of his mind, he knew he shouldn't be considering the thought that his body screamed. Yet, Fallyn didn't care. God, nothing mattered but the two of them. She closed her eyes to his approach; her lips parted invitingly.

His mouth brushed hers, ever gently, as his arms crushed her against him, sending flutters of desire down to her core. She melted completely when he finally pressed his lips against hers, his tongue playing seductively. She couldn't hide her moan, nor could she find support to hold herself up with her knees. Yet, Fallyn pulled away only enough to trail kisses from her lips to her chin and then to her neck. Slowly, tenderly, affectionately.

"Fallyn," she whimpered earnestly, her fingers twining in his hair. "Don't stop."

Kathrin knew she had said something wrong as he stiffened and backed away. He looked bewildered and ashamed, his feet almost tripping over themselves. Kathrin brought her hand to her chest to calm the flame of desire he spurned from her. "I'm sorry."

His eyes looked at hers as he continued to back away. It was an agonizing moment before he groaned, "F-forgive me, Kathrin. My actions...they were impulsive."

Kathrin couldn't imagine what he was thinking with his horrified stare, but she didn't have a chance to say anything before he added, "It shall not happen again."

Then, he left the room. Actually, he couldn't have run fast enough as he fled the kitchen. Kathrin wondered if she did something more horrible than being there.

She did, Kathrin thought after a few minutes. She had turned into a vampire.

Fallyn growled at himself for the hundredth time for what he had done. He went against all logic and understanding and, once again, let his desires blind him from the truth. She was a vampire, a blood-sucking demon! They were mindless and insane with carnage!

But even as he thought it, the other half of him argued that Kathrin wasn't any of these, even after she had turned.

Perhaps it was a trap, he tried to reason. Surely a way to protect herself from an inevitable death otherwise? But then, why would she cry once she realized what she was? Even someone who was a great actor could hardly pull that off. Before Fallyn knew where he was heading, he found himself at the edge of the woods, where he met with Hakeem. He arrived speedily, not even giving Hakeem a greeting before the gate was opened to devour him.

"Why did you not tell me she would turn vampire!?" Fallyn roared before Hakeem was even in sight.

"Did you doubt she would?" Hakeem replied without agitation.

"She is a vampire, Hakeem, not a woman plagued by spirits. You cannot correct what courses in her veins!" Fallyn growled as he stormed towards the cavern.

"Is this anger because she's a vampire or because you cannot correct it?" Hakeem pondered.

"This anger is because I have a vampire in my haven, and I cannot bring myself to kill it!"

Hakeem made a grunt of doubt as Fallyn entered the room, shifting his weight as Fallyn pulled out his sword in a threatening manner towards Hakeem.

"And I'm at fault for your path being trying?"

Fallyn roared his rage at the top of his lungs, "You deceived me! You were to tell me what was to become of her!"

"You didn't even care to listen longer than her heritage. That wasn't my fault," Hakeem countered, his own voice rising.

Fallyn hated that Hakeem was right. He stewed with his unbridled rage of self-contempt until he pierced his sword into the dry soil and began to storm back and forth in front of Hakeem. Minutes passed with his frustration before he snarled, "A vampire is an unquenchable monster of evil! I have seen the similarities. It should be no different with her!"

"Then, why is she still alive? Kill her and be done with it." Hakeem retorted flatly, although he knew that

Kathrin was more than Fallyn depicted her as.

Fallyn looked at Hakeem's thousands of eyes. Kill her. I need to kill her. But the thought of completing an order directed by the Infernal felt more like manslaughter. Even now, he could only see her in his arms, his lips on hers as they were but an hour before.

"It feels wrong to do the task," he shook his head. It angered him that he was feeling this sensation that he shouldn't be. "My hand falls away from any objective when it is in the thought of her! It cannot be this way! She is evil incarnate. She will slay thousands if I do not finish her off now!"

"Tell me what she's done to prove such demonic behavior."

Fallyn growled as he began to pace again, reminding Hakeem of a panther traveling agitated from side to side against the bars of a cage.

"If you can name them, then I'll agree with you."

Fallyn stared at the ground while he turned and followed the beaten path that he made. He shook his head finally. There were none. She didn't even know that the event was real until he told her.

"So, Kathrin has become a vampire but has ignored tradition in your mind, huh?"

Fallyn didn't reply. He knew Hakeem knew the answer already. Hakeem gestured slowly.

"Well, why don't you kill me too? I am- most certainly- from the blood of the dark. What saves me from your hand?"

" Your decision to abandon your station to aid me," Fallyn replied, finally coming to a stop within his tracks as he processed it through.

"I see. So, because 'I've seen the light,' I'm allowed to live."

Fallyn's brow furrowed at Hakeem's mockery.

"You're cursed by sin, yet you're marked a mercenary of virtue. Why can't Kathrin become the same, "Hakeem asked finally.

Kathrin be virtuous?

The question diffused any anger he had as he found his seat on a nearby rock. Why couldn't she be the same as him? She certainly didn't follow anything like the rest of the vampires. She kept her reasoning, like he did. After hundreds of years, someone was born for humanity once again.

"It is difficult to open my horizons beyond what is ingrained," Fallyn acknowledged after a few minutes.

"It always is, Fallyn. But I promise you nothing but good is in her future," Hakeem smiled.

Fallyn arched a brow, "Are you sure?"

"You know I cannot divulge such details. Yet know that in the many years to come, you will be proud of your choice today."

Chapter Fourteen

Many days passed between them in silence, Kathrin brooding on her becoming a vampire and how it had changed her involvement with Fallyn while Fallyn kept his distance from her completely. Yet even though everything between them had changed dramatically from the moment they were in the kitchen, Kathrin would never regret that intimate moment they shared. Even days later, if she closed her eyes, she could envision the feel of his lips and hands against hers. Kathrin has hoped that his detached behavior would've calmed somewhat as time progressed. When it didn't, though, Kathrin began to think the worst.

It was obviously because she was a vampire, she thought. How could he let her remain like this and not be forced to kill her? Perhaps that was why he wasn't hanging around, so Kathrin could have a chance to flee before he would hunt her down just like the rest. But where on earth would she go, Kathrin wondered. She didn't know anything about the workings of the abyss, nor did she want to know. What she wanted was to stay here with Fallyn, but somehow, she felt that that time had come to an end.

Kathrin decided, after torturous hours of debate, that the only way she could figure out what she had to do next was to come hear it from Fallyn himself. Maybe if she heard the words from his mouth, it would shock her back to reality.

When Kathrin finally found Fallyn, he was near the back of his domain, sitting on a ledge of a cliff-like abyss. It was raw and untouched, as any cavern normally would be, unlike the stone-like castle carved at the mouth of the cave. Like always, he was deep in thought, perplexed with things she only vaguely knew. She wished she could understand the man who helped her so much but spoke so little. What was between them? At times, he was so endearing, loving, and compassionate, and then, the next, so reclusive. She swallowed hard with what she knew must be done and approached.

Fallyn continued to ignore her when she crouched to sit beside him. She turned her attention toward him, barely able to see his features that were hiding under the locks of his untamed hair. Yet, she spotted his copper eyes glance her way for but a second before they turned away once more. At least he acknowledged her, she thought.

Minutes passed in awkward silence as Kathrin tried to find the words to ask her questions. But now that she was next to him, they all became a mottled blur.

"What troubles you?" Fallyn asked first.

Kathrin twined her fingers amongst themselves. It was now or never. "If I were to ask you something, would you answer it no matter the topic?"

Fallyn's distant stare didn't falter as he nodded in reply minutes later. She hoped he'd honor it.

"Well, before my turning, you taught me many things about how I could protect myself against creatures of the night, including vampires. But you knew all along that I was going to be cursed to that very fate, didn't you?"

Fallyn rose himself off the cliffside as he cut in quickly, "It is late, Kathrin-"

"- Please!" she cried, raising herself up just a hastily. "I need to know!"

When he continued to walk away, she cried louder: "Fallyn, PLEASE!"

Fallyn stopped in his tracks as he sighed exasperatingly, "Kathrin-"

Kathrin closed the distance as quickly as she could. "Please, Fallyn, I've just got to know!" When he didn't respond to her plea, she continued in a calmer voice. "You knew all along that I might become one of them, didn't you?"

With a brief pause, Fallyn answered, "Yes."

"But the vampire is what you've vowed to hunt, a monster I've seen you kill before. You've even told me they were the Infernal's greatest threat. They're horrid beasts that you despise and take pride in destroying them. So, if you knew I was going to be one of them, why train me?" She cried out with emotion, feeling the tears she hadn't meant to fall over her questioning present on her cheeks.

Fallyn just stood with his back towards her and remained silent. Not a motion, not a breath. Kathrin wished he would speak and soothe the fears that ate her up inside. "You hate vampires. Your sole purpose is to destroy them all. So, why did you SAVE ME!?!?"

Kathrin fell onto the ground in uncontrollable sobs, her tears overflowing between her fingers. This one question had been eating away at her from the moment she realized what she had become. How she wished she was back in the days when she only had to be concerned with one life. To deal with the thought of dying a second time, after already knowing how it felt the first time, was unbearable to think of. She didn't notice when Fallyn turned around to face her, nor did she notice him kneeling and resting his hand on her shoulder.

"Kathrin," he soothed. "Kathrin, your fear is for not."

This comment didn't calm her, though; it didn't even get her to the point of reasoning. She had been so concerned with this that she was practically in a frenzy while she blundered through her turmoil.

"Why?" she sobbed uncontrollably. "It's only a matter of time before I'm on your list! What if I become the monster you hunt or- better yet- the one that turned me? I don't want to kill anyone! I don't want to be like that!"

Fallyn tried to keep his thoughts collected as she became more and more hysterical. Yet, each time he tried to soothe her with reassurance, she didn't hear it and only sobbed louder. He understood it, though, recalling his own days of fear when he was first introduced to the darkness. How could he reach her, though?

Flustered for the first time in centuries, Fallyn grabbed both of her arms, lifted her off the ground, and crushed her against his chest. Kathrin's eyes enlarged in surprise at the act. Yet, although she found comfort in his arms, the tears wouldn't cease to fall.

"Kathrin, do not cry. You are safe with me. That I vow." His mouth was merely inches from her ear as he spoke in the most tender of voices.

"But what if I change? What if I become like them? It would only be right to kill me..."

His hand pressed her head further into his chest as his lips rested on the brow of her forehead. Even the sound of his rhythmical heartbeat soothed her anxiety. Did she feel a slight quiver in his arms while he held her?

"Kathrin... you are not what you fear. To even become creatures such as that, you would have to have a soul bound with some form of evil. Yours is purer than the silvered moon." Fallyn clenched her tighter, barely able to restrain his own emotions: "But even if your mind twisted to that of your fears, I could never, would never harm you.

You are too special for such a fate."

Fallyn suddenly noted that the very restraints that slipped on him before were about to do so again. So, he abruptly released her, spinning on his heels to walk away. He couldn't become the man who let his feelings blind him like they had so many years ago. If he had his naive feelings under check, then he might have been able to react more quickly and do the right thing. He could have saved them so long ago.

"Good night, Kathrin."

Kathrin was stunned by the flip of emotions, seeing the depth of him that she never thought she would again. But, when he widened the distance between them, she just couldn't fathom going back to the way they were before. No, not again. Panicked that she was losing him forever, she reached out and clenched onto his shoulder.

"Fallyn, wait," she called. But, as the tips of her nails touched the covered skin on his blade, Fallyn let out a hiss of piercing severity and fell to his knees.

"What's wrong? What happened!" she gasped as she impulsively snatched her hand away.

He squinted his eyes at the throb that bled from the back of his spine and oozed up into his skull. Then, sweat beaded his temples as he balled his fists against the pain. Stop the spinning, stop the spinning.... Even his strength weakened substantially. He hadn't realized the venom had spread so viciously. He could almost feel its pulse in his shoulder and nothing else. Looking for level ground, Fallyn needed anything to balance his dizzy head. Then, glancing over at Kathrin, his eyes began to blur. He saw her call his name but heard nothing. He felt himself falling, falling. A blackness was pulling him under. Yet, before he was swallowed whole, he could only muster a single word.

"Kathrin…"

When Fallyn collapsed onto the ground, Kathrin could hardly hide her fears. She cried in horror as she fell to her knees and shook him violently while he lay motionless on the ground. She didn't know what happened, but her mind reeled in worry. Trying to review the events that passed seconds before, she remembered touching his shoulder.

"An injury?" she shuddered as she looked over to the blade in question.

After a moment of wonder, her mind set on what she needed to do. She couldn't leave him to fend on his own if it was this far gone. She leaned across his body to tug off his coat, having it off him within minutes. Beneath, he had a soft silk-like shirt on that hid practically nothing. That was when she saw a black veined monstrosity marring his shoulder. She gasped aloud. It was almost like his shoulder was rotting off from gangrene! With that fear, she didn't give thought to the care of the remainder of his clothing as she tore the material wide open to see the wound in full.

In the center of this black infection was a swollen welt with a cream look to its texture. It was almost like a boil rising to the surface of his skin, ready to break free. She shuddered. She was surprised she wasn't gagging from the sight of it, knowing full well how she used always to find things like that nauseating. She pondered if she had to thank the vampirism for that. Yet, she didn't focus on it any further than that before Fallyn let out a groan.

Assessing the situation, Kathrin tried to identify a step-by-step process that would work best. But, in the end, all she could think of was removing the puss from the wound before she could determine more thereafter. She rummaged in the legs of Fallyn's pants, recalling seeing a dagger hidden there once before. Suddenly, a ghostly whisper echoed gauntly in the air.

"No... don't do it..."

Startled, Kathrin glanced around to see who had spoken it, but no one was there. After a moment, she grasped onto the knife in his boot and brought it over the wound when the soft whisper echoed again.

"No... it will not work..."

She glanced around again before she queried nervously: "Who's there?"

"No one is here...."

"Then, who's speaking?"

"I am the blood in your veins," the small sound soothed.

"'The blood in my veins'?" she pondered sarcastically. "My blood doesn't speak! Who are you?"

"When a vampire child is young, your blood calls to the elements for guidance. I am this."

"Guidance?" she questioned before her face paled horribly white. The knife fell from her fingers onto the floor as her hands slammed against her ears, shaking her head violently in refusal.

"No, I will not lose my sanity! I will stay true to myself! I will not be a monster!!"

"Child, I do not convert. I am only knowledge."

"I don't believe you! I'm not a murderer! I'm not a murderer!!" she screamed frantically, closing her eyes.

"Child, listen. Your ally has little time as it is."

Her shakes of refusal suddenly stopped with a lower of her hands. "Little time? Oh no!"

"Yes, but with my aid, you can save him."

"You're trying to have me kill him!" she spat, too afraid to believe that this could possibly be happening.

"No, child. I will help you achieve what you desire. I do not convert."

After a minute of thought, she tested the voice to see

if the answer could be trusted. "Then, why can't I use the knife? I'm trying to clean the wound!"

"If you use that knife, child, you will harm him greater than this infection has. Use your nails instead. If you wish, it will be just as sharp."

The answer gave Kathrin the satisfaction she needed. If this was the only help she would have, she would gladly take it. She raised her nails into her view. "My nails? How do I make it that sharp?"

"Keep in focus what you seek, believing it is possible, and it will happen."

Nodding slightly, Kathrin did as instructed. It didn't take long for her pointer nail to become exactly that.

"Well done, child. It takes most much longer to reach their goal the first time."

"I don't have time for my ignorance. Fallyn needs my help, and I know nothing of what I'm facing," she muttered, her fear of losing Fallyn turning into inner rage.

"It is a bite from a Digornath, a lesser demon- or a mutt- in the vampire society. His strength is what saved him thus far."

Wasn't a Digornath the beast that Fallyn faced the night of her rescue?

Kathrin couldn't help but pale at the thought of the injury resulting from him coming to her rescue. And to ignore it for so long in silence without complaint almost made her nauseous with guilt.

"What do I do next?" she cut in, trying to speed up the medical attention required.

"Use your nail and cut two incisions, one overlapping the first like an addition sign."

Without thought, she did as she was told, finding it odd that it didn't ooze when she did.

"Why didn't it puss?" she inquired, concerned she had done something wrong.

"This is not like that of a mankind infection. Now, lift the skin you had cut apart. You will see a white stone, that of a pearl. Do not remove it yet. You must be prepared."

"Prepared?" she asked, wondering what this spirit thought she was doing currently to make her any less ready.

"Yes. Hold your off-hand out and engrave the markings you will see on your palm with either the dagger or your nail."

"Markings?" Just as she spoke the confused words, a silhouette of runes appeared on her palm. She inhaled a knowing breath of the pain to come.

"It must be done to help your ally."

"I know," she groaned before using her nail to trace over the lines, wincing a little with each symbol she inscribed. Once completed, the voice continued once more.

"Now, be prepared to work quickly; this is a larva of the Digornath and will try to escape once released."

"A- a larva!?!" she gasped. She never assumed it was anything alive!

"Calm yourself, child. It will only consume him if you leave it. It is already close to his heart."

She swallowed hard as she felt her skin cool with uneasiness. All she could do was nod nervously as she replied.

"You will have to snatch it with your nails and quickly pull it out. You will feel it struggle, but do not let go. If you release it, it will bury further into his body, and his chances for survival will become slim to none. Once you remove it, throw it into your hand with the symbols and hold it tightly. No matter what happens or what you may see, do not release it, for this is the only way to separate its hold on your ally."

She swallowed, a bit repulsed by what had to be done before she readied her hand atop the larvae. Like a countdown inside her head, she suddenly lashed out at the larvae. She followed with a just-as-quick tug of it out of Fallyn's shoulder. The texture was jello soft. Her nail pierced the membrane layer in a gruesome pop. Fallyn let out a wail of pain in his unconscious state that almost made her lose her grasp.

"Careful, child!"

She could feel the fight of the Digornath larvae as it tried to pull away. She had to end Fallyn's pain before it was too late! Fighting against her disgust, she yanked it out with all of her might.

The larva was much larger than she had anticipated. The top of the head, where she had held, was pale white and oblong like a bird's egg while, at the bottom, there was a razor mouth of deep black, surrounded with tentacles of various sizes. In her moment of observation, the larvae let out a horrific squeal, and Fallyn began to convulse on the ground. Kathrin stumbled back at the sight, mortified.

"Quick, Child! Put it in your palm of symbols before it's too late!"

Kathrin forced the larvae into her off-hand, which resulted in the larva shrieking in agony, writhing around in her clenched palm.

"Hold it tight. Do not let go."

Focusing while wincing at the pitch of the squeal, Kathrin observed that by holding fast onto the larvae as it writhed about, the smaller it became. Once it shrunk into the size of a tooth in her hand, only then did Fallyn finally still. An eerie moment of silence passed, disturbingly quiet.

Shuddering, she moaned, "Can I release it?"

"Yes, it is safe now. Complete your task by slicing it

in two. Do this, and it will be no more."

With relief, Kathrin sighed and quite happily followed through. In that very second, a breath of dark mist escaped from Fallyn's lips.

"He shall mend now. But he needs the venom cleansed from his bloodstream."

Kathrin nodded as she returned her gaze back to his shoulder.

"What of the incision?" she queried, not analyzing the spirit's direction anymore.

"That is the final step; first, you must clean it."

Looking around briefly toward random objects that could assist her, she pondered aloud, "How do I do that?"

"Drain it in feeding."

Kathrin paled. She couldn't dare acknowledge the vampire within her. "Feeding!?! No. No. No! I am not going to kill him! I will not become a monster!!"

"Child-"

"- And stop calling me that!"

"...Kathrin, it is natural for you to feed. It is a part of your life cycle now. If you do not, you will die."

"But if I feed, I'll kill him!"

"No, Kathrin, you won't. You will only harm if you wish to harm. You will not hurt him. And don't worry about the venom. It will not harm you."

She twined her fingers in awkward terror. This

would be her first deliberate feeding. What if something went wrong? What if the voice was lying, and she would hurt Fallyn? She looked over at the wound again, then over to the side of Fallyn's face. His face looked troubled, although he was unaware of his predicament. She knew she needed to help him, and if feeding was the way to help, would she really refuse to do it?

"How- How will I know when I'm going too far?"

"Kathrin... You will know..."

She closed her eyes and nodded, then swallowed hard before she looked back at the venom in Fallyn's skin. The idea of feeding to remove the poison, tasting his blood, gave her an unusual thrill that shrilled down her spine. Her teeth began to ache with hunger, almost giving her the impulse to impale them into his flesh just to ease the discomfort. Instinctively, she buried her teeth into the skin near the incision; the hot liquid instantly filled her mouth. With the first gulp, she was wary, unsure of the unholy act. But, as the fluid hit her belly, she became dizzy with enjoyment.

The flavor was sweet and electrifying with power. It was like she was bathing in the rays of Fallyn's strength, that wondrous magic in his blood. It took everything she could to keep her head from swimming dizzily. But, amongst the succulence, there was laced a spice of bitterness and rot.

'Remove the poison,' she moaned to herself as she began to lose herself in the sweetness.

She could almost feel her fingers reaching into his mind, grabbing onto a handle of a door that he sealed away from everyone. Yet, when she turned the handle and opened it slowly, she was suddenly bombarded with many visions of his. The visions were of things in his past, but as quickly as one would enter her mind, so too would that of another. But, for once in her life, she finally understood. Everything about him made sense now as she felt closer to Fallyn than ever before.

A hand touched her shoulder gently, and she turned to greet Fallyn, who was standing behind her in his full glory. There was no hat, no trench coat, just him in the comforts of his own persona. His eyes seemed to smile for the first in a long time as he gently spoke, "It is done, Kathrin."

Hearing his words, she nodded, and the wave of their mind-link ended. In her awareness, the bitterness in his blood was finally gone. She lifted her mouth away with a final swallow. Yet, without having the spirit instructing her to do so, Kathrin licked the wounds. She couldn't place a finger on it, but she felt right to drag her tongue across each of the incisions, and- by doing so- they would seal as if they were never there.

"Well done, Kathrin. You are learning quickly to trust

your instincts."

Kathrin could feel her cells were revived as she sat back on her haunches. She scanned over where the damage should have been, but it was like it was nothing but a dream.

"Thank you," she whispered towards the spirit who helped but got no reply thereafter.

Kathrin couldn't help but feel a level of accomplishment. Why couldn't she be proud of the things she did to save him? What was better was that the price wasn't as steep as she thought it would be. She didn't have to lose what humanity she had left. Kathrin realized, then, that what the spirit and Fallyn had both tried to assure her was true. It wasn't being a vampire that twisted you, but what was in your heart. All the abilities she learned tonight were for good. If the talents she gained were not evil, then that meant that Kathrin could remain herself.

Feeling the strength that flowed in her veins, she smiled slightly as she looked back towards Fallyn and sighed, " Now to see you to bed."

Chapter Fifteen

As the day came to a close, Fallyn watched the sun as its rays gave a final kiss to his cheeks before it sunk behind mountains. She should have been here by now, Fallyn thought, perturbed. They were supposed to meet in the midafternoon to flee from their stations by ship on the eve of the night. Yet, as Fallyn glanced towards the dirt-beaten road she would have arrived upon, there was still no sign of her. Now, the ship was to leave within the hour, and he began to fear the worst. Did her family find out their plan and had bound indoors to keep her from him? As his concerns overwhelmed his every thought, he suddenly found himself racing towards her home. He needed to know what had happened. Neither the strain on his limbs nor the stumbling stopped him. Yet the closer he got to Tonia's home, the more eerie the silence became. Not even a cricket was heard. Fallyn was too focused on seeing her once more to notice.

Suddenly, a scream echoed further down the passage. It was a voice he knew as well as his own.

"Tonia!?!" he exclaimed with new-found vigor. He had never heard that level of fear before, and it cut him down to the core.

"Tonia, I am coming!! Hold on!!"

His steps were too slow, and the crest of the hill

seemed so far away. Her screams didn't seem to be getting any louder. But finally, something appeared over the crest of the pathway, and Fallyn came to a halt.

She was in but a pale gown as she stumbled toward Fallyn, her gown covered in painted sprays of what look like blood.

"Tonia!!" Fallyn exclaimed, racing towards her.

Clenching onto her petite frame, he eased what bile had reached his throat. "Tonia, what has happened?"

Her face was stained with tears and stricken horror. "My…my family… they are all dead…."

"Dead??" he questioned, too stunned to believe it. "How?? Why??"

Tonia's head shook slowly as her mind relived the madness. "Beasts… horrid man-beasts struck them down… PLEASE, we must RUN!"

"Beasts? Tonia, beasts?? It is not possible!"

"Please, Fallyn, please-" she cried until her eyes bulged open, her words becoming caught in the back of her throat.

"Tonia?!" Fallyn exclaimed. But, as he raised his arms to accommodate her falling weight, he noticed the object that had caused her stutter.

"Tonia!!" he cried out again as she slid from his grasp. Fallyn saw that a dagger was embedded in her spine.

"Fallyn…. Run-away…" she gagged, blood slipping out of the corner of her lips.

He looked around frantically to find where the dagger had come from but saw nothing. His eyes returned to hers, tear stricken, as he soothed, "You will be fine. I will not leave you!"

"Fallyn…Please…" but as her final breath escaped her lips and her body grew limp, he was devastated with the knowledge that she was no more.

"Tonia!! Tonia, wake up. Please!!" he sobbed, holding her close to his chest. "I cannot live without you!"

He held her there for what seemed like only seconds when something massive impaled his own back, making him stiffen in agony before he coughed out blood. It felt as if his body was practically in two when a deep masculine voice chuckled behind him, "A pity for you, lad, to have met this family."

Fallyn gritted his teeth as he prayed for the moment to stop. Instead, the obstruction began to spin and twine in his back. He could only guess it was something like a claw as the torture made him yell out, dropping Tonia to the ground. Then, his body rose from the earth, even higher than his own feet could stand. He was helpless as he dangled in the air at the whims of a madman.

"Why?" he coughed out, blood dripping from the corners of his mouth.

Instantly, he was tossed aside twenty feet away as the claw ripped apart what once kept it together. Fallyn squinted towards the sky as it began to thunder, the raindrops slowly finding their way onto his face as his eyelids rose and fell in exhaustion. Fallyn could hear, all too well, the footsteps approach. The slow even strides from the person who sealed his fate. Then, they were upon him, standing in the pool of blood that flowed from Fallyn.

"May the gates of hell greet you with open arms, child," he remarked, looking briefly into Fallyn's eyes before he strode away. Fallyn felt his life slipping away as the end of the rotting darkness reached for his soul. But all he could think of was Tonia. He rolled onto his side with what little strength he had, only to cough up more blood. He looked at Tonia, so far away.

"Tonia," he groaned.

He had to reach her. His arm outstretched in an attempt to close the distance enough to touch her, but he just couldn't. His eyes felt ever so heavy. He wanted to close them once and for all, and there was no more will to fight it.

Fallyn opened his eyes, somewhat stunned to be seeing his lair once more. His memory seemed so real to not believe it was happening all over again. It was a distant recollection from his youth. It rather amazed him that he recalled it with such detail even though he knew he would never forget. How could he have? It was his fault that Tonia met the same fate as her family. It was his naivete and blindness that caused her to die and forfeit the second chance for mankind. For that, he would never forget nor forgive himself. That was why he kept his emotions in check; they were the ones that hindered him when he was needed most. That was why he vowed it would never happen again. Never.

"Fallyn, you're alright," Kathrin sighed in relief as she rose from her seat and brushed the hairs that strayed onto his brow.

Startled, he glanced over at Kathrin and saw nothing but concern. Her eyes were just like Tonia's. They were as tender and soft, everything that drew him to Tonia in the first place so long ago. Yet, although their looks were parallel, Kathrin was very different and so much more. When Tonia would hit obstacles in her life, she would have felt defeated and shied away in her misery. Kathrin had already proven that she challenges her turmoil and rises to battle another. It was an admirable quality that brought beauty to her even more. But he couldn't open his heart to a woman again. He didn't want anyone to face that level of pain again like he did before.

"You are very lucky, Fallyn, "Kathrin smiled.

At that moment, Fallyn realized that he felt the best

he had in months.

"I assume it was more than I guessed," Fallyn retorted as he stared up toward the ceiling.

"Way more, you stubborn ox. You were near death. Heck, you've been out for quite some time, Fallyn."

Fallyn smirked slightly at that retort. It was the first time Kathrin had used a nickname on him, and Fallyn knew it was rather suited to him. He highly doubted the truth was exactly as she said, though. "I assure you, it would take more than venom to harm me."

Kathrin was very excited to share with Fallyn her enthralling discovery of herself and how she aided him. But she could tell by his comment that he'd probably doubt her anyhow. So, instead, she simply smiled.

"You're probably right, Fallyn. Here, let me get you some food," she cooed. She leaned over to the end table nearby to reach for a tray of fruits and pieces of bread she had brought in shortly before his awakening. Then, placing the meal beside him, she began to offer it to Fallyn when his hand snapped a hold of her own.

"What are these?" he questioned abruptly, raising onto his elbow to examine her hand more closely; it was the one she carved the symbols on.

She tried to close her hand to hide away her scars from him, but with a simple press of his thumb on her wrist, he took her strength away to fight his investigation. "It's nothing. I was just practicing-"

"These are incantations for severing possession," he stated, his stare narrowing onto hers.

Her face flushed as she averted her eyes and pulled her hand out of his palm. "It's really nothing, Fallyn, I -"

"You should realize, by now, that you are a very poor liar," he interrupted. His glare never faltered from hers, although she glanced away.

With an exhale, she tried to muster the courage to look at him once more. Yet, when her gaze returned, the words she attempted to say instantly trailed off. "I helped you get…. better…"

She could see the deep worry in his eyes for the first time in what seemed like forever. He was afraid he wasn't there in her time of need. Kathrin swallowed hard as she blushed again.

"Are you hurt?"

Kathrin stuttered, almost losing her seat as she tried to find the words to say. "Me? Fallyn, it was you who was hurt. I saved you!"

"I was not possessed-"

"Not possessed?!" She cried as she stood up, frustrated that he was denying his peril. "If you weren't possessed, then why did I have to carve these into my hand?! Why did I have to do all the things I did to take that Digornath larva out of your back and dispose of it?! But lord knows you believe enough about the venom. So, I guess all I did was suck out the poison that was festering in your body!!"

As the words spilled from her mouth, her face became stained with tears. She knew she would regret them later, but she just couldn't stop. How could she when the fear she felt before re-exposed itself just by quickly explaining everything that happened before? So disheartened, she spun around and stormed out of the room.

"Who taught you the symbols?"

"You figure it out!"

As she twined in and out of the corridors, she couldn't stop her tears. He was so close to death, and it didn't even matter. She didn't know how long she walked aimlessly around the hallways before she found herself at a dead end. Then, she sat down in the corner.

Kathrin didn't understand why his distrust was like a dagger piercing her heart. She always believed him- even if it sounded impossible- for he never gave her any reason not to. But now, the one time she wanted his faith with something beyond his control it wasn't there.

She wiped the tears from her eyes yet again, cursing herself for the way she felt. Why did she feel so betrayed? There was nothing between them beyond a kiss that had been ignored ever since. Yet, the idea that Fallyn could have died was like she was to lose her very soul.

"Why do I feel so hurt?" she spoke aloud just to hear the words.

"He's done so much for me without complaint. But all I want from him is to…to love me…" she sobbed, the answer rising as she spoke the words aloud.

She never would've realized that love was what crept into her heart in such a short time. Sure, he was handsome, intelligent, and patient towards her inexperience. But it was the moments when he made her feel so very cherished that grasped at the strings of her soul.

As the time passed on and the evening came to a close, her sobs and anguish became a numbed ache in her skull. Kathrin lifted herself from the floor and returned to her quarters, finding it the only good thing she could do with herself at this time of day. But when her steps were heard no more, Fallyn revealed himself from the shadows that concealed him, his thoughts reeling like never before.

Daimos found himself dazed once more within the confines of his thoughts as he lounged in the comforts of his domain. It had been some time since the evening when he tossed the wretched little female out of the window to her death. Yet his mind, unusually, continued to dwell upon her. Mortal life was generally so careless to him. He had slain prettier females than her before. Some of them had even meant more to him than any other person. Yet, he never dwelled on them. So why did she, a measly little thing that he used to burn Fallyn out of his hole, distract him every day?

Sitting the glass of red wine that he swirled in his hand aside, Daimos went onto the balcony and glanced at the night sky. Because of his distraction, Daimos sent servants out to search for more clues to the puzzle. It was curious for him to discover that Fallyn didn't let Kathrin fall to her death but rather saved her from the fall. Did, perhaps, Fallyn know more about Kathrin's existence than he led on? Did he know of the connection Kathrin had to both of their pasts even though she wasn't aware of it? As much as he wanted to investigate these questions, Daimos had learned at such an early age that he was unable to sire children. Years upon years, hundreds of prospective mortals he would bite and prepare for the time of their turning, but not one of them would. They would die just like the rest. Daimos suspected this would be no different for Kathrin. And so, as much as he wanted to find this woman who stumbled upon his path, he tried to forget her and continue with his life as an undead.

Chapter Sixteen

As time carried on, Kathrin kept to herself, busy with tasks around Fallyn's domain, while Fallyn watched her as she went about them. He could see how her face had grown solemn and her eyes dead of emotion. All she was now was a mirror of himself, and he knew he was to blame. He didn't like it, either.

He tried to converse with her to attempt to return her to her lively self, which would brighten any room she entered. Yet, she would only nod in agreement or shrug if she wasn't sure. If he thought his guilt was as deep as it could go, she proved that wrong as well. Her lack of interest shot bile into his throat. It was only on one of those nights when he couldn't find her within the cavern walls that he wandered outdoors in search of her. He found her leaning against the mouth of the cave, somewhere he believed in northern Pennsylvania, looking up at the stars. Her face was obviously stained with tears. He wouldn't walk away from her this time. He had always walked away. Fallyn approached her and crouched down on his haunches.

"This night is pleasant," he spoke in an attempt to strike up a conversation.

After a moment of trying to hide her tears, she answered, "Yes.... It is."

Minutes passed between them, Fallyn relearning the profile of her face. There was no mistake in her words before. They begged for his love, and he was sure it was his restraint of it that had pushed her over the edge. His eyes furrowed with confusion. It wasn't that he didn't feel the strong emotion, but the last time he opened his heart so freely, he lost everything that mattered most. He didn't think he could handle going through that again. Could he handle knowing that his refusal was killing her instead?

"Kathrin, I never imagined my injury was so severe."

Kathrin's eyes began to water again, her remorse overwhelming. "Fallyn, I'm sorry I'm such an idiot. I had no right to yell at-"

"-Do not," he interrupted almost instantly.

"But there was no reason for it. I just wasn't thinking-" she began again, wiping her tears away, when Fallyn suddenly touched his fingers onto her lips ever so softly. Kathrin looked into his eyes, confused by the touch. What she didn't realize was that her eyes also pleaded to him with all her loneliness, desire, and regret. They clawed like vines into his heart and pitted it into the depths of his stomach. With an unnerving sigh, Fallyn lowered his touch from her lips to the tip of her chin in a gentle caress.

"Kathrin, never apologize for speaking," he moaned while he bore into her soul through his copper eyes. "I never imagined a larvae was amongst the venom. It does explain the discomfort that had grown within the months, though."

Kathrin's lip trembled. "You were near death, Fallyn. I saw you.... slipping away. I was so scared..."

Fallyn nodded, "I believed myself stronger than any venom that some demon could spill. It was an oversight I am pleased that you were aware of."

Why did her skin have to feel so soft and inviting? He fought the impulse to bring her closer and rekindle the memory of their kiss that he knew they both longed for since. Grasping onto anything to distract his thoughts, he recalled the questions he had been meaning to ask her instead. He softly raised her hand into the moon's rays. The runes were still present within her palm, even though the incident had long since passed. "Who showed you these symbols? I have never taught you these..."

Kathrin partially chuckled, feeling rather foolish to even be repeating it as she replied, "It... was a guidance spirit. It told me it helps young vampires learn their talents. It showed me how to heal you, and then you disappeared. I know it sounds unbelievable-"

"No...it does not," he soothed in a deep accented voice that almost spellbound her to his lips. Kathrin felt the tension thickening the air in that instant. "I, too, have had assistance from a guide. It would explain why the text is that of Theseus. Only spirits would use runes so old."

"So old?" she queried, unaware of the severity Fallyn implied.

Fallyn nodded as a smirk rose onto his lips, "None are stronger than the runes of the first vampire. For you to use them without harm is quite unusual and lucky."

"I didn't realize..." she trailed as she gazed at the symbols. It was hard to avoid the eagerness that arose in her belly. But, when she suddenly comprehended the vastness of what Fallyn meant, she stuttered. "Wait! Was the spirit trying to kill me?!"

Fallyn lowered his head with a shake before a small chuckle reverberated from his chest. "No. A guide would never try you further than your ability. But let us not worry about these questions. Come, let us return to our training for this eve."

Fallyn rose onto his feet and offered his hand to her. Kathrin looked toward the ground instead, shaking her head in slight refusal. "I'd rather not... I just- I don't feel very well."

Fallyn's eyes narrowed. It was improbable for her to be ill like some common mortal. "What is wrong, Kathrin?"

She smiled weakly, "Honestly, nothing's wrong. I've just had a lot on my mind, considering, and I think you would cream me to the floor if I tried to fight you."

After a pause, Fallyn nodded and returned through

the cavern entrance, adding, "I shall be in the library if you are in need of me."

Her reply, though, wasn't the truth at all. It was more than her thoughts. Although she was grateful that he placed distance between them so she could avoid her weakening desire, she hadn't fed since his injury, and, at that, his blood was contaminated. So, she needed more nourishment. She knew it wouldn't be of concern for Fallyn to be the host for her needs. Her predicament was the connection they would share as a result. Now that she finally realized how deeply she loved him, sharing something intimate she knew would crush her emotionally, knowing the feeling was not returned. She wanted him to love her. God, to hold her in ways only her fantasies were aware of. But the horrible reality was that whenever things became too steamy, he would run away like she was the plague.

Kathrin sighed with a final resignation and entered the cavern. She had to choke back her discomfort to get her sustenance. No one said it would be easy, but her cold, weak body needed it more than her lonely isolation. So, she searched for Fallyn, where he said he would be.

Once she arrived, Kathrin braced herself with the wall to maintain her balance and called out for him. Fallyn slipped out from behind some library shelves, raising his head as he closed his novel to glance up at her. The simple fact that his hair hugged his rigid shoulders coiled her belly tightly. She exhaled, trying to ignore it.

"What is it?" he coaxed, walking around a stocky desk as he waited for her reply.

Kathrin paused hesitantly as her face flushed. Oh, how she could hear her heart pleading to be near him! Could he see her desires even now? "I- um... I need to ask you something."

Fallyn placed the novel down upon the desk and closed the gap between them, aware of the disturbance in the air. "What ails you?"

"Noth- Nothing's wrong. It's just - just," she stuttered when Fallyn arrived at her side, ever close. All she wanted was to feel his touch. He obliged her unknowingly when he lifted her chin so he could stare into her turquoise eyes that flickered brightly, bathing in their innocence and uncertainty. He could see she struggled with some unspoken thing, worrying about his response. It was the last thing Fallyn ever wanted from her. Yet here she was, stuttering like she was pleading for salvation.

"Say whatever it is, Kathrin. I assure you I will not be angered."

She inhaled deeply as she tried to soothe the butterflies that fluttered in her stomach. She closed her eyes before she blurted meekly, "I need to feed."

There was a pause, almost having Kathrin wonder if

she should have thought her words through before he snickered, "Is that all? I pondered how long it would be before you would ask."

Stunned at how trivially he placed concern on the problem, Kathrin replied, "But…it's somewhat invading."

Fallyn's eyes flashed electrically, hues of gold lacing in their copper depths as he countered softly, "You speak of the connection. I am sure there was much I would have rather kept hidden from you. But if not for it, how else would I have seen what spills from your heart? There has been much we have kept hidden from each other.…"

Registering what Fallyn admitted, Kathrin turned a thousand shades of red. She didn't think that the bond went both ways. God, did he know she loved him? How could she ever face him again, knowing what he knew of her? Fallyn ignored her humiliation as he shifted the collar of his shirt aside, tilting his head to offer her his throat.

"Here, Kathrin."

She was barely able to ignore it as she saw the offering, his pulse calling to all her senses like a drum pounding in her ears. A silhouette of his veins traced over his neck, his blood thrumming at her hunger. Unbeknownst to her, her eyes dilated, and her teeth elongated to their full form. She could even recall how succulent it tasted before. Her hands reached for him, placing one on his chest and collar to stretch up into the crook of his neck. Her longing blinded her from Fallyn's arms twining around her back. He held her so tightly he could almost take her breath away.

When her teeth buried deep into his neck, taking her first strong tug from his opened vein, he whispered in her ear, "Realize, Kathrin, I would do anything for you."

Her head swam with the words of his vow before the blindingly delicious vision took form like before. Yet, this time was much different than the previous. Instead of a door within blackness, Kathrin was surrounded by a field in the autumn sun. The leaves of crimson and bronze danced playfully in the cool breeze as she looked across the land. Then, when she found Fallyn wearing only black denim jeans that left nothing to the imagination, she was overwhelmed with heady desire. She couldn't help but admire him as he approached. But she knew what he was after: her. He pulled her close, his arms twining around her. It was like he was in control like she had entered his mind, and he tuned the strings of their delightful bond. But it didn't matter who patted out the details of this lovely visage. When she reached up and pressed her lips against his, her belly swooned.

How could she deny her love for him when he could whisk her away like this so easily? Fallyn parted his lips from hers. She could see the desire that loomed in his expression. But why did she see hesitation, too? Her eyes furrowed with curiosity. It was only seconds later, though, before something must have changed in him, washing completely away his reservation to only leave his hunger in the wake. He smiled handsomely, "Let me show you my desires outside of our minds."

She nodded, shuddering with passion. Fighting the drunken haze in her soul, she brought the ever-crisp vision of beauty to an end and drew her mind back to reality. Her mouth was still fastened onto Fallyn's neck as she felt renewed, barely able to hold onto his collar to brace herself from her dizziness. She was already ready for him, and it took all of her will to plane back into her body and lick the two-pronged wounds shut.

When Fallyn offered his neck to Kathrin's hunger, he had no idea of the electric vibe that would shoot right through his body and down to his sex. But when her teeth punctured his vein, her hands upon him like butterflies resting on a pedal, his want darkened from a slight stirring to a hardened throb. His jaw clenched as her audible suckles had him nearly thrust her against the table and take her where she stood. But Fallyn was doing this for her need, not his own crazed desire. But as the vision of longing formed in their link together, Fallyn had to find anything that could balance him back to his reasons to keep her at bay.

He couldn't love her. He just couldn't. To love her

meant she would die. Something would happen, and she would be taken away. The thought that he would be without her made him numb to the point of wanting to crumple onto his knees. In that shattering recognition, Fallyn realized it was already too late. Kathrin was his, and he belonged to her.

When her head cleared from its fog, she looked up at Fallyn to see if he, too, had felt the same beautiful moment but was cut short. His fingers traced her jawline, cupping her face within his palms, and guided her into a kiss more exquisite than their first. The scent in the air, his soft lips demanding, it all drained her of her vigor. Her knees gave way, which only brought her body deeper into his arms and belly flat against his hardened member. Her groin ached. His tongue parted her lips and delved into her mouth hungrily, a growl escaping from the rumble of his chest as she became pliable to his every whim.

Why was he melting her into her every desire after being reclusive for so long? Kathrin couldn't think further than the question before she was pulled, once again, into her erotic fantasy. Her hands held firm onto the collar of his linen shirt, unable to help but follow his silent directions. And Fallyn clenched her tighter against him, his own passion overtaking his senses.

No more denial, no more ignoring the calls in his heart. She was his aphrodisiac, and he would never have enough of her.

Kathrin couldn't prevent her moans as her body prickled at Fallyn's fingertips, exploring her body, vibrating with heady anticipation as they caressed her neck and collarbone. She had no idea that he had steered them into his bedroom, only realizing the fact once her calves pressed against the mattress. But his fingers told her what he intended. They traced the buttons on her blouse and pushed the fabric aside to expose the pale, tender flesh of her breasts. Kathrin shuddered.

"Be calm," Fallyn coaxed as he caressed her breast bound only by the lace of her mist-colored bra, "I will give only what you desire, but I cannot deny I want you with every fiber of my being."

She never wanted anything as much as this, either. Fallyn lowered his head to nibble on the crook of her neck, bracing her lower back as he fondled her. It was funny how one action could wreak havoc upon her skin while the other could soothe the goosebumps he created.

"Please, Fallyn," Kathrin panted as she reached down to stroke his hidden member. "Please make love to me."

Her plea had Fallyn eagerly push her blouse off her shoulders onto the floor, her bra close behind. Kathrin tried to do the same with him, but it was more haphazard than the grace he seemed to have. Fallyn arched her body against him as his lips trailed toward the exposed flesh of her breasts. Kathrin gasped, her fingers twining into his mane. He made her feel so empty inside, and it was something she knew only he could fill. His breath heated her chest, groaning as his tongue circled her nipple.

"Unbutton your pants, "Fallyn rasped finally. "Let me see the beauty God bestowed upon you."

Mesmerized by the order, Kathrin followed mindlessly as she loosened her bottoms to have them fall from her waist to the floor. It was only a slight tug of her panties before they, too, followed. When Fallyn stepped away to admire her, Kathrin instantly blushed. His eyes lowered onto her legs and slowly drew back up to her eyes, noticing the small chestnut curls between her toned legs, her feathered hips, and the fullness of her breast before he moaned aloud, "Beauty such as an angel."

When he tugged her against him once more, his mouth laying claim with his tongue, she forgot why she was even remotely embarrassed. Then, slowly, he laid her on the mattress. She marveled at how, even though she was falling delicately onto the disarrayed sheets, his lips never parted from hers as he followed to kneel above her. His hands explored her; his lips devoured her as he brought her to the tips of insanity. He was fully aware of it, too. Her womanly musk burned like a wild spice into his nostrils so much that he barely understood why he was holding himself at bay. He wanted to be sure she experienced nothing as blissful as their lovemaking and to remember this moment forever. Hell, he wanted to hear her scream.

Fallyn rolled off, bucking his pelvis into the air to remove his pants before he sat next to her.

"Come here, Kathrin. Straddle me."

Kathrin rose to her knees and crawled over to him. Then, he assisted her when she neared, slowly sitting her onto his lap to mount him. She vibrated with anticipation, yet Fallyn still took his time. Reclaiming her mouth, she assured her that the time would come, but only when it was right.

His suckling lips and fingers continued for some time, kissing and caressing before Fallyn brought his hands to her behind and guided her on top of him. Kathrin moaned. With her eyes closed, holding onto him for support, his body began to gently move. Then, with one of the small thrusts, he gained entrance. She couldn't miss Fallyn's audible sound of satisfaction amidst her gasp of surprise and pleasure. Then, Fallyn began to rock into her, bracing around her back onto her shoulders to rock forcefully deeper, reaching her hilt. She held on, drunk with a wonder she'd never felt before with another. She wasn't new to sex, but how could he make her feel like everything else before was inferior to him? But it was.

Christ, she was sure she was about to explode. He fondled her breasts with each thrust, teasing, suckling, and caressing. At first, his pumping was in a slow, rhythmic motion. But as their passion became heated, it progressed faster and stronger with his need to make her his own.

Mine.

Kathrin cried aloud as her nails dug into Fallyn's shoulders, him pinning her with his arms to accept all of him. Her climax rose like a tidal wave being held at bay with floodgates, but even the gates were deteriorating.

"Fallyn, I'm - I'm building," she cried, the pressure growing larger.

Fallyn glanced up at her, his eyes full of primal energy as he gritted: "Give into it."

It didn't matter that as he looked at her at that moment, his eyes were their golden slivers. She could only hold on until she thought she couldn't bear it anymore. But then her climax burst forth, Fallyn joining her in the magnificent explosion.

"I love you, Fallyn!"

Kathrin collapsed into his arms as she shuddered with satisfaction while Fallyn continued to pound into her. He was far from done with her. Fallyn needed to have her again, completely. There was no more denial. She was his.

He rolled her onto her back, still lodged deeply within her as she, in her languid delight, accepted his silent commands. He slid into her softness over and over, pistoning deep into her. It wasn't long before her hands returned to his back, her nails digging into his skin, as he knew the torrent of energy was returning for her once again, and he wanted it. Nothing could describe the feeling he had at that moment to be the only one for her. He gripped her hands and pinned them above her head while he devoured her mouth. It was then that the words she had spoken finally sunk home.

She loved him. She was his.

His body began its incline once more as Kathrin panted at her nearness, too. Her own teeth punctured her lips as her silver eyes begged him for release. A small trickle of blood slipped down her lip, and Fallyn thoughtlessly licked the trail with his tongue. He couldn't deny himself the opportunity to taste the lilacs and sweet honey of her blood when it was so readily available. The blood tickled his tongue. Yet suddenly, his senses tuned into her and everything she was experiencing. Her desperate eagerness as another climax built, the thrusting of him into her void, everything she felt joined with his own mounding desire.

Exquisite.

Within seconds of the succulent taste, Fallyn's body detonated, and the sound of their release reverberated within the walls of his home. He held onto her with the final quivers of satisfaction; his seed buried deep within her. His head felt drugged, intoxicated by her as he adjusted to lay beside her.

Was he tasting her power? Is that what had affected his senses?

Fallyn cradled Kathrin's back into his chest as the questions whisked away as quickly as they entered. They both quickly fell into the throws of slumber before any words passed between them. And as dawn approached ever slowly- and even though nothing was resolved between them- what happened in this moment, they knew, would be between them forever.

Chapter Seventeen

As Kathrin rose to Fallyn's deep breaths of slumber upon her neck, she relived the wonders of their lovemaking. Even thinking about it now made her flush. Yet, as much as she loved him, she began to question if it was their connection in feeding that transferred her desires to him. It would explain why he would be so reclusive one minute and then become so passionate the next. When she suddenly realized she blurted her devotion in the throes of passion, she blushed profusely. He didn't even return them. What did she expect? He didn't have to return her feelings. Yet was everything she felt with him truly just one-sided? Was even this intimacy something taken advantage of in a frenzied moment? Unable to avoid those questions, she couldn't prevent berating herself over and over. What if that was the only time they would share such an intimate act? After all, he had his taste of her. He could, very well, find her boring...

Tears burned her eyes at the thought. She never wanted to change how they were for the worst, but now she pondered if she had done just that. How would it be for them now, after this? Would it be too awkward for them to even be near each other now? Wouldn't such discomfort drive them further apart?

Attempting to fight back her tears, her chastisement

slowly slipped Kathrin out of Fallyn's arms as she attempted to sneak back to her own quarters without rousing Fallyn. Yet, with the faint movement of the mattress, Fallyn's hand clenched around hers like lightning. She gasped in shock. Then, with one simple command, Kathrin discovered how alert Fallyn was.

"Do not leave."

She should've figured he would have keen senses all around with the lifestyle he had lived. Kathrin instantly forced on a smile to conceal her actual sadness. "Go to sleep, Fallyn. I'm just gonna' head to my room. I don't want to burden you with lack of sleep or something."

Fallyn's eyes enlarged with astonishment as he repeated: "'Burden me'? Kathrin, you have never been such a thing."

She couldn't find it within her to believe him as she examined his eyes ever thoroughly. But as Fallyn tugged her gently back into his arms, she knew that it was all too real.

"You amaze me, alhaja. Did you believe I could bond with you in such a splendid manner to feign it later as nothing more than a vulnerable moment?"

Boy, could he hit the nail on the head? Kathrin couldn't help but blush as she averted her eyes from his stare. When Fallyn spotted her ever-clear behavior of doubt, Fallyn kissed her lips tenderly and returned her gaze back to his.

"Kathrin, I would never share something so wonderful with you to be ignorant of it later. What, on earth, would drive me to do so?"

Her eyes blurred with tears. Why could he read all her fears and esteem issues so easily? She didn't even have to say anything for him to know it. Yet, even with his steady assurance, she couldn't accept what her own emotions denied. Why would such a talented, very amazing man ever consider her for more than sexual relief? She was nothing like him in knowledge or capability. Heck, even in strength, he could pummel her to the ground, she thought as she matched his stare. "Everyone has needs, Fallyn. And it's only natural to want it without ties. I just assumed that was the case with me."

Fallyn's face instantly went stern, unimpressed with her retort as he bore into her soul. When his arms crushed her to him with a growl, she cringed at her idiocy. "Do not ever say that again. Is that clear?"

Kathrin swallowed hard but nodded as he held her even tighter.

"I have never been a man to bed a woman 'without ties,' nor do I intend to." Then, within minutes, he sighed, easing the tension of his embrace. "Why do you doubt your self-worth so, Kathrin? Hearing you speak like this saddens me. Have I ever given you cause to believe such things? Have I ever shunned you with words of disgust?"

Kathrin remained silent as she tried to find the moment when he had done such a thing, but there was none. He never shoved her away with words of hate or made her feel like a burden. Seeing Kathrin couldn't answer his question, he added, " I know my words are few with you- even evasive to your inquiries when you ask them- but none could ever express what you mean to me."

Kathrin almost doubted she was hearing him correctly at all as he returned her gaze. Yet within seconds, his lips pressed against hers as he rolled over top of her to have her beneath him once more. And he promised her with this barrier-melting kiss the sincerity of his devotion. Her core rattled; her belly flipped as she melted to his touch.

"You are my life renewed, alhaja. I love you so very deeply."

Her eyes watered uncontrollably as he smiled handsomely. "Do not forget that."

Then he kissed her again. And as their kissing led to their passionate lovemaking, Kathrin finally understood the equality of their love.

※ ※ ※ ※ ※ ※

Kathrin glanced around the water-eroded cavern at the many stalagmites that surrounded the edges of her battle ground, keenly. Fallyn had been determined to spar with her for some time now in attempts for her to learn her own capabilities. But, with the recent obstacles that had come between them, this idea fell to the wayside until only recent. But Fallyn was sure that there was a war approaching, and he wanted her at nothing less than her full potential when it arrived.

Kathrin dressed accordingly in a combo of white tights and a long black sleeve top with a silver belt. She was surprised when Fallyn gave her one of his katanas to use during their duel. What was more surprising was that he only made one rule crystal clear: gunfire was explicitly excluded. Fallyn sported the other katana, his only attire being a pair of slacks, which Kathrin was sure was just to distract her in their brawl.

"You have learned the key elements of battle: offensive and defensive," Fallyn began, quickly breaking her concentration. "But, now it's time to apply these theories so that you can discover through your own strengths and weaknesses what works best for you."

When Kathrin saw Fallyn's emotionless stare, she knew all too well she couldn't help but smirk.

"Kathrin. This is not intended to be easy. I want to see everything you have; Restraint is not an option. Understood? The only way to know how far you can push yourself is by doing so when your life is on the line."

Kathrin grasped exactly what he was trying to say.

So, showing him she comprehended what he meant, she unsheathed the katana with her right hand and took a stance. Fallyn approved with a stance of his own.

"Let us begin," Fallyn said as he awaited her next move.

Although her anticipation had her jumping within her skin, Kathrin didn't move. What did she want to do, tell Fallyn she hadn't been listening to a single word he'd been telling her? The first move was always the most defenseless. But, God, all she wanted to do was get this ball rolling! When Fallyn saw that the move would have to be his, he began to pace sideways with a smile of approval for her choice. Kathrin followed suit, keeping the distance equal between them while they strode around clockwise.

Then it happened. Fallyn hunkered down onto his knees and lunged toward her; his blade readied for a downward slash. Kathrin instinctively jumped as she parried the attack, the force of impact between the two blades pushing her a short distance away. She barely balanced herself with her free hand as her head shot up to find Fallyn, yet she was surprised that he was already in mid-air above her. She sprung out of the way just as his sword plunged down to the earth.

Kathrin staggered back to widen the distance while Fallyn returned to his feet. Then, he removed the tip of his sword from the ground.

"What the hell, Fallyn?!"

Fallyn's steps became ever steady once more. "I said there was no restraint."

Kathrin's jaw dropped open. She knew what he said, dammit. She backed away further with a growl, "Yeah, I heard you. But I had no idea trying to kill me was part of the fun!"

Fallyn lowered his blade as his expressionless face contorted with concern. "I would never kill you, alhaja. Yet, I cannot say you will be unharmed if I catch your weakness."

How the hell could Fallyn differentiate the two?!

"Kathrin, an injury we can mend. You know of my abilities."

She knew he had plenty of talents, that's for sure. But she never saw anything that may help her right now if it came down to it. Yet, nothing was going to happen if she backed out now. So, although her mind was wary, she swallowed hard and raised her weapon again.

Fallyn smiled as he complimented: "There you go, alhaja," before he, too, returned his sword to stance. "Show me what you are capable of."

Kathrin nodded briefly before she sprung toward him, arms raised above her head to strike. Kathrin knew how vulnerable of a position it was, but she hoped Fallyn would take advantage of it. As she closed the distance between them and Fallyn lowered his blade accordingly, Kathrin smiled inwardly.

When his blade swung toward her mid, Kathrin adjusted her blade with just seconds to spare. A loud clash echoed throughout the cavern as the swords connected. She used the momentum of the impact to spring over his head with a flip. Landing, her body arched and drew the blade toward her bosom to impale it into his now-opened back. But in that instant, she paused. She couldn't strike such a critical blow onto him; the thought practically disgusted her. It was with that second's delay that suddenly forced her back into the defensive. His katana slid toward her from between his arm and torso.

Kathrin dropped in attempts to miss the strike and countered with a roundhouse sweep towards Fallyn's legs. Unfortunately, Kathrin couldn't evade it fast enough as the tip of the blade sliced the side of her arm. She winced. When her leg swept the floor, though, Fallyn was already gone. Kathrin gasped aloud as her deficient speed had her lose sight of the fact that Fallyn was already behind her, sending her sprawling across the cave with a kick. The force knocked out a guttural groan the moment she impacted against a stalagmite on the far corner.

Her body trembled as she stumbled onto her feet. Drearily, she glanced up to locate Fallyn but had to rise her sword reflexively again to parry another blow. The impact was like being slammed by a freight train as Kathrin was sent flailing yet again from the blow. With some new-found vigor, she spun her body around in the air to land her feet on the wall. I can do this, she repeated. I need to show him I'm strong enough! She sprung off the wall toward him in a wave of onslaught. But Fallyn was far too fast and strong for her to ensue any critical blows. She would just line one up only to be thrust into the defensive once more.

Yet, knowing the odds, Kathrin didn't give up. She almost couldn't. She felt that if she did, it was the same as failing Fallyn. Even when her body became scarred, the bruises beneath the skin already turning purple, or when her body became sluggish, she didn't quit.

With another toss to the floor, Kathrin trembled warily on her hands and knees to get up yet again. This time, she coughed up blood. Her eyes blurred in and out of focus as she glanced dizzily towards Fallyn. Fallyn didn't move. He only watched her battered, limp body stumble warily to her feet.

"That is enough for now, Kathrin," he started as she leaned onto her good leg for support. "We can try again another time."

Each word stung her insides. In his eyes, she already failed him. Her face lowered to hide her tears of frustration. How could she fail him? She just had to do this for him. She had to do it for herself.

"No," Kathrin gritted through her tears, glancing at Fallyn as she took her stance once again. "I'm not gonna' give up!"

Fallyn admired her determination, although they both knew the outcome. "If you insist."

Kathrin tried with all of her might, but, once again, she couldn't out-beat Fallyn. Within minutes, she was sprawled on the earth, this time with a slice on her cheekbone. Fallyn resented his decision even more as her arms quivered to even raise from the floor. "Kathrin, there is no shame in defeat. I have had many years to tune my abilities."

"No," Kathrin whimpered, her vision blurring to the sense of inferiority that overwhelmed her. She hated herself for her weakness.

Fallyn tried to approach Kathrin, but when she quickly barked at him to stay away, he felt obligated to listen.

"This was only meant to call to your vampire blood, not to kill you."

Although she knew his words were true, Kathrin was still too enraged with herself to listen. She would only burden Fallyn if this was how she fought. It made her feel as if all of the cuts and wounds on her body were well deserved. Damn you, Kathrin gritted towards herself. I hate you for what you are! A cool breeze arose to Kathrin's attention as a faint and familiar voice announced his presence.

"Kathrin, if you desire to be more, you need only find it. The power already lies within you," the spirit guide spoke softly.

Within her. She groaned. Once again, it was something about her that was the hindrance. Her rage mounted till she felt like she was nothing more than the emotion itself, not even worth the immortal existence granted to her. But amidst her self-loathing was a desire to prove her worthlessness wrong. It sparkled like a pebble trying to change the course of a river. She refused to accept it. It called upon the very core of her soul for proof of a sealed door that had never been opened before.

Kathrin rose to her feet as a wave of cool electricity swelled throughout her veins. Her muscles felt renewed, her body alive and on fire. She felt like she would burst into flames from it! Glowing silver saucers glared up at Fallyn from under her bangs. Her pupils were nothing but mere dots. It felt like billions of atoms were exploding within her.

Fallyn's eyes widened at the aura that instantly began to pour off of Kathrin, swirling around her like a cool breath on a crisp winter's morning. Never had he seen such a vast level of power. It was almost like a greater deity had awoken within her. "Kathrin?"

Kathrin smirked devilishly as she challenged in a thunderous voice, "Fight me, Fallyn. I'll prove I'm not weak."

Fallyn gazed hard at Kathrin. If this was the beast he wanted to awaken, he was greeted with far more than he could have expected. Even with all his past encounters, he had only heard that it was possible. He raised his blade again, this time, the idea of their sparing finally intriguing him. It had been some time since he had a challenge.

Kathrin looked down at the katana she wielded and tossed it aside with a sneer. It was a faulty weapon, something her claws could do so much better. Then, she elongated her nails to almost double the size of her fingers. Even their density thickened to fine steel.

She smiled sinfully as she walked towards Fallyn, almost provocatively. She could foresee what moves they would each play in this onslaught, which would come like an overlaid shadow on Fallyn's body. The shadow, dark and hallowed, lunged at her, passing through her like a cloud of smoke. When Fallyn raised his blade to follow through with what the silhouette acknowledged, Kathrin's speed instantly surpassed his own, so much so that he lost track of her. She leaped from side to side, phasing in and out of reality like it was but a paper curtain in her way as she approached Fallyn.

With a blink of an eye, Kathrin was in front of him. Wisps of her hair loosened from their bind, fluttering hauntingly in the air like a demon's wings outstretched to capture its prey. Fallyn's hand reacted involuntarily as he swung his sword. The strike couldn't have been any more precise. Yet, with an evil flash of her eyes, she phased out of reality once more just as the edge of his sword severed through her neck. Fallyn's eyes enlarged with bewilderment.

The second the sword's edge passed through her hallowed skin, Kathrin returned to her physical form. That was when her bound hair became caught by the edge and fell detached onto the ground. Her dagger-like nails instantly speared him in the left of his chest. Fallyn choked on haggard breaths as proof of her accomplishment began to flow out of the wound.

She stared triumphantly at her nail within his flesh. Her nose flared; her fangs enlarged with the sweet smell of his life draining from him. A hunger stirred. The moment was exotic, blinding her from everything but the sinful craving to see her victim's eyes before he slipped away. But when she looked up at Fallyn as he cringed in the aftermath, Kathrin paled deathly white. Her rage for triumph blinded her to who she was against! Fallyn dropped his katana.

"Oh my God!" Kathrin cried out, her eyes watering

with horror as they returned to their turquoise self. "My God, Fallyn, I'm sorry! I'm sorry!"

The moment she pulled her nails out of his chest, they returned to their original state. He grunted as he stumbled back, his hand covering his wound while Kathrin tried to support him. She couldn't stop her tears as she repeated over and over her apologies. Yet Fallyn slowly collapsed onto the ground to ease his weakening body. He smiled weakly as he looked back at Kathrin.

"That was incredible, Kathrin," Fallyn wheezed.

She shook her head in refusal. "No, it's horrible! I never wanted to hurt you! I'm so sorry!"

Fallyn tutted her slightly as his other hand came up and rubbed her falling tears from the side of her cheek, "This is but a scratch. You did exactly what I asked of you." But, when she shook her head in denial, he continued. "You accomplished something I have never witnessed in my lifetime, alhaja. I only wished to bring you to a level similar to your older brethren, and here, you surpassed anything I could have imagined."

"But at the cost of you!" Kathrin sobbed as she hugged him closely.

Fallyn chuckled lightly as he shook his head. Then, he pushed her away. "'The cost of me?' Alhaja, I am fine. See for yourself."

"You're not fine! The wound is -" but Kathrin's words

trailed off as Fallyn removed his hand from where the injury should have been. There was blood still coated around the skin, although the gash was gone. Her fingers touched the place in disbelief before she looked puzzled towards Fallyn for answers.

"-How did you?"

Fallyn smirked slightly as he repeated: "You know of my abilities." But, as he also glanced to places in which she should have carried injuries herself, he added, "But it seems that you are now discovering your own."

Kathrin followed Fallyn's gaze to what he referred to while Fallyn began to play with her now short hair. Yet now, there was an unusual streak of bright silver hair that was quite longer than the rest. Examining for more abnormalities, he also found that now her eyes had changed, too. The once deep green ovals were now speckled with pearls of blue and silver. How very beautiful.

"You carry marks of one awakened. Undoubtedly, you must notice a difference within yourself. Am I correct?" Fallyn inquired as Kathrin tried to calm herself while she wiped her tears away.

"I- I don't know," she muttered thoughtlessly. She honestly had to think about the question. "It feels like everything inside me finally found peace. I don't feel so scattered... I don't know... Maybe even in control of what's happened to me. I guess I'm not so afraid of being a vampire now."

Fallyn nodded, a beam erupting from the corners of his lips. "Well spoken, Kathrin. I could not have said it any better myself. This was what I wanted to achieve from this. To connect the two halves of yourself: The woman you are and the vampire you have become."

"But... I hurt you! I don't ever want to be mindless like that again." Kathrin groaned, averting her gaze as she rubbed her anxiety from her arms.

Fallyn argued, "It always takes much more to initially attune your body to your vampirism. Yet, what was used to awaken you will not be required again. It should be second nature now. Does it not feel that way?"

It did. Every power she had was at her disposal. She nodded slowly as he stood up on his feet and offered her a hand in assistance.

"Then my ambition was for not." He smiled handsomely as his accent soothed her panicked thoughts like it always did.

Kathrin accepted his hand as he lifted her from the floor. "Okay...but... Can we never do this again? I don't think I could handle it without kicking your ass to the floor."

Fallyn couldn't hide his hearty laughter as he shook his head in humored disbelief. "I shall keep this in mind. I would hate to be throttled by the likes of you, *alhaja.*"

Chapter Eighteen

Daimo's eyes widened from his morning slumber as the electric connection with his sired child screamed its presence. He had long since pondered before this moment as to why his mind kept wrapping itself around the female, Kathrin. But now, as the energy reverberated between them, it was proven more than ever.

Kathrin was an awakened vampire, and he was the one who fathered her.

Daimos sat up from his bed in the blackened room, a wave of fascination flooding his veins. Out of all the hundreds of years of trying, Daimos finally found a person strong enough to handle his curse. But what made it even more spectacular was the fact that there were only a handful of vampires who had ever been awakened, including himself. Yet now, Kathrin was one of them, too. He couldn't be prouder. His only child, surpassing any of the vampire spawns of the current generation.

But, as his mind was awed at this insight, other visions began to burn into his mind. Visions of what seemed like a duel. Powerful, strenuous, Kathrin battling a man...no.... Fallyn! She impaled his chest to what seemed like his doom. But... she was saddened by it?

Daimo's brow furrowed. Why was she not driven by her need for blood and carnage? It took awakened vampires time to calm the blood rage, most commonly weeks. Even his own thirst was often, but Daimos had, with time, learned to control it.

That was when another memory appeared; Kathrin was within Fallyn's arms while in the throes of intimacy.

"Blasphemous!" Daimos growled as he slammed his fist onto the mattress. "A vampire bedding that... that... Filth!"

Daimos flicked his hand in the air, and a candle in the corner of the room suddenly burned with fire.

A woman was draped across the bed, drugged from the previous feeding Daimos had performed hours earlier.

"What's wrong, sugar?" she slurred as her figure slid over to his seat on the bed. Her naked body pressed invitingly against him while her hands reached onto his leg.

Daimos growled unpleasantly before he removed her hand from his thigh. "Leave it be, wench. It's none of your concern."

She giggled slyly as she raised onto her knees, flattening her breasts against his back. "Oh, baby... If it's thirst that's bothering you, then yes, it is."

Daimos looked over his shoulder with frustration as he recalled the hours prior with their own need. Pounding, clawing, feeding on her neck in their passion. She asked for it time and again, which was the only reason she had lived this long. It was few who could tempt him so. But only for a few hours, a day at max.

She was a busty, toned blond. But even now, no appearance could sway his mind as her arms hung off his shoulder. She nibbled his neck.

"I said, 'Leave me be'. I'm not in the mood."

She swayed as if intoxicated as she tried to pull him back onto the mattress.

"Come on. I want you, and I know you want me," she whimpered.

Daimos growled, reaching the end of his thread. With uncanny speeds, he flipped around and pinned her against the mattress. His eyes beamed silver as his fangs lunged for her neck and crushed her throat under his mouth.

He was far from caring as he devoured her, what little blood she had left departing into his mouth. It was more than this worthless mortal that he wanted dead. As the female's arms flopped onto the mattress with her final breath, Daimos seethed with the knowledge that his child shamed him with her impulsive actions. It was something he planned to correct. Either with Fallyn's death, Kathrin's torture into enlightenment, or, if need be, her death too.

All the options did sound rather appealing to Daimos.

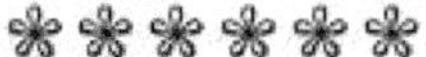

Kathrin was in the kitchen cleaning what dishes they had used for Fallyn's morning meal while Fallyn showered up from the night before. Or, at least, that was how she assumed she should explain it. Kathrin couldn't even explain her day herself. Since her turning, her days awake were at night, and her nights asleep had been at daybreak.

But, the thoughts of their intimacy still plagued her, even now, as she dried the plates and pots. Demons, rescues, and a ruggedly handsome hero, although even he was a member of the dark. And within the months, her hero was now her lover and life mate. That was clear whenever he sat next to her while she studied more books. His arms reached for her waist just to draw her near or simply smiling with that twinkle in his eyes that told her he was thinking about her.

Kathrin began to giggle at her fond memories when suddenly, like the searing of a cattle prod upon her mind, a horrid vision shot into her mind.

Fangs impaled a woman's neck, blood gushing into her mouth as she could feel the jugular crushing under her teeth. The woman's screams for help were gurgled as they bubbled in her own blood. Her hands frantically grasped at Kathrin's shoulders.

There was another flash of the devil's eyes glaring at

her; all the while, she could feel this woman's organs in her palms.

"Dear...God..." Kathrin gasped with horror as the plate she was drying slipped from her fingers and smashed it upon the ground.

Were these her thoughts? Were these things to come?

She could hear bones snapping, an urge to instill violence in anything and anyone setting in. This woman's death permeated like an aphrodisiac, making her hungry. Heart beats, pulse, gore.

Her body quivered uncontrollably as her fangs enlarged. What was this temptation? She needed it, craved it. War, anger, hatred to all. They were only cattle. Kathrin was paralyzed by her vision of madness as it called out her demonic blood.

Turning around the corner into the kitchen as he pondered what had happened, Fallyn instantly observed Kathrin's torment. She stood there clenched, struggling with something internal that Fallyn assumed was quite strong. Even now, the tales of her vampirism were vibrant. Her silver-illuminated eyes and enlarged fangs gasped for air like she was being strangled.

It was her demon, just like he himself faced when he was weak. But the demon's temptation could be a fine line; a small suggestion could result in a turning point in one's humanity. Was Kathrin losing hers?

Fallyn frowned, hating the thought that he had reached within a few short moments. If her will was too weak, she could still become like the rest of her brethren. He still may have to kill her.

Be strong, Kathrin. Please be strong, he pleaded to himself, not daring to approach her in her current state.

She convulsed her head, her mouth outstretched as she looked at the ceiling of the room. Her pupils were almost gone when a lone tear escaped the corner of her eye.

"I... won't be... a monster," she whimpered before a roar of rage bellowed out from her.

Her hands slammed onto the counter enough to make the surface shift, and Fallyn prepared for the worst. But nothing came. Kathrin stammered around like she had just awoken from a dream. She glanced at her hands, then looked towards the kitchen sink with confusion before she looked over to the entrance way.

Although she was unaware of them, her silver eyes and protruding fangs were still present while she looked toward Fallyn. So, in noticing her uncertainty, Fallyn acted as if nothing was out of the ordinary.

"What happened, Kathrin? I heard the plate break and ventured forth to find you." Fallyn smiled softly.

She paused for a minute before she stuttered, "I-I

don't know."

Just as he thought.

"You are not hurt, are you?" Fallyn replied as he witnessed Kathrin's fangs receding.

"No-no, I don't think so."

Fallyn nodded as he approached her. He stepped over the broken plate and escorted her to a dining room chair.

"Perhaps you have been on your feet too long. Let me tidy while you rest."

"O-okay, Fallyn," she moaned weakly and began to rub her head in confusion as he began the cleanup of the debris.

Chapter Nineteen

Sitting in the darkness of the living room, Kathrin scrunched her eyes against the constant pounding of her skull that hadn't let up for days. Why was there such a noise in her mind?! It was like someone was endlessly chattering, suggesting things she'd never imagined before. Yet this voice, which Kathrin had begun to believe was carnage itself, had been tormenting her for a few weeks. She was lucky enough that, at first, it was only in mere whispers. She wished she could say it was like that now.

Kathrin didn't want to burden Fallyn with her troubles, though. After all, they were still endurable enough to handle on her own. What boggled her, though, was why it had only just begun in the last few weeks. Was it because of her awakening?

Unbeknownst to Kathrin, Fallyn had witnessed her torment a handful of times already. Each time, she won the call and continued as if it had never happened. But Fallyn feared the day when she might lose.

So, for many mornings while Kathrin slumbered, Fallyn researched whatever he could about her current predicament. Unfortunately, there was nothing to be found. Book after book, chapter after chapter, and not one morsel of information resembled her uniqueness.

Frustrated, all Fallyn knew was that he needed to find the answer soon.

So, with a small kiss to the side of her cheek, as she tried to relax in her lounger chair, Fallyn assured her he would be home before dawn as he went on a hunt once more. It was later on in the evening, while he watched the gluttonous actions of vampires within a club, that Fallyn noticed something much different than all of his other times.

He was being watched.

Fallyn stood across the club from a group of three vampires who were sinfully choosing out their prey. The blare of music and the flickering of colored lights deafened any noise beyond the couples beside him. But, from the corner of the hall, Fallyn felt the eyes upon him as thoroughly as he waited for his moment to strike. Slowly, as Fallyn's head remained fixed on the vampires, Fallyn's eyes traveled to the man he suspected.

A tall, brooding man leaned against the wall next to a hallway with his arms crossed amongst themselves. His posture, relaxed and focused, seemed like he couldn't be bothered with the whole scene around him. He was here for one specific reason.

Him.

Fallyn looked back towards the vampires as they fondled women who passed, attempting to grab their attention enough to lure them into their control. This tactic had only worked for one thus far. He still had some time.

The eyes practically burned his skin, lingering upon him like insects crawling down his neck. Fallyn knew that he should've acted oblivious to the situation, but his irritation got the best of him after only a few minutes.

Fallyn turned his attention blatantly back towards the man who watched him. The assumption of the man spying on him was proven in mere seconds as he quickly rolled around the corner and out of sight. Fallyn growled in annoyance as he reverted to the vampires. Two women were now within their control. Only one more victim until they would depart.

Though his head remained stationed at the vampires' table, Fallyn watched the corner of the club again until the man returned from his hiding. He was sure to remain in the darkest shadows of the room, leaving him a mere silhouette in the already darkened club.

The chain of investigations was short-lived as the last vampire claimed his victim, and the three began to depart. Fallyn followed in suit.

The man is no more than a setback; Fallyn tries to cool himself. While he followed his prey, Fallyn considered thrashing the man where he stood.

Fallyn swerved around the tables and the dance floor. The dark presence surrounded him, keeping the civilians at bay as he focused on his targets. They exited the doors with Fallyn near enough to track them without their unwanted attention. Fallyn knew that the prowler followed, as well.

Exiting the entrance doors while he trailed the entourage, Fallyn took to the rooftops in a blink of an eye. Two stories were nothing to Fallyn, and now, with its advantage, he could watch them in a more discreet manner.

The demons, with their arms clung around their prey, were assuring the women with their manipulative powers that they were merely returning to their homes, though Fallyn knew the truth. They were looking for a dark alleyway to fill their hunger.

Fallyn pursued them into the alleyway, and when the three vampires were about to turn on their own prey, he flew down from the rooftops in a tornado-like flash to disperse each of them before they knew he was upon them. The women, still dazed by their hypnotic orders, simply watched, unaware of the horrendous battle of teeth and blades before them. The guttural cries, the snarls, and hisses, even the blood splattering across the walls of the buildings that gave notice to the unholy deed, didn't snap the three innocents out of their hypnotic reality.

As the wail of the final vampire trembled into Fallyn's ear, he looked at the three women helpless in their control.

Fallyn's eyes glowed their bestial yellow as his voice thundered an order into their weak-willed minds. "Travel to your homes. Forget this night has ever sought you."

The three of them turned and departed, exiting the alleyway like nothing was amiss. By the time they were out of sight, the three husks had dissolved into the night's air.

Fallyn's mind trailed to his own memoirs as he sheathed his blade. Why couldn't he have been able to save Kathrin from her fateful bite like he did for these three women? If he had, then the world's survival and her humanity wouldn't be hanging by a thread.

The hairs on his neck prickled, and Fallyn knew he was being watched once again.

Instead of looking towards the man he knew was there, Fallyn darted out of the alleyway and onto the rooftops once more. He ran for a few miles, the person following beginning to become a nuisance. All Fallyn wanted was to be left to himself, and it seemed all he was getting was the pestering of a man who he knew was beyond the civilian public. Not a vampire or a demon, such as himself, but someone who was tuned into the darkness.

He jumped from building to building, looking for the next monster to find as he tried to lose his stalker. But it seemed that whenever Fallyn paused to smell out the area, that looming feeling lurked down his spine once again.

Finally, he spotted one through a bay window of an apartment across the way. A vampire was threatening a comrade who came at the wrong time. Angling down from his thirteen-story perch, Fallyn aimed his silenced M1911A1 at the vampire. His skin began to crawl. Once again, the eyes were upon him.

'Blasted soul,' he muttered as he pegged the vampire through the window with a bullet square to the head.

Without pausing to see the vampire fall, Fallyn whirled his gun around to face the prowler behind him. Fallyn's trigger was clenched, aimed, and readied on the target who hid behind the emergency exit. The smell, yearning and earnest, permeated within the breeze. His eyes altered, glowing out their golden fire from under the veils of his hat.

"Best you show yourself if you desire to live another moment," Fallyn growled, obvious of his frustration.

A second passed, Fallyn's eyes narrowing on the corner where he knew the man was before the dragging of feet could be heard, and the man turned from around the corner.

"Fallyn, don't shoot. It's me," the voice spoke up, his hands raised as he came out defenseless.

Fallyn recognized the voice instantly as he returned his gun to its holster and examined the person more closely, "Why do you stalk from the shadows, Eli? It does not befit you."

The man chuckled, his hand coming into his hair to fan it out of his face as he replied, "I guess you can call it safety."

Fallyn examined Eli closely for the remark, realizing that he wouldn't make such a comment without cause. "What brings you to me, Eli? Surely this is not a friendly reunion?"

Eli coughed, knowing full well that he couldn't hide anything from Fallyn. He hadn't been able to since he first met him almost thirty years ago. "I wish I could say it was, Fallyn."

Fallyn sighed at Eli before he leaned against the emergency exit wall, crossing his arms. Fallyn would never have guessed that Eli, out of anyone from their order, would be the one to search for him. Not that Eli and he were enemies. Fallyn figured quite the opposite. After all, Eli was a child; he had been rescued years ago when his family was turned into vampire minions or undead husks. Eli was only six then, terrified and unsure that he was alive himself. Fallyn helped him. He got him away from his former parents before he destroyed them in a ball of fire and then took Eli to an Infernal's haven to find protection. Fallyn eyed the man who stood before him now and acknowledged that he had, indeed, become a true warrior to the cause. He was a mere reflection of what he once was. His lean build frame, shaggy brown hair, and goatee were fashionable in the era. Even the sword that hung from his hip suited him well like that was his destiny all along.

"Tell me what complaint the Infernal has with me."

Eli seemed rather puzzled at the insight, "who said anything about it being a complaint?"

"You need not evade the issue, Eli. I have been with them longer than any member. I know of their tactics," Fallyn chuckled as he shook his head toward Eli.

Eli cleared his throat as he leaned over the ledge of the rooftop and gazed down the stories before he started, "Fallyn, the Infernals have heard disturbing news recently."

Fallyn nodded. He was prepared for the words he knew were going to follow. "I am sure they have heard much."

"It has to do with a vampire," Eli added, turning his eyes towards Fallyn.

Fallyn shrugged, "What of them? I have rid the city of many."

Eli lowered his head, hating that he was the one to confront his own childhood hero, "God, Fallyn, please don't make this harder than it has to be."

Eli pulled out a pack of cigarettes from the back

pocket of his jeans, flicking a stick out to light it in his mouth. Fallyn merely watched. With one deep inhale, he looked over at Fallyn again.

"Is there not more deadlier things that could end your life than those?" Fallyn interjected.

Eli smiled slightly at Fallyn's sarcasm before he shook his head over the topic switch. "No, I'm serious, Fallyn. This is important."

"I have never doubted that, Eli."

Fallyn remained cool and collective, which only unnerved Eli even more. "They heard you came in contact with Daimos."

"That I have, many times, but I have yet to rid the earth of him."

"They also heard he fed from a mortal in one of your meetings."

Fallyn nodded, "He did."

"But you didn't kill her after he left."

Fallyn remained silent. What was he going to say? That he saved her from her death, assisted with her awakening, and came to love her? No, no one could understand the emotions between them like he did.

Fallyn's silence had Eli ask again, more pressingly, "Fallyn, tell me, please. You're the person that inspired me to become part of the Infernals. I want to know, need to know if it's true."

"So, that is why you came as the messenger? To find validation?" Although Fallyn knew he should feel offended by the man's desire for the truth, could only question him.

"No, it's not like that. I mean, if it wasn't me, then it would be a far cry worse."

"So, you came to protect me?"

Eli scrunched his eyes out of frustration as he inhaled another puff of his smoke. "God damn it, Fallyn! Is it true that you took her in?!"

"Yes."

Eli was unprepared for that answer as he saw Fallyn's golden glowing eyes watching him closely. "You took her in?"

Fallyn's stare didn't falter. "Yes."

Eli began to pace, upset and panicked by the news, as his cigarette became smaller and smaller. "Did…. did she die from the turning? Tell me she died from the turning…"

"Would it ease your mind if I did?"

Eli growled at Fallyn's game, which he was toiling. "Just shut the fuck, up and answer me!"

"No, she did not."

"So, you are protecting a vampire, a blood-sucking freak?!" Eli couldn't hide his aggravation towards the knowledge he prayed was all a misunderstanding.

"I assure you she is much different than many vampires I have met before."

"I don't care if she is the fucking Queen of England! She's a vampire, Fallyn! They stop at nothing to feed their hunger! You, of all people, should know that!!"

Fallyn watched Eli storm back and forth as he yelled his irritation. There was so much displeasure towards him. But Fallyn wasn't here to impress anyone.

"Do you not realize the power she possesses!?! She a child of Daimos! He had never spawned children before because his blood was so pure!"

"Eli," Fallyn raised his voice in an attempt to grab his attention, "I have faced these questions since my choice. These observations are not new to me."

"She's a fucking killer, Fallyn, not any better than the ones you slay on the streets!"

"Do you honestly take me as a fool, Eli? Do you truly believe I would harbor a monster if that, indeed, was the case?" Fallyn countered, his voice matching Eli's in volume as he tried to defend himself.

"I don't know what to fucking believe! For all I know, you very well could be under her control!"

Fallyn forced himself off the wall and ripped the collar of his shirt aside harshly enough to snap off the first few buttons, "Look! Do I carry her mark? Am I now acting like a man possessed by the will of a lunatic?"

Eli looked at Fallyn, recognizing that Fallyn was an emotional man when it came to his faith. If Fallyn truly believed he was in the wrong, he would not defend himself with such passion. Eli looked at his neck, which he now bore; it was naked of any scars that a vampire would leave. Eli couldn't say Fallyn would have even spoken with him if he was indeed under her spell. With that, Eli couldn't help but feel a glimmer of hope.

"- I...I see nothing, Fallyn..."

Fallyn adjusted his shirt and coat as he approached Eli. Deep inside, he knew that Fallyn had no ill intent.

"I have disregarded the code. I acknowledge this. But she is nothing of the vampires I have slain in a mire of the city. I believe she is the evolution to vampire intellect. If more are born in this manner, I would even implore that they could fight by our sides as comrades of the Infernal."

"Oh my god, Fallyn. You're not serious!"

"I do not fib, Eli. None of her humanity was lost at the time of her turning. She remained such as you and I. She holds the fear of her darkness, which gives her strength to hold it at bay. Death has not once laid upon her hands." Seeing Eli's difficulty in grasping the words Fallyn spoke, Fallyn could not prevent the praise that followed as he announced, "if it was not for her care, my body would now be used as a shell for a Digornath."

Fallyn was never one to admit when he needed help

or ever announce when he had received it. This was Fallyn's pride that sheltered him from comrades and friends. But, to hear his words commend another struck Eli with the realization that Fallyn held her as valuable as he alleged.

"What?" Eli questioned.

Fallyn nodded as his golden eyes pleaded for Eli to believe him, a man who perhaps knew him closer than any other within their organization. "She saved me, Eli. Could you honestly tell me a vampire that we commonly know would do the same?"

Eli looked at Fallyn briefly before he cursed and lit another cigarette as he began to pace once more. "Shit! This is... this is too much, Fallyn. You know... to digest all at once."

"Nor should you even think twice about his sack of lies," a voice cut in, coming into view from his own hideout.

Fallyn and Eli both looked towards the spy as Fallyn was the first to speak up, "I wondered when you would come out from the shadows."

"Don't even talk to me, you traitor!" the man barked as he approached Eli.

Eli fumbled with is words, almost ashamed of the emotion he had felt for Fallyn, "Kent, he... what if what he says is true? ... he didn't turn on us yet."

"Don't tell me you actually believe this shit spilling from his mouth," the man, called Kent, growled.

Eli lowered his head. Fallyn saw that Eli wanted to defend the father figure that he held but didn't want to rebuke his duty.

"As for you, shit head, I should fucking kill you where you stand! Acknowledging the deceit of our brotherhood, admitting you protect a vampire, "he growled, shoving Eli behind him when he got close enough.

Fallyn didn't try to defend himself, knowing that Kent had already made up his mind. Fallyn merely stared at the man who passed judgment.

Seeing that he hadn't picked Fallyn's rage, Kent chuckled, "I guess it doesn't really matter, though, for she is but a few moments away from her death as it is."

Fallyn's skin crawled to ice. "You lie."

Kent laughed at Fallyn's expression as he added, "oh, you would like that, wouldn't you? No, unfortunately for you, we are surrounding your hideout as we speak. I only wish I had permission from the Infernal to pop you off right now. But they would like to be filled in on your traitorous actions."

Fallyn looked towards Eli in the hope that he could tell him Kent was wrong. But all Eli did was give a sympathetic look. Fallyn cursed soundly as he dove from the thirteen-story rooftop to the ground below. He had to reach his haven fast enough to save Kathrin.

He sped through the night on his motorcycle, more reckless and distracted than ever before. He needed to find her, to reach her. And, although he was racing at speeds that even the motorcycle could barely handle, it just didn't seem fast enough.

Be safe, please be safe.

The roar of his motorbike didn't compete with the bellow that followed as he shrilled to a halt within the cavern entrance, dust sputtering in a cloud as his bike almost spun to a stop. "Kathrin! Where are you!?!"

He jumped from his motorcycle, ready to lunge down the hallway in search of her, when he heard the one thing he thought he wouldn't.

Kathrin darted around the corner in alarm, her voice practically a balm to his panicked mind. "What is it? What's wrong?!"

He froze, scanning her from head to toe to confirm his disbelief. She wore a silk off-the-shoulder blouse and a knee-high flowing skirt. No scars, no scrapes, nothing. She was perfectly fine. It was all a ruse to have Fallyn give his hideout away. But, even if any other person had followed him through the entrance he used to return home, none of them would have been able to follow him through it without his previous consent. It was the magical warding infused into the entrance that gifted that. But, with all his concern, it was only now that he realized the improbability of such a threat.

Chapter Twenty

When Kathrin heard the roar of Fallyn's panic from the comfort of her lounge chair, she was sure they were in the middle of a full-out war. So, it was to no surprise that she impulsively lunged from her seat and dove for the entrance to see what was going on. But, as she turned the corner to ask him the very question that jumped in her skin, his wracked face of fear froze her in her tracks.

He eyed her like he was staring at a ghost as if he didn't even believe she was there. And, although his eyes unnerved her in their golden glory of fire, it wasn't because they appeared full of aggression. He looked scared.

"Fallyn? What happened?"

He didn't answer her as he closed the distance between them, crushing her against him in a mouth-devouring kiss. It confused and stunned her. But, as he coaxed her lips into his frantic need of realization, she could only wantonly follow his silent directions. Her knees buckled almost instantly as her mind swam in the desire for his masculinity. He was far from tender as he commanded of her, almost violently, what she was willing to give.

Fallyn slammed her up against the table, tugging passionately off her blouse to expose her lace bra, as his hands practically bruised her flesh as he grazed, gripped, and tugged. It lit her core on fire. She was barely able to coax him out of his own jacket, him too determined to have his way to assist her before he rose her skirt. Kathrin inhaled in shock when his hands began to tug on her panties.

"Fallyn, I-" she moaned in hopes of assisting him.

His only reply was a guttural groan, "We shall get you more."

They were off before she could make another response, him already lifting her onto the table to spread her legs. He took her there, unbinding only enough to enable the act. He pumped hard and strong, Kathrin clinging onto his shoulders as she rode the furious torrent Fallyn bestowed.

And, as her mind wallowed in his glory, she couldn't shake her curiosity about what could have caused it. He snarled his need, grinding into her forcefully deep as Kathrin gazed at him in her hazed state. She studied his features that, even now, seemed tormented with untold fear. It was then that Kathrin noticed a single tear fall from the corner of Fallyn's golden eye. What was he afraid of?

Was he afraid for me? Did he think something happened to me?

It was those questions that had her hold him closer to her bosom as she rode the passion that Fallyn tried to find appeasement from his tortured mind. She could feel the pressure of her climax and, by the deepness Fallyn pummeled, was sure that his own was approaching, as well.

"Fallyn, I'm here. I'll always be here," she moaned amidst the mounding pleasure.

Fallyn coiled her into his arms in a bear grip as he cradled her head against his neck. His climax ripped through him then and filled her deeply. Even after the edge subsided and their pants of exertion became mere whispers did, he hold her there.

It was then he moaned into her ear the surety he required. "I will make sure of that, Kathrin. For even eternity would not be enough to have you by my side."

She smiled slightly as she was confused by the words while he adjusted once more to collect his attire. His eyes softened towards hers as he lifted her from her seat, raising her discarded chemise back over her shoulders.

"Forgive my impulsiveness, for I believe you should be adorned in a more eloquent manner. Here, let us sit by the fireplace," he smiled roguishly before he wrapped his arm around her waist and escorted her to the hallway, "But first, I believe we both could enjoy bathing in some water. What is it you call it?"

She chuckled lightly, "a shower."

Kathrin watched with dismay as Fallyn prepared for the evening's hunt, filling his ammo clips, sharpening his daggers, and arming himself with his Katana's. It wasn't that long ago those weapons used to make her squeamish. Now, it was more than a part of her life. What made her feel more helpless than those was her having to watch him drive out of the cavern exit practically every night while she stayed behind. Kathrin sighed as she leaned on the table to bid him farewell once more.

Fallyn was about to strap on another one of his handguns when he looked over at her. He had been noticing her level of displacement for some time now, but now that he had prepared for another night without her, it made him feel guilty for leaving her all over again. He hated seeing that face on her. So, with a small inhale to confirm he knew what he was doing, he handed her the belt and firearm instead. At first, she looked at it dumbfounded, not realizing what he meant by it, and she apologized, " I'm sorry, I didn't know you needed me to hold it for you."

That made him grin, " I do enjoy your assistance, but this is not what I am implying."

" I- I don't understand, Fallyn," she mumbled, looking at the M1911A1 as she tried to mull over the offer.

"Go ready yourself, Kathrin. Tonight, you shall hunt with me."

"What?" she stuttered in shocked, her face beaming within seconds.

He chuckled at her brightened mood as he repeated, "Yes, Kathrin. Hurry."

She looked into his smiling eyes only for a moment before she darted out of the room. Fallyn was unable to hide his laughter as he watched her scurry to their room. Then, he leaned down and retrieved a sack he had dropped aside from the day earlier and opened it up. He laid out a collar-darted leather coat, knuckle gloves, leather firearm belt, a couple of hunting knives, and her own personal Glock17 semi-automatic onto the table. He was going to give them to Kathrin soon enough. But, since she was about to join him tonight in his excursion, Fallyn figured now was as good of a time as any.

She was quicker than he assumed she would be, turning the corner, sporting a pair of figure-flattering denim jeans, a tight emerald green t-shirt, and a pair of brown hiking boots. She clasped her hair out of her face, the one lock of platinum silver hanging down onto her shoulder in obvious view.

"This is good, right?" she questioned as she glanced for his approval before she moved any further in.

Fallyn nodded, his own desires kindling with the faint glimpse of her.

"It is perfect, Kathrin. Yet, I do think you are missing

a few items. Come collect them," Fallyn assured her as he motioned over at the items on the table.

Her eyes widened, "Oh my god, Fallyn! They're great!"

She wasted no time throwing on the garb designed for her. She buckled the firearms onto her hips. The knives followed thereafter, hidden under the veils of her leather jacket. Once her outfit was complete, Fallyn could agree that she was ready for a night as a warrior.

"Let us leave, Kathrin," he motioned, heading towards his bike.

"Okay," she answered and climbed onto the bike behind him as the engine roared to life.

❀❀❀❀❀❀

Kathrin couldn't express how happy she was as they zoomed towards the capital of British Columbia. Fallyn finally thought she was good enough to take out and fight the darkness. He better have thought that Kathrin found herself answering herself, they had been sparing for some time now as it was.

She was sure Fallyn enjoyed their practicing, too, because when they were done mending each other's battle wounds, he always had this thick grin just barely hiding behind his eyes. Fallyn knew she was ready for battle from the first moment she awoke, though. He simply cared too much for her to want to have her face the odds that far outweighed them. But now that the Infernal had shown their interest in their situation, Fallyn felt it even safer for her to be by his side rather than hidden away.

"Kathrin, last night I was faced with disturbing news," he began as he turned his head to speak over his shoulder.

"I guessed as much; you were pretty shaken up," she replied. The memory of their primal connection flashed into their mind again, which had her slightly blushing.

Fallyn agreed as he continued, "the Infernal came to me last night."

"The organization you're with? Are they coming to help you out?" she yelled over the noise of the streets.

"Quite doubtful. I have been pronounced traitorous. Undoubtedly, by the month's end, I will be on their warrant list."

"Are you serious?! What the hell have you done that makes you traitorous? Every frickin' night you're out here killing monsters," she growled, appalled with the idea.

"It is not the demons I have destroyed that is the cause. It is the one I let live that has them question my intent."

"...Me..." she added. Her heart suddenly sunk from the joy she once had. It was her fault he was going to be hunted by the Infernals. "I knew I was a bigger burden than needed."

"I refuse to listen to you say that. I do not regret my choice. If they heard my argument, they could see you are a helpful ally. They must simply allow it."

"But how do I prove that? It's easier said than done, don't you think?"

Fallyn nodded, "It is indeed. Yet to prove it would be simply doing what you do normally. Be yourself and fight alongside me as my partner. Do not doubt that your actions will fall to their ears."

She knew Fallyn was right. Frankly, Kathrin didn't care what fell onto who's ears. As long as she was with him, helping him by any means she could. She wanted to be part of the legacy he was weaving. She wanted to fight against the things she always seemed to run away from. These were the things she cared about.

"So, what's the plan tonight?"

Fallyn hid his smile at her determination. Her defiance to stand against the world was so admirable. After a thousand years, it finally gave him the strength to face it yet again himself.

"I have heard rumors that a creature torments the shorelines of the city. If I am correct, I believe it is none other than a Briacci. I assume it is a decent place to begin our night. If things go well, I have another rumor to follow, a little more hazardous."

Kathrin chuckled, "ah, so you're testing me out, eh?

Don't think I could whip your ass to the ground again?"

Fallyn chuckled as well, "A woman's scorn I would rather avoid. But I am sure you had only 'beginners' luck' on your side."

"I can prove that wrong, you know."

"I cannot wait for the moment, Alhaja." Fallyn smiled, thinking he was going to enjoy the night even more now that she was around.

Chapter Twenty-One

It was only the skylights from the city buildings that reflected into the murky water of the blackened docks. Kathrin's nose curled slightly at the moldy stench that wafted from the damp wood. She was quite aware that now wouldn't be the time to start a conversation, and Fallyn was already giving her the signal that a Briacci could be nearby. She watched Fallyn as his eyes blazed into their yellow glow while he led the way, having her follow the idea by reverting her own into their silver-heightened form. Kathrin couldn't see anything out of the ordinary, although they both drew their weapons in preparation. After some time, Kathrin began to wonder if there was anything here at all because even their keen senses didn't give them any clues of where it could be.

"Do you think it was a false lead?" she whispered over at Fallyn, who was only a few feet away.

Fallyn shook his head, still scouring the boats docked among the harbors. "This is the worst of the hunt, Kathrin. The wait."

Kathrin sighed but accepted the answer as she followed close behind. Then suddenly, an odor permeated of the worst rot she could imagine, and Fallyn announced what Kathrin had already assumed.

"The scent, alhaja. It is close," he whispered,

glancing into each of the shadows cascaded by the waterfront and ships to find it.

Kathrin didn't see it at first, but her prognostic awareness showed her where it would dart to in mere seconds. She quickly pointed in the direction of the malformed goblin for Fallyn to see before she phased out of reality and darted away. Fallyn cursed at Kathrin's action. She shouldn't take off now! They'll lose it for sure! Then, he noticed the movement of the Briacci from the corner of his eye. He tried to fire a shot to paralyze it from its escape but missed it by a hair as it lunged out of its hiding spot.

Fallyn tried to locate Kathrin as he retrieved his katanas, but to no avail. Gritting, he darted for the Briacci instead. He had to put faith in her, he reminded himself. It had been a long time since he had a partner. He had to trust her instincts if they were ever going to work as a team. The Briacci squealed its fear as it scrambled away, losing sight of Kathrin just as much as Fallyn had. Though it was mangled and bone-like- Fallyn didn't underestimate its speed as he gave chase. He jumped over the docks and through the ships in his attempt to catch it.

Where would she have gone?

The Briacci reached the edge of the waterfront cliff where houses of the finest design stood above. It tried to climb its way up the cliff-side only to fall onto it's back. Squealing, it attempted again. Fallyn raised his sword to strike the finishing blow when Fallyn heard the whiz of a bullet brush past his ear, followed by the guttural cry from the little creature who tried to flee from him.

Fallyn turned around the moment Kathrin phased back into reality and witnessed, with much surprise, her claws impaling a much larger monstrosity within the chest that hid behind Fallyn. As the larger devil snarled on its final breaths, Fallyn glanced at her with awe.

"How did you know of the mature Briacci," Fallyn marveled at the fact he wasn't even aware of it, yet she was.

Kathrin shrugged slightly as she placed her Glock17 back into its holster. She casually stepped over the beast as it began its dissipation. Returning to the shoreline, she washed her hands. Kathrin eventually replied, rather lightly, "One of the books you had me read explained that once the Briacci begin to attack it meant there is more than one to their pack. Also, the stench is more horrible if the creatures are near an adult or of the mature nature."

"Well done, Kathrin," Fallyn remarked, keen towards the knowledge she retained with her tutoring.

"Okay, you're gonna' make me all embarrassed or something," she blushed, wiping her now clean hands on her denim jeans.

"You need not shy from a compliment, alhaja. It is my pride that speaks to them."

"Well... then thank you," she answered. Fallyn adored the soft speckle that flushed her cheeks.

"Are you well enough to resume, alhaja?" Fallyn grinned as he sheathed his blade onto his back and gestured to her towards his motorcycle parked at a playground nearby.

She motioned her willingness, but not before asking the one thing she had been curious about for some time. "That nickname. You've been using it for a while now. What does it mean?"

By the sudden expression he showed, Kathrin knew that he was waiting for the day she would ask. "It is an endearment, Kathrin. In the language of my birth, Spanish. It means jewel."

"Jewel," Kathrin repeated as she pondered the nickname.

"For you are mi joya preciosa, my precious jewel." Fallyn acknowledged as he escorted her towards their ride.

"Okay, okay. Now I really am embarrassed. Where to next?" Kathrin groaned in an attempt to change the topic. Fallyn, seeing the blush speckling her cheeks once more, was less than offended by it. He grinned at her distraction.

"I have heard of a lair that needs investigating. It is from your brethren."

They arrived at a shutdown factory near the center of the city. All the blocks around it were like a barren wasteland, although they were in the very heart of the capital. It was almost saddening, Kathrin sighed. Why did these parts become so lost in time? Fallyn distracted her thoughts when he clarified what he had planned for the event to come.

"It has been said that your brethren have been using this area to assemble. As can be concluded, when vampires collect in mass volumes, mortals go missing at a much-accelerated rate than they should to avoid human involvement. So, it would be best if we take out this shelter in one fatal swoop."

Kathrin nodded with approval as she followed close behind. But, before they made it to the factory, Fallyn stopped short and turned around, "I shall scout first. Please wait for me here. I shall retrieve you once I learn of their numbers."

"Okay, Fallyn. But you better come back. I'll kick your ass if I find out you are trying to do a 'One-man-show' here," she snickered, but somehow Fallyn knew that there was some truth to it.

"I promise you, Kathrin. You are my partner now.

Companions work together on the battlefield." His hand caressed the side of her jaw lightly before he parted ways.

Kathrin leaned against the alleyway wall and looked at the worn-down buildings nearby. Kathrin never had a reason to travel to the city's center. Her previous employer and condo were on the outskirts of this massively populated area. But this was disheartening. It was such a desolate wasteland. The boulevard she looked across was grimy, with broken windows and signs of businesses that no longer existed littering the sidewalks. That was a pale comparison to the homeless citizens who huddled together on the other side of the road. Hundreds of them were waiting for a turn to have a single warm meal for the night before they would try to sleep somewhere.

No one wanted these people. Not even society would give them a chance as they tried to live until the next day. It was no wonder that people would randomly disappear in this vicinity, Kathrin thought. They were so easily accessible for the vampires, and no one would care if a few more would be off the streets.

Heartless.

Kathrin felt something reverberate within her. Her skin prickled, and her palms became clammy. Someone was approaching her, and their thoughts were carnal and deadly. No, not someone. A Vampire.

Her muscles spazed as they suddenly became

heavy inside her. Her body was claimed with another gruesome image of death. A man… a homeless man, was having his throat crushed under a mouth of a demon. Kathrin, curious, glanced over at the crowd across the way. These were not her images, she finally realized after so long of dealing with them. These were what some other vampire was doing right now.

The call was too familiar within her. She knew who it was; she could see his deeds through his eyes like they were her own. And, as the blood coursed into his mouth, he gave witness to her presence too. He looked at her from the mass of poverty and grinned.

Run! You gotta' run!

Kathrin wanted to with all that she was, but her body was sluggish; Her blood like anvils in her veins. He snapped the neck of the homeless man and shoved his way through the crowd, tossing the body to the floor without care from anyone else.

Her mind blurred with all the evils he had done the closer he approached. Her blood boiled. Her eyes and fangs responded involuntarily with what he did to her. She had to get him out of her mind!

He was thirty feet away. Her body convulsed as she remained stationed where he wanted her to be.

Twenty feet…Ten feet. Death, curiosity…Daimos.

"What a most pleasant surprise to finally meet you,

my daughter," Daimos called, examining her demonic features and the awakened tells they carried.

She felt burned by his presence. Her mouth outstretched to hiss the heat that bubbled within her. He was drawing the evil from her and Kathrin was losing her control.

"Stop…it," Kathrin grimaced, the reins on her rage slipping.

"What, dear child? The hold I have on you or the innate call that your body cannot resist?" Daimos sneered.

Kathrin couldn't answer him, for her mind, what wasn't tormented by his visions of madness, was using every inch of her will to maintain control. Watching her helplessness, Daimos chuckled.

"Why do you venture out in the mire of the city by yourself?"

Kathrin growled. The mass level of heartbeats called out at her senses. He was elevating her desire to feed, wanting to throw her into a frenzy. She almost knew he would find pleasure in the thought of her being just like him.

"Fuck you."

"Aww, now that isn't a way to talk to your father, Kathrin," Daimos smiled, though he tried to sound offended by her insult.

"You're not … my father."

"In death, your blood became mine, so yes… in the realm of the dark, I have sired you. But I wonder why you are all alone out here?" Daimos glanced around the surroundings, towards the many faces. It wasn't a guess who he meant. Fallyn.

"Doing my…own thing…. what does it matter?" Kathrin gritted.

"Hmmm," was his only response as he returned his gaze to her. Within a minute, he continued, "Why not come with me and let me show you the ways of our society? It would be only fitting to learn the ways from a second generation."

"…Bugger off…," she seethed. She needed to find anything that could help break his hold on her.

Daimo's powder blue eyes glared at her as they turned into their own silver glow. He growled his displeasure with fangs, "I warn you; I will not have a child sired from my blood be connected to a heathen such as him…"

Kathrin could see what he meant as his visions of her death crept into her mind if she didn't give up her place with Fallyn. She felt the approach of two other vampires. Daimos must have called them with a thought. They crawled out from behind the dispossessed crowd and business alike. Even with more danger approaching, she couldn't break his ties to her.

"Let… me go!" Kathrin's face was the purest, carnal demon it could reach, her restraint a hairline from complete annihilation.

When the other vampires were upon them, they hissed their own lecherous need towards Kathrin as they circled her. Daimos threatened her with surety, "Last chance, daughter. Come with me and leave the menace you stay with, and I'll spare your life. If not, I will kill you where you stand and have these vampires absorb your blood into their bodies."

She couldn't answer him, or she refused to. Daimos wasn't sure of the situation as she resisted his temptation. She was a strong-spirited one, something he could find pride breaking even if she came involuntarily. Daimos glanced down at her comely physique and thought that he would even enjoy fucking her with or without her consent. She would be a desirable mate to have chained under his control.

Kathrin shuddered, feeling like she was beginning to choke on her own breaths. Gasping, she closed her eyes to the strength she held on to by a thread. Kathrin felt the arrival of someone else. Cool and electrifying. Please be someone who will help her. Please be Fallyn.

❄ ❄ ❄ ❄ ❄ ❄

Fallyn had begun his return for Kathrin with his discovery that the warehouse was abandoned in a hurry.

There were no signs of vampire or human activity. It was nothing but a dusty, scattered mess. They must have caught wind of his hunt. He had hoped he would've been able to dispose of a large source of them in one sure strike. But, seeing the outcome of his search, it wouldn't be tonight.

When Fallyn turned the corner of one of the apartment complexes to meet with Kathrin, a strange and girdled heat began to bubble within him. It wasn't his own pain or anger, Fallyn recognized as much, but whomever it was, there was a force that was breaking down its will. Fallyn reached for his katanas as he snuck closer towards the unnatural sensation. With each fateful step closer to the origin, more bile rose into his throat.

When the cool breeze of the early morning carried the scent of honeyed lilacs and pungent decay, Fallyn was affirmed it was Kathrin's mind that he was feeling. She was confronted by her brethren. He peered around the corner at the vampires who threatened Kathrin with nothing but soundless stealth. Three of them, one of them was Daimos, and Kathrin was battling a frenzy once more. Undoubtedly, because of Daimo's presence, Fallyn judged. She was a hairline away from losing everything.

Without a chance to be detected by the three, Fallyn charged out and beheaded one of the lesser vampires. With the growl from the other two, Fallyn swung towards the second. He knew it was better to leave the toughest enemy for last.

Daimos remained behind Kathrin in her struggle for humanity as he cursed towards the interruption he wasn't prepared for. Fallyn had to be killed. Daimos growled, looking at the battle that was pursued. He glanced back at Kathrin to determine a fitful demise, and a sinfully pleasant idea suddenly came to mind. If he couldn't have Kathrin agree to join him, then he would give her a reason to.

With her willpower at the end of its thread, Kathrin pleaded to any higher being to ease her internal chaos. She couldn't see past the bubbles of death, but she knew that Fallyn was assisting her. But, if she slipped even a fraction, this rage would turn on him and Kathrin was horrified with that possibility. Suddenly, Daimos inched his way near Kathrin and began to whisper in her ear. Daimos was casting a spell, and Kathrin panicked with comprehension.

Daimos words echoed in her mind in the language of Thesius, jabbing into her sealed thoughts like a snake pushing its way into a burrow. Kathrin understood them clearly. "Power's pleasure, fury's rage. Haunting devils, take thy page. Bubbled blood that spurns from mine let her form, and thoughts entwine."

Kathrin gnashed against the torrent of shadows, the

many hands that were sealing her mind away into a blackened chamber. He was taking her over!

"Fallyn…shit! Stop the…curse! I can't…I can't…!"

Fallyn's eyes met Kathrin and understood instantly. By thrusting his sword into the vampire, Fallyn released his katana, whirled his M1911A1 out, and fired a bullet toward Daimo's head. But, before Daimos escaped the deadly promise, the final words of the incantation escaped his lips.

"Battles wills of child be, let her body belong to me."

Daimos disappeared as he withdrew in a cloud of purple smoke. Fallyn felt the oozed-layered sludge coat Kathrin's aura. Her body stumbled into a heap on the floor. He studied her as her eyes dulled completely white. He failed. Kathrin was under whatever means Daimos had subjected her too.

"You are much stronger than this, Kathrin. Fight the spell." He searched her for some level of familiarity. He had to reach his angel shrouded in the fleece of wolves.

Kathrin trembled with convulsions before she rose to her feet once again. Her nails enlarged; her face expressionless. She hunkered down in a primal, undeniable preparation of battle.

"Kathrin, hear me. I am here to help you. This is not who you are."

She paused. His words were reaching whatever

speck of her that could hear.

She phased out of reality. But, before Fallyn found where she was, her nails buried deep into his back. He grimaced.

"Kathrin...fight him." Fallyn groaned.

He couldn't raise his blade, not when his heart belonged with her.

"Kathrin, I am here for you...Te quiero, mi joya preciosa."

Kathrin's nails withdrew, and Fallyn fell onto his knees. He exhaled an even breath. He waited for another crucial blow, but nothing else ensued. Confused, Fallyn glanced behind him. Kathrin, too, was slumped on the floor, her own tears staining her face and hands.

"Kathrin?" Fallyn wheezed.

"I am a monster...I almost killed you... again."

Fallyn couldn't help his moan of relief as he crawled over to her on the ground and drew her into his arms. He comforted her as her tears dampened his trench coat. He understood her pain. It was difficult to accept the possibility that someone could control your every motion with a few empowered words.

"You are no monster, alhaja. Those actions were not of your own will." Fallyn soothed, the muscle and sinew binding itself together in his gaping wounds.

"The rage.... I couldn't control the rage he called

from me…I don't think I'll be able to handle another bout if it happens again…" Kathrin sobbed aloud, pouring the fear she'd been keeping secret for weeks.

"You have been fighting much lately, alhaja. I have witnessed your battles," Fallyn admitted as the skin itched to its mended form.

"You… you have?" Kathrin pondered alarmed.

Fallyn clenched her even closer. "I fear I may have wronged you to have awoken your blood."

Kathrin glanced up in awareness to the lightning of the sky as dawn approached. She shook her in denial. "It's Daimos I've been fighting… I now know that the murderous images I've been having are his."

Aware of the time remaining as well, Fallyn lifted Kathrin from the alleyway floor and carried her toward his motorcycle. Fallyn heard the theory that a bond was formed between father and child within the vampire society, but he never truly knew the gravity that it entailed.

"That is unfortunate, alhaja. For I do not know of ways to mend such connections."

Kathrin slung her arms around his shoulders in thought. It was perturbing to think of the power Daimos had on her. They departed in silence, Fallyn unable to reply to the predicament while Kathrin tried to think of anything that could prevent the path, she was heading down from happening. When he sat her down upon on his

Kawasaki, Kathrin spoke up.

"Fallyn?"

"What is it, mi joya preciosa?"

"Thank you for helping me." Her gratitude was evident with her words.

"It is a pale equivalent to what I am indebted to you."

"-And... I love you too." a small smile curved the corner of Kathrin's worried lips to give reassurance.

Fallyn smiled vaguely at her awareness. "Come. We shall return to our haven before dawn scars your flesh."

Chapter Twenty-Two

The instant it was destroyed, Daimos roared aloud from the severed bond with Kathrin, shattering a historical sculpture of him in his youth in a violent hurl. She was far too strong for the likes of a child, Daimos seethed. No vampire of a lesser generation should be able to break the ties to their parent under incantations such as that. She should have completely been under his control until he decided otherwise. But, in only a few short minutes, she had pushed him from her mind and locked away the key.

Daimos stormed the room with agitation. He was in a mansion designated for all first-born vampires; his own abode littered with the treasures he collected along the hundreds of years of existence.

Why was she able to resist his manipulation?

Although Daimos couldn't think of the answer himself, he somehow knew that something was different with her than other vampires. It itched the back of his skull, picking to the corners of his knowledge. Daimos paused next to a table that held objects from the 16th century and closed his eyes.

He recalled the atmosphere that came with the possession. Blurred and hazy, dizzy. It felt as though he was in a bottle relearning the basic functions of the human body. But... it was warm. A sensation that he hadn't felt in eons. Daimo's eyes opened with a flash, the realization slamming against him like a tidal wave. Then, a faint sound appeared, quiet but constant... then another.

"It can't be," Daimos gasped, " It's impossible."

But it was and Daimos, after a few minutes, realized the advantage of the extraordinary miracle. Kathrin would be his alive, and her ability would be used to the utmost. Then, there would be no question of generational strength. There would be many awakened vampires in the eras to come.

Within their bed, Kathrin yawned lazily as she rolled over to embrace Fallyn. Within seconds, Kathrin realized Fallyn wasn't beside her. Kathrin leaned up on her arm and scanned the room as she rubbed her eyes. He never left the bed, let alone the room, without alerting her in some form or another.

Because she wasn't notified at all, Kathrin was a little uneasy. It was only within a few seconds of scouting their quarters that she noticed the whispering orb on the bedside table. The last time she saw that, it was in the library. Kathrin twisted her legs off the side of the bed and reached for a candle to light. Once the flames danced playfully on the wick, she glanced back at the orb and suddenly felt defeat. The fluid bubbled wildly within the restraints of the glass in a most vibrant of red.

"Oh, Fallyn," Kathrin sighed, dismayed. With all the wild whirlwind events that they've gone through, Kathrin forgot completely about the curse that drove Fallyn out of the cavern.

She dressed for the evening, carrying the orb along as she went about. She forever gazed back at it while she attempted to read more bound novels or tidy what she could. But, when the orb didn't lessen from its boiling fury by the end of the night, Kathrin's anxiety grew even further. How long would it be before he returned safe? After a while, she caught herself pacing at the entrance to their home, averting her eyes now and again in hopes of finding him there instead. What, on earth, was he facing? What demon plagued him that he was so afraid of? Did he need her help, even now? Glancing down at the floor in thought, her silver lock of hair bounced into her peripheral view. She looked at it and thought of what it represented. Suddenly, Kathrin came to the most reckless idea she had yet.

She was an Awakened, and quite frequently showed Fallyn how good she was at it. So, Kathrin reasoned by this that if she was able to defeat Fallyn before, it shouldn't be difficult to do so again, if needed be. So, ignoring her vow to Fallyn, Kathrin rushed to collect some belongings of his into a sack. She figured he may need his clothing, at least. Kathrin did a final scan of the entrance and noticed both

Fallyn's and her weaponry. No, she argued to herself immediately. She wouldn't possibly use them against him. With a swallow, she rushed fearlessly into the blackness from the cavern's exit.

She didn't know where she was heading, but she knew enough by Fallyn's explanation that all she had to do was think where she wanted to go to get there. By her desire to find Fallyn, she knew she would be taken to him. She craved to be there for him now. After all, there were countless times he had been there for her; it only seemed fit to return the favor.

The blackness bled into droplets of reds and greens like she had stepped onto a canvas, and she was the prism to the colors among it. They bounced and shimmered with each of her steps as they expanded into different hues from the previous until all schemes of the rainbow had dabbed onto the mural at work. Then, the vision took form as features and figures took their place. The swashes of green became a thick, overgrown forest, and the reds bled into the navy sky like northern lights until she no longer walked amongst the drippings of paint but within the mural of reality.

The chill was sharp as Kathrin noticed the frost coating everything around her. Kathrin clutched the sack onto her shoulders. She had to keep focused.

It wasn't long within her travels before faint

whispers alongside the snapping of twigs under her footsteps drew her attention. They were what appeared to be little devils of minuscule size. They peered around the plant life up to the new stranger.

"There rides a vampire blood with us."

"Yes, a vampire. Tasty flesh, have they."

"Forever has a vampire dared to enter this land-"

"-By chance, she, too, can meet the fates like all the rest."

"And then her flesh we shall consume."

The taunts were eerie as they shrilled one after the other, threatening her with jeers as they scrambled away from her. Kathrin was taken aback by the fact they roamed so openly within the forest. Why didn't they hide like normal devils did from humanity? They continued to follow her with chortles of her death they believed followed. But when a fowl stench swarmed upon the breeze, they froze in their tracks. What was that horrible smell?

"Go no further," they hissed as they sunk behind the trees.

"Stay away from the destroyer."

"Our lives will be spared."

"For we are not as foolish as the vampire is."

Kathrin turned to press for an explanation at the label 'destroyer' but they were already gone. A sound similar to an exhaled breath loomed over the woods ahead, faces of perverse insanity taking form among the shadows and leaves. Kathrin swallowed hard, a cold chill of fingers fluttering down her spine. Kathrin never read of a devil being referred to as 'the destroyer,' but the name itself gave away that it was known for killing even lesser demons. It truly must be untouched by compassion if madness and carnage were its only focus. Kathrin couldn't help but shudder as she stepped closer to where she knew she had to go. Something innate inside told her so. Then, a howl of overbearing agony drummed sharply against the trunks of the trees, and she recognized it instantly.

Fallyn's howl was panicked; suffered. Was Fallyn in the clutches of this 'Destroyer'? Was he battling something even worse than his own monstrous curse? All the questions of dread echoed in her mind as she raced to the source of distraught.

"I'm coming, Fallyn! Hold on!" she hollered.

It seemed like only seconds when she arrived at the edge of the forest's foliage, halting near a clearing of a shifted meadow. That was where she found him in amidst the crumbling rocks that broke the meadow's smoothness.

Carcasses of things unidentifiable laid amidst Fallyn's naked body in bloodied horror, each of them gored in manners that were less than humane. She couldn't pull her eyes away as she watched Fallyn shifting back into his mortal form, hardly any depiction of the beast he once was except for the bristled hairs still edging his hands, torso, and feet. His face was winced in a primal snarl as he knelt on his hands and knees. Holy hell, Kathrin thought, she barely recognized him. Was she sure about this now that she looked at what was left of his actions before? There were dozens of carcasses around him.

"It is never wise to find your own demise, young one," his voice roared, deep and snarling, almost God-like in its supremacy.

Kathrin's eyes bulged in shock as he rose to his feet, his own golden eyes flickering like fire now that the feral demon maintained its hold onto Fallyn. She didn't even notice he caught wind of her.

Fearing the powers he thus could have, Kathrin fumbled the bag off of her shoulder as she stuttered, "But, I've brought your belongings. I thought you would need them."

A haunting chuckle emanated from Fallyn as he gleamed with sadistic pleasure, "A gift for me? I do not need such mortal things, el chupacabra."

He chuckled some more. Kathrin remained motionless in hopes to avoid a wrath otherwise tested. "Why not pass these belongings you speak of to me so I may mock what you mere vampires hold so dear."

Hesitantly, she did as ordered and tossed the sack high into the air to fly into his outstretched arm. He glimmered with humor at her actions before he lowered his head to begin his investigation. Kathrin waited anxiously. She wanted her Fallyn back, that she knew was trapped within this demon. She couldn't handle seeing him succumb to this.

"Does any of it look familiar to you?... Do I look familiar to you?" she mumbled, knowing no other way to confront the questions.

His eyes darted viciously away from the clothing back onto her within seconds as he knew what she attempted to do. He dropped the bag deliberately while he still held onto Fallyn's trench coat, the ingredients sprawling onto the ground. Within a flash, his hand was around her neck. His grip was unbearable as he raised her from the ground, lifting her above his head. She grasped instinctively at his fist.

Her body innately attempted to phase out of his grasp in her shroud from reality. But, when her power should have responded, a metallic weight clamped down like liquid metal, filling her legs from the inside out. Why isn't it working? She panicked. Why was she trapped in his grasp?

Kathrin gasped for breath, coughing to dislodge the

suppression of her own larynx. His grip was so fierce it was as if he wanted to squeeze her own head off her body like a dandelion. She couldn't speak. She barely received enough air to remain conscious as she hung at his whim. He glowered his rage at her; his intentions were very clear.

"Nothing in his life has meaning to me, nor does witnessing what he cherishes most sway my hand any less! I do not live with guilt for my pleasures, even if it means tearing out his heart!"

Her mind swam into emptiness as her resistance slowly diminished from her limbs. Her mind almost slipped into a much-needed slumber. His eyes were then drawn to the horizon. When he returned his gauntly stare back towards hers, he loosened his grip on her throat just enough for her to breathe.

"Mayhaps I can make his heart crumble a little more. For your foolish desire to save him has put you at a vicarious position yourself. Look and see your death impending," he smiled wickedly as he spun her body around to show her what he spoke of.

As Kathrin panted desperately to fill her lungs, she could barely look toward where he directed. Her skin began to itch with untold knowledge. She noticed the sun cresting over the mountains in the distance, at that moment, and her eyes bulged in horror. Mortified, she tried to squirm out of his grasp, unable to break his hold on her as she felt the flickers of her skin sting from the rays of the sun. The moment her body began melting from its curse, the demon that held Fallyn's body captive winced. He shielded his eyes from the brightness of the sun in a hiss of pain, dropping Kathrin so she crumpled in a heap onto the ground.

His form adjusted as the final bestial grasp slid out of his body. The bristled fur that nestled on his limbs and torso receded, the feral features of his face and eyes easing into the person they had hold of. And, as Fallyn staggered into his control once more, he confusedly looked down at his hand that held his trench coat.

How did that get here? He couldn't remember a thing. The only probable answer suddenly flooded his mind in a spike of dread. He spun his gaze around in search of her when he found Kathrin standing before the sun. His eyes widened in alarm as he witnessed the sun crumbling her flesh to ash. She returned the gaze in agonized recollection, knowing somewhere that this would be their last meeting.

When Fallyn winced away from the sun and dropped her to the ground, her nerves began to ignite on fire. She couldn't run or move herself from the paralyzing anguish that swept her body. Her skin was crisping away. Tears streamed down her marred face; she knew this was where she was going to die. Nothing she could do could save her from the promise the sun bestowed. Kathrin shuddered violently as she forced herself onto her feet, her skin peeling away into pungent ashes to reveal the muscles and sinew below. If she was to meet her fate for her ignorance, she wanted to, at least, see her Fallyn just one last time.

Their eyes met. Fallyn bewildered with her presence which turned to sudden terror, Kathrin loving him with the knowledge that there would be no more words of endearment between them. When the skin on her face began to burn, Kathrin winced again before she spoke, "I love you, Fallyn."

"No," Fallyn gasped as he refused to accept what Kathrin already had.

His blood ran cold. His insides were torn apart. He flung his coat around Kathrin to shield her from the sun as she fell limp. Then, he raced away with her in his arms. All logic was gone while his mind tortured itself with the pleas to spare her life as he ran. Nothing mattered but her safety. Even as the devils skittered with hisses at his sight, he not slow.

"Do not die now, Kathrin! Hold on for but a few more seconds!" he hollered at her lifeless body. There was not one God he didn't pray to.

Only until he flooded them with the darkness of his cavern did his panic ease ever so slightly. "Why were you there, Kathrin?! Why did you come!?"

Even though his words were as vicious as the edge of a sword, Fallyn was more frustrated with himself that he didn't prevent such a fatal occurrence from happening. He placed her gently onto the mattress as he cursed what his trench coat revealed. Her flesh was boiled, the mere sight of it nauseating his stomach, although he witnessed far worse hundreds of times before. He, almost thoughtlessly, slit his wrist and pressed it against her blistered lips.

"Drink, Kathrin," he groaned with urgency. But, when nothing changed with her within seconds, he growled far more hastily, "Drink!!"

His fingers massaged her throat as he tried to force his sustenance into her limp, frail body in desperation. Still, the minutes passed, and nothing changed.

"I vow to myself," gritted Fallyn, tears glimmering in the corners of his eyes at the mere thought he could be at fault for this, "I vow if her death is upon your hands, I will feed myself to the very depths of hell…"

Waiting for a sign of her well-being felt more helpless than any trials he faced before. His fingers gripped the duvet, convulsing with unbearable grief. He needed to know something. Anything. When he couldn't fathom anything else, he averted his eyes into their higher plane of sight. He knew it was pointless for him to try methods used to identify a person alive. They wouldn't work on someone undead, but he had to try something. Yet, unlike any vampire he'd faced before, her body was much different. Her heart fluttered in her chest; she had a pulse. Only at this point did he see her weakened breath inhale into her lungs. He closed his eyes to restrain his emotion.

"Thank the heavens!" he moaned, glancing towards the foot of the bed as he tried to collect his composure.

With this averted glance, he spotted something that paled him with utter shock. He stumbled on his own feet as he stepped away from the bed. He glanced back to Kathrin's face for answers even she couldn't explain. And, for once in his life, he felt like he was faced with something no books could prepare him for.

Chapter Twenty-Three

The sky wept as Kathrin walked up the cobbled pathway that led to the ossuary at the peak of the cemetery, glancing upon the graves. She knew who waited for her at the crest of the hill from the call of her blood. Scanning each of the tombstones where bodies were buried, she saw the spirits of the dead howling at her to save them from their eternal unrest. They were trapped in their corpses because of the way they were killed, all gifted by the very person she now approached. This was the same fated intended for her if not for Fallyn's intervention. Each of her motions now, though, were marionetted by this demon, her feeling his fingers guiding her from within. He even filtered her rationale and fears.

"Come, my child," he hummed within her mind.

His voice was hypnotic, gruff, with a fateful promise that Kathrin couldn't avoid. She pressed further, the transparent hands of the ghosts clawing at the ground on which she walked until she reached the large wooden doors of the gauntly decorated cathedral. The gates opened on their own accord, whining their weight with the swing. Then, Kathrin saw the man of a massacre, her creator, as he turned around to greet her. He grinned almost seductively as he offered her a gesture of greeting with a bow, a formality.

"I've been wanting to speak to you, daughter. Please, come closer to me," Daimos smiled with a motion that couldn't hide the dangers of his character.

She wanted to tell him where to go, almost made her lips bleed with her effort although all she could do was follow his commands. Her hands folded among themselves as she elegantly walked to him, her head bowed towards the floor in forced submission. He manipulated her presence; even the empress-style gown of velvet wine that she wore was all affected by the whims of this vampire. When her steps drew her close enough to him, her hand rose to his involuntarily. He escorted her to the pulpit's stairs.

"My daughter of the night," he began as he guided her to the skull-decorated wall embedded with candles of silver and white. "You've passed your trial, something I haven't seen in centuries. But, as the first to accept your destiny in some time, you also are the first in a birth of evolution."

She felt the hold on her mouth finally loosen to allow her to lash out her bitterness. "A trial?? That's what you're calling your carnage? Call it what it really is in the eyes of God, a sadistic sin which means any less to you, however the outcome."

Daimos smiled slyly as he motioned her to sit on a

pedestal, "I'd figured by now you would've realized that God turns a blind eye to us."

Kathrin fought to remain on her feet, but he forced her down with his will to sit on the very pedestal he directed. Frustrated with her lack of self-control, she was at least grateful with her unguarded tongue. "If he truly cared less about us, then why is it vampires are cursed to the night? Why do you cower in shadows as you wait for your time to come? God's might comes in the most peculiar of ways, but we will all witness it in the end."

Daimos did not seem the least bit affected by her words as he paced a few steps away. As he gazed towards the skeletal candelabra hanging suspended from the ceiling, his eyes beamed with enjoyment.

"Your views are not far from where I was in the years of my youth, Kathrin. For I, too, believed an end would come to us and humanity would be saved. But, as I lived in the shadows, waiting for the Armageddon of my fate to come to greet me, I witnessed the rise and fall of man time and again. War after war, plague after plague, the deaths of my loved ones happen time and again. I witnessed the evils of man expose itself even in the babes I saw grow from shelters beside my own. It was with this repetitious nature of man that made me realize that humanity brought forth their own damnation and not from what lurked in the night. If there is a higher being that truly means to cleanse the world, then why do they- themselves- flood the gates of hell with their souls? No, Kathrin, our God merely watches the world's distraught and we merely have the privilege to withstand their destruction. We simply can deliver them to their fates earlier without the pain they would have otherwise."

His comments enraged Kathrin. How could he view the hundreds, if not thousands, of deaths as nothing more than 'delivering them to their fate'? "I will never hold life as careless as you!"

He laughed, "'As careless as me'? Look around you. Are all the stabbings at night by man a proclamation of their love for life? Each gunshot to someone's heart, each bomb fired to helpless countries, is that the actions of a race that holds any value to life?"

"Stop it," Kathrin moaned, her awareness of the man's flaws drawing tears to her eyes. "Nothing you say will ever sway my heart to accept what time will bring, unlike you, who will always hide like a coward until he flushes you out of your hole!"

With that growl from Kathrin, Daimo's eyes returned back to hers, "That's right, isn't it? You're also the first to sway the hand of the very one we abhor. It still amazes me that he shelters you, knowing what you really are."

Kathrin paled when she realized how her candid tongue gave away what she was trying to hide from him before. Kathrin turned her eyes away to hide her fear of his knowledge. But he returned them slowly with his fingers on her chin.

"Tell me, how is it to bed the very person who hunts your kind? To find ecstasy in the hands of a destroyer?"

'Destroyer.' Kathrin gasped at the title she had heard only once before but now finally understood its meaning. The destroyer that the goblins in the forest referred to was not some other demon, as she thought, but the very one she loved. She cursed herself for her naivety as she growled through her teeth, "What do you want, Daimos?"

A noise of bittersweet amusement escaped his lips as he rose to his full height once again, "Tell me where he is."

Dumbfounded by the request, Kathrin paused for a moment before she laughed out, "I think not. Why the hell would I ever tell you where he is?"

Honestly, Kathrin couldn't answer the question anyhow. She didn't know where, exactly, their hideout was and every time they departed from Fallyn's lair, they appeared someplace new. It was never close enough to civilization and never the same exit that was used before. She'd never let Daimos know that, though, and wouldn't correct whatever he chose to believe. What stunned her, though, was when he joined her in her laughter. His chuckles were deep and reverberating with some sort of evil scheme.

"I knew you'd never tell me if I threatened your own life. After all, you've already admitted you would accept your death when it arrived. I also know you'd never give away that knowledge to save Fallyn cause we both know he doesn't need to be defended. I assumed you'd offer it to protect something a little more personal."

Kathrin examined him, looking for the secret he held hostage as he motioned her to her feet. Those were the only two methods she knew would sway her enough to answer, so if neither of them was what he intended to use against her, then what would it be?

When Daimos saw the curiosity in her eyes, he smiled softly. "When I told you that you were the first to a new line in evolution, I meant that because of your uniqueness, something I figured you didn't know about yourself. Vampires are creatures of the dead; all our organs cease to function when we turn. But somehow, yours have remained very much alive. You breathe, your heart beats, you continue to maintain every aspect." And as his hand pressed firmly against her abdomen, he made it quite clear what he referred to as he spoke, "even the aspect of procreation."

Her limbs went numb, astonished by the idea he led her to believe. She couldn't be pregnant, could she? It was impossible for the dead to conceive. She wanted to believe he was tricking her, trying to manipulate her to give him what he desired. But even as she tried to make herself believe those words, somehow, she knew they were all wrong.

Daimos grinned at her, distraught, hoping that now it would drive home her sense of survival as he smirked, "I doubt Fallyn would make a respectable father."

"Shut up," she moaned, pushing his hand away from her abdomen as she spat, "I've had enough of your bull shit! I'll never tell you, even if what you say is true!"

With her vow of silence, Kathrin began to fight the strings that held her like a puppet. She had to cut the ties to this nightmare. She backed away from him as if ripping off the sections of skin where each thread secured her. Daimos watched her, almost delighted with her effort as her face winced slightly.

"Haven't you learned, by now, that your blood is beholden to me," he scoffed as she stumbled on her toes. "You can only leave if I see fit."

Kathrin glared viciously towards him. She refused to believe that. Fallyn had told her plenty of times how it is the will of the mind that can free you from any conundrum you may enter. Kathrin grasped to this thought as she was intent on proving that no beholden 'calling-of-the-blood' would change that.

The candles that flickered on the wall beside them

began to bleed wax of blood as she stepped away some more. Her stress pressed into her raspy voice, "You'll never control me, Daimos. Neither me nor any child I conceive."

Kathrin could hear a call of her name echo in the distance. It was a voice of security that was searching for her. Daimos growled with frustration because of it.

"You seemed concerned, Daimos," she grimaced as the ground began to shudder into hues of black.

Daimos snarled back, irritated with her response, "I will find you, Kathrin. He won't be there to save you forever."

As the ground opened to swallow her whole, Kathrin knew those words were very much true.

❉ ❉ ❉ ❉ ❉ ❉

Kathrin opened her eyes with a start. Her vision was so real, she almost forgot what brought her to that place to begin with. She was burning before the sun. But then her confusion settled in. She should be, in all sense, dead. The sun's vow was already quite prominent upon her flesh when she fainted. She turned her head to its side and found her hand resting parallel to her shoulder. She wasn't burned at all. Kathrin didn't need to think twice about who had saved her, for he always had a tendency for coming to her rescue in the nick of time.

She gave a small stretch before she slowly eased up

in her bed. She didn't even have a chance to ponder where Fallyn was before she found him resting in a chair across the room. She couldn't help but grin as she watched him focused on his revere once again. Undoubtedly, fixed on the recent ordeal. His arms rested on each of his legs, his head bowed towards the floor. She watched him for some time, simply observing his actions before his gaze finally met hers with a lift of his head.

At first, he was stunned to be meeting her in an awakened state. But, when it finally dawned on him, she was coherent; it didn't move him from his chair. In fact, he stared at her with so much perplexity through the hollowed pits of his eyes and the gauntly color of his skin that it told Kathrin she was much more important to him than she thought.

"Fallyn, what's wrong," she moaned after a distressing minute of them staring at each other.

The corners of Fallyn's lips curled in attempts to smile, although his features remained perplexed. "Why did you come, alhaja?"

Kathrin flushed with guilt as she looked at her lap, embarrassed by her irrational thinking. When the moment was there, she had hundreds of valid reasons why she should go to his side. Now that she awoke from the aftermath of her actions, none of them seemed suitable enough to even use. She still tried to recall one to mind, though. But, when her eyes returned to speak it, he interrupted her argument with one simple sentence.

"You swore to me, Kathrin."

Her words were lost, blushing with humility. She knew she had hurt his trust in a way she wasn't sure she could mend. The only thing that could mean anything more than dim-witted excuses from her childish mind was the apology that repeated itself within her, "I- I'm sorry, Fallyn."

Fallyn looked back towards the ground with his hurt. "I made you vow to me for a very justifiable reason, alhaja, exactly what occurred. You were only minutes from your demise, but you had given up. I saw you give up."

She tried to interrupt as she spoke up, "It was excruciating, Fallyn-"

But he would hear none of it, "What pains me more is that I cannot recall, for the life of me, what happened. Was it by fluke I arrived there? Did I hold you to that peril? It is only blackness, Kathrin."

Though his last question was the correct one, Kathrin refused to acknowledge it as she assured him, "You didn't do anything, Fallyn. It was you're curse; it even spoke to me as if he was a different person."

His eyes returned to hers, his face tormented. "Do you not realize that 'curse' is a part of me? No matter if I remember or not, I am still at fault for whatever horror it bestows upon you."

With that agonized reply, he drew himself over to the bedside to sit next to her. His hands grabbed hers gently as he was unable to dampen the turmoil swirling within his mind ever since they returned to his lair. "But I would not have been at fault for only your life. I would have been at fault for two lives. When were you going to tell me of this phenomenon, Kathrin?"

His hand caressed gently the covers where her belly was, having Kathrin gasp at shock that even he knew of it as well. She felt like she was the last one to know of this miracle, and it was her body. She blushed profoundly as she stuttered, "I didn't know until now, Fallyn. If I knew about it, I'd never done such a reckless move."

"You should not take such reckless moves for your own life! I cannot always be here for you, but do not throw your life away over perilous thinking!!" Fallyn bellowed. Clenching to collect his composure thereafter, Fallyn glanced at the mattress with a deep breath.

"I'm sorry, Fallyn," Kathrin choked, her own guilt squeezing her chest with cold realization.

Fallyn simply nodded, squeezing her hand tighter as he self-acknowledged that she was all alright. But Kathrin was still perturbed with her nightmare of Daimos'. It ate away at her surety. And so, even though she was remorseful, she thought it was much wiser to announce the conversations the two of them shared with Fallyn.

"While I was recovering from my burns, Daimos came to me in my dreams."

Fallyn returned his gaze; his own anxiety washed away the instant he heard the name of the vampire leader.

"What was it he sought?"

"He wanted to use me to find you. He knows that I am different than the other vampires. He's the one who enlightened me to my pregnancy, Fallyn. He threatened the life of our unborn child if I didn't tell him. He wants me, Fallyn. He's going to stop of nothing to get me...."

Fallyn sighed. He knew it was going to be difficult to keep her safe, as it was once the secret got out. But he really hoped it wasn't going to be so soon, nor by the likes of her master... "Undoubtedly, to use your ability of conception to strengthen your elder's brethren army. Was his threat for the knowledge of my haven?"

Kathrin nodded without hesitation, "It's fortunate that I honestly couldn't answer the question myself. But we already knew he's been wanting to corner you to take you out. But Fallyn, even in my dream, he controlled me like I was nothing more than a puppet. The only thing I could do was speak. He already tried that once when we met him before. What if he does it again the next time we face him? If he can do that with me, what does that mean for our baby?"

Fallyn wished he could answer both questions, but he, truthfully, didn't know. He had never heard the politics and dealings of vampires, and all he did know was sheerly speculation from encounters with them. He was sure, though, they'd search high and low for her. It was a dilemma that he would have never thought he would face if he was approached by the information a year ago. And here Hakeem knew all along, he thought dismayed.

"I cannot say, Kathrin. You are the first of your kind. I have never heard of a vampire's ability to conceive…."

Fallyn's words trailed off as his mind recalled texts from his own tribe of demons, something which was predicted hundreds of years ago. The signs were practically identical…

"What's the matter, Fallyn?" Kathrin asked as she leaned into him.

Fallyn shook his head, avoiding the alarm with a smile as he assured, "It is nothing, mi joya preciosa. Something I have read once before has come to mind."

Kathrin narrowed her eyes to his evasive answer as he added, "In my lifespan, I have never seen such might from a vampire. Perhaps you could defend yourself from such manipulation such like you had before."

Kathrin bit her lower lip and nodded, hoping Fallyn was right about her willpower to resist. But Fallyn's mind reeled with the possibility that their predicament was following a foretold event. He had to meet with his tribesman again.

"What do we do now, Fallyn? I can't live with this knowledge of what will happen if they capture me. We gotta' defeat him, but how?"

Fallyn glanced at his hands as his muttering trailed his thoughts aloud, "his talents are much older than mine. I am wary to admit it would be almost perilous on my behalf to challenge him on my own. For him to maintain his region of control, he must have made barters with other spirits and demonic for such. With that said it would be wise for me to attack the aids who empower him first. Only then could it be possible for me to confront him fatally in a pared fight."

When he raised from his muttering to scan Kathrin, he was a little taken aback by her stern face of frustration. He didn't understand what he said to spur it on, but she didn't give him much time to think of it as she stormed, "How dare you, Fallyn."

With a pause, he questioned, "What illness did I speak? I simply described what must be done if I am to thrust down Daimos."

"You, Fallyn? What about me? I am in this as much as you are. You've trained me for this very reason. If you so much as think I'm going to sit around and hope for the best, I will kick your ass to the curb," she spoke sternly.

"Kathrin, this is life or death we speak of, not a challenge of wills. I will never subject you to this, knowing my child lays nestled in your belly."

Kathrin's stomach flipped at the thought. She carried Fallyn's baby, his baby, and he cared for her so much that he would protect her away from the horrors to come. "If you cannot defeat him, then we're both as good as dead. I won't let them subject me to life of rape and murder. So, if we are going to take Daimos out, we'll face it together, no matter the costs."

Though amazed at her choice, Fallyn respected it and simply nodded. But, before all things, he needed to meet with his clan to seek their advice.

"We shall 'lay low' for some time. I am sure if we tried to disperse of his guardians now, it would make him aware of our intent. I, also, am in need to speak with my brotherhood. We shall need any assistance possible for our goal to succeed."

Chapter Twenty-Four

Three months later...

The earth crumbled and sunk under the steady footsteps of Fallyn and Kathrin as they climbed the mountainside of Nevado del Tolima in Colombia. It had taken them some time to locate Fallyn's tribe. The clan commonly relocated every few years to avoid interest from any demons that may be hunting them. When Kathrin tried to ask questions about Fallyn's clan, she discovered quite quickly that he didn't like speaking about it, in the least. She could only guess it was because if he showed interest in their haven and lifestyle, it meant that he would have to acknowledge what he tried so hard to hide. Kathrin didn't care less either way. She was simply curious as to what she should expect. After all, she was the biggest black sheep with her own brethren as much as he probably was with his tribe.

Fallyn turned around in a pause to confirm how Kathrin was fairing. Kathrin glanced up at him with a faint smile as she stepped onto the platform Fallyn stood upon. She readjusted her clothing briefly before she waited for Fallyn to guide her further on.

" How do you feel, mi joya preciosa," Fallyn asked sincerely. His concern for her was more prominent than ever since their discovery of her pregnancy. Her stomach now well bulged with the knowledge.

"I'm fine, Fallyn," she smiled as she tried to hide her exhaustion.

He examined her fully to approve of her answer before he turned to continue up the mountain, offering his hand as support before he replied, "It is only a short way further."

Kathrin nodded as she accepted his hand, following his assistance up the mountainside. Fallyn informed her what their intentions were so they could meet up with a shaman-of-sorts first. Fallyn wanted to clarify some issues brought up recently, as well as see if he could ask for their support in what was to come. It wasn't long after that they arrived at the cavern entrance.

Fallyn was going to recommend that she come in with him, but as he looked at her pale features, which were obvious of her exhaustion, he decided against it.

He closed his hand around hers as he pulled her closer, his soft, endearing accent breaking the silence between them, "Mayhaps you should rest here, alhaja. I cannot say how smooth this shall go and I would prefer for you to evade stress when it is not needed."

Kathrin smiled vaguely and nodded. Kathrin was quite pleased with the suggestion because she was aching rather a lot in the small of her back with the tiny weight of her offspring-to-be. As Fallyn escorted her to a makeshift seat on a rock against the entrance wall, he kissed her forehead endearingly.

"I shall be but a moment, mi joya preciosa," he replied before he entered into the darkness, a cream-like sludge enveloping him in its grasp as he walked into its pit.

Fallyn felt the chill of the mired-like barrier as it encased him, the smell of stagnant air filling his nostrils as he walked through the water-like barrier that hid his clan's sanctuary behind it. For a brief moment, it felt like cold, clammy hands pulled at his insides before stepping onto the other side, flooding himself with light. His eyes squinted slightly in adjustment before he witnessed the bodies of people before him.

The hot breaths of moans and grunts filled the air as many naked, glistening bodies twined amongst themselves in primal rutting of lustful passion, men grinding and pounding into the women who opened to their desires. Some of the women panted out their satisfaction as they were pinned between two men, swallowing the staff of one while the other drove deep from behind. Others collapsed in exhaustion as the men nipped and bucked into them to find relief of their own. Men watched headily in temptation as they awaited their turn on the woman of their choice, stroking their manhood in an unaware action to the erotic scene.

Fallyn watched in disgust at the orgy before him, unable to draw his eyes away from the passion as he thought how pleased he was to have Kathrin waiting outside. His witness to the orgy was short-lived when a man amongst the rutting stood up with a curse, "How dare you enter this cavern! You are not welcome here!"

The man's body glistened with sweat and tension, each muscle etched with a throbbing desire to find the appeasement he was disturbed from receiving. His hair was wet and stringy, his face frustrated, and even his manhood stood erect before him as he glared into Fallyn's eyes. It was this man's furious bellow that parted the bodies of passion, slowly, one by one, sneaking further down the cavern to flee from the conflict arising between the two men.

"My presence is for Amun, not for the likes of you," Fallyn glowered, watching out of the corner of his eye the people fleeing.

"I'm the one you must deal with first, outcast, and I will not have you jeopardize my clan with your rebellious act of disregard!" His comment was testy, attempting to rile Fallyn's temper because of his own unfulfilled frustration.

Though the comment did accomplish what he hoped for, Fallyn laughed at his response as he jabbed, "My disregard? If I were anyone with ill intent, I could have wiped the clan of Hai-tuk from creation. Despicable! Mating like mindless dogs, men who only think with their erection rather than the minds that God bestowed. The only one who endangers his clan is its lustful chieftain!"

The man's rage was all too evident as each word dug at his shameless behavior, barely able to hold his ground. "You are not welcome here!"

Their eyes shot daggers toward the other when Fallyn glowered, "It matters not what you feel, Nozomu, for I am here to speak with Amun."

Nozomu was unimpressed with Fallyn's arrogance towards his authority but was interrupted from telling him so when the person Fallyn sought entered the chamber, announcing his entrance with a snarl, "Nozomu, these matters do not concern you. Tend to your pack in the depths of this cave."

This man was like he came from historical fiction, showing that some concepts of literature were not from the imaginations of lunatics. Though his body was broad and precise as a hard tuned man, his feet and head were like that of a dog, all too familiar to the images of Anubis in the Egyptian culture. The coat of his mane was speckled with hints of cinnamon and gray as his form held an elegance unable to be described. He was much taller than even Fallyn's six feet, towering almost two feet above Fallyn's broad form.

Nozomu grimaced before he stormed out of the room, giving Fallyn a deathly glare before continuing down the path that the shaman instructed. The conversation didn't continue until both men were confident Nozomu was truly gone, only then bringing Amun's attention towards Fallyn.

"Why is it you disturb me this night?"

Fallyn's tension eased slightly as he cleared his throat, "I have brought a female in, which I believe is from our prophecy. She awaits outside."

Amun looked outside the pit of blackness as he willed to be able to see through its protection at whom Fallyn referred about. It was only a moment before he noticed her against the entrance. He examined her closely as he reiterated, "She is a vampire, awakened at that."

Fallyn nodded at his awareness, knowing there was no need to add information to Amun's scrutiny. After a minute of his investigation, he returned his gaze back towards Fallyn, his eyes narrowing, "An awakened vampire's hunger would be strong and ravenous in its nature. How often does her need for blood call? How many times in a moon's cycle does her hunger drive her blindly?"

"She has never lost her mind to bloodlust. She remains rational whenever her hunger is present. Mayhaps once a week she is in need."

"Preposterous," Amun spat as he adverted his focus back to Kathrin, "no vampire can avoid the pull of their hunger as often as that without blind rage oozing from their minds."

"It is true," Fallyn argued, "I have had many wounds in her presence since her stay with me and she merely coddles them out of concern. She avoids the traits commonly held by vampires."

Within a moment, Amun's glare returned to Fallyn's, a possibility coming to mind that he disgustedly asked, "Have you fed her?"

Fallyn nodded slowly, "Yes."

Amun bellowed his rage. Fallyn's thoughtlessness went against all rules within their brethren. "You have disregarded all consequences with your actions! There are reasons we have laws against such atrocities! She can destroy you for your ignorance!"

It was some time since Kathrin sat by herself at the mouth of the cave, waiting for Fallyn's return. She couldn't imagine what conflict was happening between Fallyn and his people. A tender flutter tickled her abdomen, which instinctively brought Kathrin's hand to her belly in a soothing rub for the unborn child hidden within. She wasn't exactly sure because she wasn't able to see anyone with medical knowledge since her discovery, but Kathrin believed she was within her second trimester, about four months pregnant. She pondered how it all would come to pass. After all, she had never heard about the technicalities of pregnancy and labor beyond what was learned in high school. But she avoided the concern that welded up in her, realizing that the birth of their baby would happen only if they were able to destroy Daimos.

Yet, as she pondered how the two of them would deal with their troubles, Kathrin felt something more alerting flood to attention. Her stomach wrenched in cramps as an eerie coldness covered her body. Then she felt dizzy, raw, like her nerves were on fire, but relaxed as her hands became clammy. The nauseating tug was too well-known as she leaned onto the stone-like wall for support. She wrapped her arms around herself, weakening to a force she prayed she'd never feel again as she moaned out what resonated within her, "He comes."

She tried everything to stand up to find Fallyn but was unable, her convulsions pinning her down. She heard the earth crumble with the weight of the man who approached. She could smell his evil, rage, and deceit with each nearing step. As she glanced towards the black membrane beside her, where she knew Fallyn was, a voice which wasn't whom she thought announced his presence.

"Why would a vampire be this far from home?"

Her head weakly turned towards him, her eyes

blurry as she tried to see the man who reeked of Daimos. When her eyes focused enough onto the tall, shadowed figure, she suddenly paled. This was someone she only met through Fallyn's mind. She didn't know anything else but his face, but she knew, deep within the recesses of her soul, that he was pure, unadulterated evil.

"Who…are…you," she choked, trying to shake off the weariness he bestowed.

She didn't receive an answer as he closed the distance and jerked her viciously by the front of her winter coat up to his eye level. She couldn't resist his grasp. Then, drawing his nose close to her nape, he drew a deep breath, chuckling his surprise. "I never thought he sired a child. You reek of him."

She narrowed her eyes dizzily upon him, "As…do you."

His face became grim at her awareness, "I have no need for a pathetic little mouse to announce that anytime soon, either. So, why don't I shut that testy little mouth of yours."

She swallowed. She knew what those words promised, but her frailty to the stench of her sire denied her any ability to defend herself. And, as his mouth snarled and malformed, his teeth enlarging into serrated points to clamp down onto her shoulder, she shrieked out with anguish with only one thought.

FALLYN!

He heard Kathrin's panic clearly as he buckled by the resonating pain through his shoulder. His hand clenched the spot with a wince, knowing, although unfathomable, that it was her pain he felt. And even though Amun was in the middle of berating him for what he had done, Fallyn didn't think of anything else but to get to Kathrin's side. He pulled his gun out and dived into the blackness once more. The cold chill of the membrane couldn't match the dread that tore across his insides. When he surfaced on the other side, a torrent of blinding rage washed over him as he saw Kathrin in the clutches of someone else.

Her body was lifeless as it dangled in the grasp of a massive man; his jaw fastened onto her shoulder. It was one of his brotherhood, and Fallyn knew it was possible that it was an act of distaste for what she was that drove him to pursue the deed he'd done. But, with Fallyns instinct and core driven rage that spilled over him to be witnessing Kathrin as she was, he couldn't sway his hand to still.

Fallyn bellowed his fury as he pulled the trigger, the bullet speeding into the side of the tribesman's neck. He howled with agony as his teeth ripped out from Kathrin's shoulder, peeling away what skin was lodged in his mouth.

Her body barely winced with the rending, but it assured Fallyn that she was still alive as she collapsed in a motionless heap onto the earth. The male's hand clamped onto his neck as he backed away, cursing. Fallyn rushed towards Kathrin, crouched down, and lifted her into his arms, although his firearm never faltered from his obscured enemy.

The man hissed before he charged Fallyn, the cocking of Fallyn's gun the only thing that froze him in his tracks.

"Come no closer," Fallyn gritted in a deathly tone that could shrill goose bumps on the bravest of souls, "Even you know of the Achilles' heel we are beholden to, and I assure you, these bullets will instill that harm. You may even feel that doom flowing through your veins as we speak."

A slight chuckle rumbled from the shadowed man as he spoke raggedly, "You must be none other than the legendary Fallyn."

The voice was unforgettable, hauntingly picking at a depth of his mind he couldn't recall for the life of him. But he knew this man wasn't an ally; he was sure of it. And, as his steps brought him into the beams of the illuminated moon, Fallyn faltered with disbelief. The words this man cursed him with so long ago repeated themselves like they had a thousand times before.

'May the gates of hell greet you with open arms, child.'

"You…" Fallyn trembled with shock, dumbfounded by the presence of the very man who sealed his fate eons ago. His hand quivered as he relived the visions Fallyn was sure, until now, that he had overcome centuries before. But now, as the man that nearly killed him stood before him very much alive, Fallyn was paralyzed by his fear of it all over again. It seemed like ages he remained there, his weapon trembling like a rookie gunslinger. It was only the drops of Kathrin's blood that trailed down her body and onto Fallyn's arms that phased him back to reality.

"How could you? How could you obliterate an entire lineage without thought?" Fallyn growled, hating the time wasted here when Kathrin was so close to her end. But he needed to know; he had to know for his own sake.

The man merely smirked, shrugging his broad shoulders as he jeered, "You must clarify which lineage you're referring about. I've seemed to have lost count of the humans that I've laid to rest. But, perhaps, I could ask the same question to you. How can you bring yourself to protect an aberration of nature?"

Fallyn gritted at his carelessness for life. He could almost see the clans of society plummet one by one because of him. He shook his head involuntarily in disbelief and disgust. Fallyn knew he could never view him as a brother amongst demons.

"I need not answer to the likes of you! You shrug off existence like it is only slugs covering the earth. No person of brethren law could treat life that carelessly. You serve only yourself!"

His face grinned, Kathrin's blood trailing down from the corner of his mouth, "If you say so, o' holy one."

But as he chortled at Fallyn's disgust, Kathrin began to shudder weakly. They were mere flutters, her head not even raising in the attempts, but they were enough for Fallyn to notice. Fallyn squeezed her close as he leaned in.

"Alhaja, hold on for but a few moments longer."

Her moan was but a whisper as she struggled to reveal something that he knew was vital. Yet, they were simply too muffled. They were hazed into one creeping sound in her half-conscious state. Fallyn wished he understood her, he just had this knowing that what she would say would enlighten him on what he faced. Frustrated, Fallyn moaned.

Oh, how I long to hear you, Kathrin!

He serves Daimos.

Fallyn's eyes widened at her response, hearing her voice crystal clear though her lips never parted to speak them. She heard him as clearly as his thoughts had heard hers. Never had he fathomed that a psychic bond could fuse two minds together like this. His awe was short-lived when her words finally sunk home.

"You follow Daimos," Fallyn seethed, a comment that had the male pale, ghastly white.

It made perfect sense, finishing the pieces in the puzzle that were always missing. That's why Kathrin didn't defend herself. Daimos' presence before could paralyze her, so it wasn't that hard to believe even the scent of Daimos that smothered this slaughterer would affect her just the same.

"How do you know that-" the bulky man stuttered, shocked to hear that Fallyn knew his age-long secret.

Fallyn drew Kathrin up from the earth, the care he once had for the unexplainable events in his past meaning nothing anymore. He simply wanted to be away from the despicable creature in front of him. His aim never wavered as he carried Kathrin into the black liquid wall, keeping a cautious eye on the man who birthed him to his fate. When the man became furious towards Fallyn's incite, he wanted nothing more than to silence them once and for all. His unintentional step landed him a bullet square in his forehead.

His body rebounded back with another howl as Fallyn whisked Kathrin into the depths of the cavern. Without any words, once both Kathrin and Fallyn stumbled onto the other side, the ooze-like barrier became as solid as stone and rock. Amun sealed it with the strength of his own will. Fallyn glanced at Amun briefly with a question, unknowing whom he could trust anymore. After a second, he understood Amun was remaining impartial to the situation.

Amun grabbed a leather hide from the corner of the room and laid it down for Fallyn. Fallyn gently laid Kathrin upon it. Fallyn's heart was lodged in his throat, unsure he could speak if Amun wanted him to as he saw the excessive blood pouring from Kathrin's gaping wound. It was deep and serrated. He tried to remain calm and disinterested in the person he tended to be helpless beneath him but couldn't. His own emotions were on his sleeve as he grabbed the cloth Amun passed him to staunch the bleeding.

It didn't take a rocket scientist to see the affection Fallyn had for the dying woman, Amun could see it as clear as day. What troubled Amun was if Fallyn's love was a true sensation of the heart or something her vampire blood had inflicted as part of his feeding her. Amun couldn't tell for sure. Amun also wasn't sure whom his allies were neither, after overhearing the shocking conflict between the males outside the entrance. He only watched because of Fallyn's sudden bolt out of the layered gate.

"She- is not mending..." Fallyn choked as minutes passed without her powers innately responding.

The cloth he held against her shoulder but moments before was already sopping with her blood. Fallyn's eyes glistened at something Amun echoed was a possibility.

"Perhaps she is too far gone-"

"No," Fallyn denied, shaking his head violently in refusal to accept it. She couldn't die; he wouldn't let her.

"Amun, help me! She carries my offspring!" Fallyn pleaded, at a loss of what else he could do.

"She is pregnant?" Amun gasped, instantly recalling the scripts he had studied for nearly a millennium.

Fallyn could only nod as he looked back towards Kathrin's pale face, pleading for her to talk to him once more.

Please be well, alhaja! Do not die!

It was a moment of dread that past before her voice whispered weakly in his mind. Fallyn…I'm weak…so very tired….

I know you are, alhaja, but I beg you not to give up!

…I thirst, Fallyn…I must feed…

Fallyn nodded. He knew blood was a necessary part of her survival. It was the center of her lifecycle. But Fallyn also knew that Amun viewed her thirst as a deadly sin. He looked at Amun with conflict as he begged, "I cannot shame you with this deed, Amun; I beg of your leave so as to avoid witness of her feeding."

Amun scrutinized the command with complete

solemnity, "It is blood she seek?"

Fallyn nodded, "If I do not feed her thirst, she will perish."

Amun gave a slow nod in answer, and Fallyn responded quickly to inflict a wound. But, when his blade arrived at his wrist, Amun halted his action, drawing Fallyn's eyes back to his.

"I must, Amun!"

"I am not denying she is in need, Fallyn. I wish to do so myself."

Amun's hand outstretched to retrieve the dagger, which threw Fallyn's mind back in disbelief. The shaman wished to feed Kathrin, a vampire he only, minutes ago, cursed to be a plague of the earth. Fallyn could not deny him of his request. So slowly, with confusion, he handed Amun the blade. Amun followed through with the action Fallyn intended, slitting his wrist rather deeply before he tilted it over Kathrin's parted lips. Moments past with Amun feeding Kathrin while Fallyn tried to connect the reason for Amun's request before Kathrin's shoulder began to heal.

"Thank the heavens," Fallyn sighed in relief.

Amun covered his wrist and moved to the side to give Fallyn his moment with Kathrin. Fallyn watched as the cells on her shoulder multiplied and expanded, the muscle taking form before her skin smoothed itself into its milky softness. Hearing her heart pounding within her chest was the most liberating thing he could have wished for.

Fallyn moved closer toward Kathrin and drew her into his powerful arms as her head swayed lazily to the side. Her eyes opened slowly, groggily looking up at the man she knew had saved her as a lazy smile curled the corners of her lips. But, within a minute, Kathrin's eyes furrowed slightly.

"Are you crying, Fallyn?"

Fallyn chuckled at Kathrin's concern, the irony of her worry easing his own tension. "I believe it is proper to have such emotions whelm forth."

She smiled, almost humiliated, as she turned her gaze to Amun across the room. She noticed him stiffen with her glance. She observed his form and wisdom that poured off him from an era not much farther than Fallyn's as she raised herself into a sitting position.

"Thank you, noble shaman, for what you did. I can only imagine what you must be thinking right now for me even being here, "Kathrin moaned, vaguely remembering a blurred vision of Amun's thoughts through the taste of his blood.

Amun didn't say anything, almost wary to speak, as he feared his action could have doomed him all together, but he nodded. Fallyn looked over at him in confusion as he braced her back. He knew Kathrin was always determined, but she was far from being renewed. Fallyn still couldn't unravel the connection they shared, unaware of the deeds that were done that linked their minds. In curiosity, he called to her again.

Tell me my thoughts did not deceive me by imagining your words.

Kathrin's eyes glanced back towards him as she smiled with comfort.

You're not deceived, Fallyn; I can hear you as much as you can hear me.

How can this be? It does not make sense.

Neither does us having a child or the bond we share in the most peculiar of times, but, nonetheless, it happens.

Fallyn's hand slipped to her abdomen to give a gentle squeeze to the bulge, an endearment of concern as he thought, How fairs, our child? Was it harmed?

No, Fallyn, the baby is spunkier than ever, I promise you.

Fallyn smiled as he thought he felt a slight tickle on his palm before Amun shuffled in his seat, drawing an apology from Fallyn for his negligence. "Forgive me, Amun, it was not meant to ignore you."

Amun simply nodded as Fallyn found an object to prop Kathrin into a sitting position. With Fallyn staying ever close to Kathrin's side, they waited for Amun's questions to arise.

Amun eyed Kathrin for some time, confused with her, although he tried to remain cynical. It was many minutes of him boring into her soul before he broke the silence.

"Whom do you serve?"

Kathrin glanced towards the floor, flustered with how she should answer such a weighty question. "I'm not sure what you mean by that."

Fallyn was about to explain it for her when Amun's hand raised to cut him off, "the question is something you should answer with your heart. No one can give you this answer, nor can anyone lighten its significance. So, tell me with whatever floods your thoughts. Whom do you serve?"

Her voice caught in her throat as a thousand different things came to mind all at once. There was the answer everyone thought she served; then there was the answer she felt. Fallyn's hand tightened around her own, and Kathrin realized that no matter how she replied, he would still be supportive of it. With that affirmation, she was able to clarify her words.

"I've been burdened with Daimos' blood. He tried time and again to get me to submit to his malevolence and the bloodlust that follows with it. And I've fought it every single time and will continue to do it. I refuse to become part of his regime. I'm not about to be a pawn in their plot for destruction, and I'm not about to let them influence my unborn child. I will fight teeth and nails to protect it at any cost. My place is with Fallyn, and nothing will change that."

When Amun's gaze didn't flinch, she finished, "So, who do I serve? I guess you can say I serve what's right."

Amun nodded, "And what if everything you live for is taken from you? What if, in this battle, you lose Fallyn, your baby is killed, and you are left all by yourself? What then?"

The query constricted her throat. She had thought of the very same issue herself. She couldn't bear the thought that she could lose everything that was precious, but she still knew it was a possibility. Holding back the tears that were trying to escape, she choked, "If everything's taken from me and all I have left is myself, I would.... I would...."

She didn't think she would continue; the thought made her want to curl up into a ball and hide.

"Give up?" Amun added.

Kathrin wiped her tears that began to fall but she shook her head. She may believe she would become only a shell of what she once was, but she could never give up. If she did, then Fallyn's noble legacy would end, and the Abyss would win.

"I won't give up... I would continue for the people I've lost... and I would fight for everything they believed in."

"Who would you turn to in this time to accomplish that?"

"The Infernals."

"And why not the demons? Why not us?"

Kathrin swallowed as she knew what she would say would insult the shaman, "Because they are mankind fighting for mankind. I'm not sure I can say that either vampire or your clan fight for anything but themselves."

"So, then, why are you here now?"

"Because I have faith in Fallyn. If Fallyn believes that you will stand for what's right, I will remain by his side to the end, even if it means I'm killed for my naivete."

Amun nodded again, his arms crossing upon his chest as he remained fixed on her. Minutes passed on quietly, this time, the tension thickening it.

"Do you even know what Fallyn is?"

Fallyn cringed at the question. Why did Amun have to ask that? Kathrin had the right to know what he was, even if he feared it would push her away in the process. He looked at Kathrin's face, which, even though tears still stained it, remained emotionless.

"His title is 'The Destroyer'," Kathrin began, to Fallyn's amazement. "I have seen the monster's hunger firsthand in his own blind rage."

"And how did you see it, vampire?" Amun sneered, doubting her words.

"Because he refuses to harm anything humane, Fallyn seals himself away in a world I'm not even sure is earth when his curse is upon him. Out of concern for him one night, I traveled there, and I saw the bodies of demons laid to rest by his hands." Kathrin argued, innately knowing that Fallyn's eyes were fixed on her with the knowledge she admitted.

"There was at least a dozen of them."

"And how did you come to speak the tale unharmed?" Amun scoffed.

"I was harmed," Kathrin began, recalling how Fallyn had said he couldn't remember it in the least. "He held me there to burn me alive with the dawning of the sun."

Fallyn's gut wrenched at the acknowledgment Kathrin had avoided to answer prior. The day she was there and collapsed from her burns was because of him. He had almost killed her.

"I fainted at that moment, and when I came too, Fallyn had brought me back to safety."

"So, you saw him in his bestial form? You saw his carnage?"

Kathrin paused before she shook her head, "I saw the aftermath of his destruction, and Fallyn was returning to his human form when I arrived."

"So, you don't know what he is."

Kathrin huffed her indifference towards Amun, "He

is a creature of the night, just as I am. In vampire society, he and I should be fighting to the death to slay one another, a hatred bred from the beginning of time. He kills when he cannot control it. What more do I need to know? What matters to me is the actions he does take to protect what's right and moral."

Amun glanced at Fallyn's discomfort before he asked, "Do you want to know what he is; what demon rests in your belly?"

"I know what Fallyn is... and if I had the option to change what has happened, I would kick the ass of the person who offered. I'm proud that I'm carrying Fallyn's baby! It's the greatest honor imaginable for me!"

Fallyn began to wonder if that would still be the case if she really knew what he was. She didn't truly see him, simply what he was capable of. But Amun was finished with his interrogation. He rose from his seat, stating finally, "Fallyn, you are correct. She is, indeed, who was mentioned in the scripts."

Fallyn nodded, unable to find words to speak with all the remorse and fear that was running through his veins. Kathrin lifted herself off of the floor as she asked rather sarcastically, "So I passed?"

Amun glared towards her and replied curtly, "It seems as much."

Kathrin dusted her bottom off. "Then will you help

us? We need to take out Daimos if I am to be sure the child
is safe."

"Children," Amun corrected.

Kathrin numbed. "What?"

Even Fallyn was bewildered as he stared at Amun.

"You carry twins," Amun added, "'One child for each
bloodline of the parents.'"

Kathrin never imagined that twins were a possibility.
When she looked over at Fallyn's ever-solemn face to be
sure she wasn't dreaming, he, too, seemed unsure of the
words.

"Well..." Kathrin paused, flustered.

Fallyn returned to her side, easing his arm
possessively around her waist as he collected his
composure. "The number of offspring we carry is pale to
the security we must assure for them."

Amun agreed with the statement, "There's truth to
that. If Daimos is given reign over her secret in the
vampiric society, the children will undoubtedly become
the harbingers of destruction."

"Will you help us then?" Kathrin almost pleaded
with the question.

"That is variable..." Amun retorted.

Kathrin cringed at the bargaining Fallyn had warned
her was about to come. Fallyn told her that the hierarchy
of demons was built upon them. But, most commonly, it

was a price so steep that many wouldn't even consider it as an option.

"Speak of your request," Fallyn demanded, having Kathrin sense that even he was wary of the comment to come.

"It is two demands. First, the child of Fallyn's bloodline, I want to personally tutor with the ways of our clan," Amun began.

Without a second for Kathrin to mull it over, Fallyn answered, "Done."

Kathrin bit her lip in anxiety at what she was unsure of, but she knew Fallyn wouldn't have been so quick to answer if he didn't have faith in the man.

Amun continued, "And, secondly if you want our help to take out the minions who empower Daimos, that you are induced with the birth of your children tonight."

"What!?!"

Kathrin shook her head in panic, confused and alarmed with the ultimatum. "Oh, no, no. You can't! I don't want to kill them; it's too early!"

Fallyn coaxed Kathrin into his arms to hush her worries, but Amun began his reasoning for the request. "If Gurath was, indeed, a servant to Daimos, Daimos will, undoubtedly, learn that you are planning an onslaught with our assistance. As such, the chances for success will become minimal if we wait for the natural birth of the offspring. Tonight, while you are in your labor, I can discover who each of his servants is and send several factions out to kill them and nullify the bargains that strengthen him. With this time, you will have a period with your new-found family until we send word that the task is completed. Then, it will be your turn to destroy Daimos."

"Then-then, why don't we wait till you guys are done to induce the labor?"

"Kathrin-," Fallyn called to assure her but was interrupted with Amun's reply once again.

"-If we induced the labor before your battle, you would surely die from the conflict in your weakened state. Also, the longer they are subjected through your blood to Daimos' corruption, the more likely they will become tainted."

Kathrin writhed her fingers together. Not only was she going to be a mother of two but by the end of tonight?

"What does it entail? Like, what's gonna' happen if I say yes?"

Amun explained, "The labor would be induced with magic, but it would not mean that the two would be born prematurely. The incantations simply speed up the process of maturity. So, instead of waiting four months to deliver, it would become four hours, and both would be such like they would if born naturally."

Kathrin hadn't realized, until that moment, how much

power came with magic. The ability to speed up her pregnancy? Fallyn saw her insecurities and assured her, "These tactics are commonly used within the tribe, mi joya preciosa. This spell is not rare."

Fallyn understood her fear clearly, for he felt the same reverberation in his soul. Letting the babies be born naturally would psychologically prepare them for their arrival. But, to force the labor to a few short hours was still too much of a shock that neither of them was prepared for. Unfortunately, if she refused, then they would completely lose the support of his tribe and would have to battle Daimos and his minions themselves. Fallyn knew he couldn't ask for the support of The Infernals, not when they were questioning if Fallyn was a follower of the abyss. Kathrin glanced at Fallyn for the answer. Fallyn smiled lovingly to ensure her that whatever she decided, he would stand behind her.

Kathrin sighed fearfully before she concluded to what had to be done.

"Okay, I'll do it. I'll have the babies tonight."

Chapter Twenty-Five

Kathrin panted out another wave of convulsions while drops of sweat beaded her brow line. With the starting of the labor, only a single woman was added to their numbers. She was an older, salt-and-peppered-haired female who had a presence of calming tranquility. She didn't seem to be phased once she discovered through Kathrin's illuminated eyes and fangs that Kathrin was a vampire. She simply smiled comfortingly and assisted her again with making her as comfortable as she could be. It stunned Kathrin to the lack of racism, but was glad for her support with what Kathrin didn't know.

Three hours passed since the incantations had begun, and now, by what the midwife had announced, Kathrin was near the end of the labor. The contractions were in shorter intervals, and her water had broken about fifteen minutes prior.

Another contraction pulsed and Kathrin gritted her teeth to the involuntary urge to push down.

"Pace yourself, child. They will come in due time."

Kathrin returned to her repetitive breaths as she clenched to the furs that supported her. Though his face showed no emotion, Fallyn paced the room, pausing only enough to witness her anguish to the sharp agony before he would continue his aimless wandering. Amun had left and returned many times throughout the span. But now that it was determined that the birthing was close, he remained fixed in a seat on the other side of the cave.

The woman glanced over at Fallyn briefly before she lifted from her station beside Kathrin, smiling, "I'll be right back. I'm just going to grab some fresh water."

Leaving, she approached Fallyn, who paused at her arrival. Leaning in, she whispered, "She's ready to deliver them, but the woman needs your support. Her fear is what's stalling their birth."

Fallyn glanced over towards Kathrin as she panted out her anguish again, the dread that the midwife spoke of evident in her features. Fallyn nodded and approached Kathrin's side. He knelt beside her and lifted her head and shoulders onto his lap before he smiled handsomely. Her eyes hadn't returned to their turquoise self since the labor had begun, her fangs only slightly present with her distress.

"Hello, mi joya preciosa."

Kathrin tried to smile between her pants but couldn't get past the spasm. She looked at Fallyn's delightful eyes and moaned, "I'm... I don't know if I can do this, Fallyn."

Fallyn lifted a washcloth from a basin that rested beside them and dabbed her forehead. "You are very strong, mi joya preciosa. You have battled many things and were triumphant. This will be the most joyous one imaginable."

"But what if something goes wrong? What if I'm a bad mom?" Kathrin whimpered before another spasm gripped her body.

Fallyn returned the cloth to the basin and embraced her trembling hand, raising it to rest on her chest with his own.   "They are well, Kathrin. Do you not think my brothers would have discovered such warning if something was amiss?"

With that, he leaned down and kissed her brow tenderly, "And, as honored as you were to carry my children, I am fulfilled to know that you shall raise my offspring with your acuity. I could not have begged for a more fitting mother."

Kathrin's eyes watered. Those words meant the world to her. Whatever concerns she had before then whisked away. She nodded, barely smiling, and she whispered, "You'll be a great dad too."

The midwife returned with some furs, blankets, and another basin of water. Fallyn knew with the items collected that now it was time. He returned his gaze to Kathrin and announced, "I believe you may listen to what your body demands. They are prepared to deliver."

The midwife nodded at his insight, lifting Kathrin's knees apart and curled to begin. Kathrin bit her lip with worry, her face becoming concerned again, but she nodded. Fallyn smiled as he held her hand tighter in his palm.

"Estoy aquí para usted, mi joya preciosa. Conseguiremos con esto juntos."

Those words in English meant I am here for you, my precious jewel. We will get through this together, but somehow the wariness remained in her eyes. Fallyn was her pillar of strength in her own weakness. When the contraction arrived again, instead of resisting the urge to push, Kathrin listened to it and grunted with all her might. The pain that she had previously encountered was like nothing to what she was experiencing now.

"That's right. Keep pushing; one's almost here," the woman called, supporting the infant that was almost out.

With another push, an infant's cry made aware that she had succeeded with one of the births. It was powerful and moving, tears of relief etching Kathrin's face as she looked toward Fallyn to see his own joy. But he simply stared at her with his handsome smile.

"It's a boy," the midwife announced as she bundled the baby in the blankets and furs once the nose and eyes were cleaned.

Fallyn only then glanced to his eldest born, one he never imagined he would have in his life, and was awed at how beautiful he was. His wail echoed down the cave, a hearty cry of anger to be free from his previous home. Fallyn's heart bounded with joy as he returned his gaze to Kathrin once more.

"Wonderful, alhaja. He is as beautiful as the moon."

Then her body convulsed again to deliver the next, Fallyn encouraging her all the way. Within minutes, another wail echoed in the cavern, just as hearty though only slightly deeper.

"Another boy," the midwife spoke up with even a smile crossing her face to the miracle of life, "They are both as healthy as their parents."

Fallyn kissed Kathrin's brow once more as Kathrin leaned down to reach for one of her sons, the woman offering the youngest born to her grasp once he was prepped for her attention. The firstborn was offered to Fallyn's arms without request, and he accepted him nervously.

They quieted down with the warmth of the furs, a content slumber covering each of them as both Fallyn and Kathrin admired their features. Both sons had their mother's chestnut hair but had more predominant characteristics from Fallyn's sharpened features, including the length of their future height-to-be. Fallyn beamed proudly, looking to the face of one, then the other, before he leaned in to kiss Kathrin. She made this miracle possible.

"I'm still in shock," Kathrin giggled when the infant squirmed slightly in her arms.

Fallyn nodded in agreement with the statement. Only then did Amun rise from his seat and approach the commotion. Fallyn knew exactly what now was entailed. He would now examine the infants from the prophecy. Fallyn stood up with his bundled son, somewhat offering his child to Amun. Amun began to weave a spell upon the infant. Within a few minutes of the enchantment, Amun replied, almost bitterly, "This child is of vampire blood."

Amun motioned for Fallyn to raise him to his chest, where he then exposed the son's bare splotchy shoulder. He carved in a demonic symbol whose bloodline was his, vampire, and the infant wailed his discomfort, which dug into Fallyn's heart. Once completed with the marking of the baby, Fallyn covered the infant's shoulder with his palm to absorb the pain with a spell of his own, only leaving the engraved tattoo on his shoulder as it was meant to be.

Amun turned towards Kathrin, who warily coddled her child deeper into her arms. "It is a marking of genetics."

Hesitantly, Kathrin looked up at Fallyn, who only gave a bow of his head with reassurance. Kathrin sighed, nauseated, and sat up to offer him her son embraced in her arms. Amun knelt down to repeat the same incantation as done so for the firstborn before he announced what was already known, "His blood is of our own."

Kathrin repeated the actions Fallyn had for Amun to engrave another symbol onto her youngest son's shoulder blade. His own deepened cry, shouting throughout the room. When Amun was finished, Kathrin snuggled him close to her chest to soothe him. Amun turned to speak with Fallyn.

"The child of your blood will begin his tutoring at the age of five. I will have him such like mortal schooling would dictate, and this shall continue until his eighteenth birthday, where then he will know of his birthright."

"His name is Roland, "Kathrin interrupted as the midwife continued to assist with the aftermath of birth.

Amun's brow furrowed, unimpressed with her decision, as he corrected, "It is Fallyn's right to name the children what he so desires."

"It's my right too. They are my babies as much as they are Fallyn's," Kathrin argued, indignant at Amun's perspective.

Amun gritted his teeth as he tried to maintain his irritation. "The naming of a child is given to the father. No vampire female will decide the-"

"-His name is Roland," Fallyn interrupted with a growl, the degrading sneer from Amun prickling Fallyn's temper to the worst it could reach, "Kathrin's choice of name holds as much weight as would my own. But, if it shall please the skeptical opinion of the shaman, then 'Roland' is the title I have chosen for the son held in the vampire female's arms."

Kathrin felt vindicated from Fallyn's correction, pleased to know that he cared enough to intervene in a confrontation that she wasn't about to give up. But she knew that Fallyn would have stepped in anyway. Amun lowered his head at his error but was unable to rectify it when Fallyn gritted again, "Her name is Kathrin. If you desire to preserve my trust and admiration, you shall avoid such racist behavior toward my mate."

It was a moment before Amun begged, "Forgive my brazen tongue."

Fallyn's glare didn't falter from Amun for some time until he finished, "This child in my arms shall be called Zayden."

"Their names will be known within our tribe. You can stay till night falls. Until then, Mayiana will assist with the caring and bathing needs of you and your offspring."

Amun motioned towards the midwife, finally giving Kathrin the name of the woman to be thankful for before he exited to the chamber below. Fallyn returned to Kathrin's side as Mayiana began to teach and aid both parents with the care of their babies. This was something that neither ever thought they would see the day, and both relished it now that it was finally here.

Chapter Twenty-Six

Seven weeks later...

Kathrin didn't understand why she seemed to give Roland just a little more attention than Zayden. It wasn't that she didn't love or adore Zayden. She always cuddled and laughed at the cute little squirms he would make just like Roland would, but somehow, it just seemed a little different. Perhaps because Roland was of Fallyn's blood, she thought to herself. But, whatever the reason, Roland always got that second kiss at night before he was tucked in.

Tucking her babies to bed was the only moment Kathrin felt like she did something right; everything else seemed like she barely mottled her way through. When she became frazzled with the wails of her sons, she thought she was failing; Fallyn would swoop in. He would give a tender kiss to her forehead as he told her that she did wonderfully, then gathered the two infants into his arms and walk away, giving Kathrin the alone time she needed to collect her composure. Sometimes, she would use this to fall into a much-needed sleep, others to relieve her stress by cleaning the built-up clutter.

When Kathrin woke from a nap on one of these evenings, she snuck into the nursery to see Fallyn cuddling the infants before he laid them into their crib.

Tiptoeing behind him to wrap her arms around his, she smiled down at Roland and Zayden. It seemed like there wasn't an issue at all from before she had her rest.

"How do you do it, "Kathrin whispered questioningly as she looked at her two little angels.

Fallyn smirked and leaned his head onto hers, wrapping his arm around her as he escorted her out of the room. "They are simply too exhausted with their complaints with you to continue them with me."

Kathrin giggled slyly as she nudged him with her elbow, "Oh, that I doubt."

His deep chuckle could be heard as they closed the door, and gave her a tight squeeze with his arm. With an accomplished sigh, Kathrin turned to face Fallyn.

"So, what would you like to do-"

Her comment was silenced as Fallyn pushed her up against the wall and consumed her lips with earnest demand, startling her for only a few seconds before she melted like a pile of mud on the floor. His hands grazed her skin as his lips commanded hers with a need that hadn't been there for what seemed like forever.

Their personal life went to an abrupt halt with the two children, and even though she loved them to bits, there were nights where she would cry to sleep because of it. The last time Fallyn touched her this intimately was the night before they went in search of Amun. Even as she thought of the time that spanned, it was almost like an eternity. Fallyn mirrored her regret.

"So long, mi joya preciosa," he grumbled against her lips, "It has been a punishment of hell to be with you but unable to touch you."

Tears collected in her eyes as he pressed her tight against his chest. His hands roamed to her bottom to grind her hips to his already swollen staff. Her arms wrapped around his neck and held him against her mouth, almost afraid that if they parted now, this would never happen again. Her observation was answered with an auditory growl that rumbled deep in his throat. He scooped her off the ground and practically slammed Kathrin against the wall, her complimenting the motion by wrapping her legs around his hips. He ground against her, un-phased by the restrictions of their clothing, while Kathrin panted at his mouth. When his tongue trailed down her neck to her collarbone, Kathrin barely understood the words that purred against her skin.

"Forgive me. I need you so badly. I cannot compose myself any longer."

"I don't care," she gasped breathlessly.

He tugged her covered nipples into his mouth. He acted like he could devour her, that he wanted to devour her, and at that moment, Kathrin wanted him to, as well. Jerking at his shirt, Kathrin moaned aloud to his sucking demands. As he carried her to their room, Kathrin giggled slyly at his persistence and almost laughed as he kicked their door closed with his foot.

"You find my need humorous?" he groaned, exasperated.

She chuckled with a shake of her head, "No, I'm enjoying seeing this. It's nice to feel cherished again."

Fallyn paused with a furrow of his brow, returning her to her feet. "I never ceased to cherish you, mi joya preciosa."

"I know… but you must admit it has taken its toll."

He was about to argue the point but then, knowingly, sighed and nodded, "That it has. But never again. I will not hold you at bay unless you ask it of me. Trying to be the gentleman and consider your exhaustion has seemed to make us both more saddened than rested."

Kathrin smiled lovingly as she grabbed his hand to pull him towards the bed. Reaching the foot of the mattress, she turned around and began to undress. There was a time when Kathrin could recall being shy towards him. But now, after all they experienced, she knew there was no reason for it any longer. For he loved her, maybe even greater than she loved him. And, as each item of clothing dropped to the floor, she watched his expression. Fallyn's eyes blazed fiery gold with passion. He relearned the woman he hadn't touched in what seemed like forever.

It was no surprise that, in her own silver saucers, Fallyn saw her desire, as well. When she finally stood naked before him, she smirked devilishly as her hands turned to him.

It took an immeasurable amount of strength to restrain from shoving her onto the bed to making love to her. But he wanted her to have her enjoyment. She tugged his shirt over his shoulders, stopping only to swirl circles around his taunt nipples before her tongue trailed lower to his abdomen. He gritted aloud, and she chuckled again.

"Aww, am I being too cruel?"

"You will be the death of me, Kathrin."

She giggled as her hands went to his belt buckle.

"Oh, but I'm far from done, Fallyn." Her mouth curved playfully into a pout, having Fallyn want nothing more than to latch onto the lower lip and suck on it before she whined, "Are you going to stop me from having a little fun?"

Fallyn almost hissed at the sugared purr that oozed from her as he braced his hands at his sides. "I would never dream of withholding your pleasures from you."

She chucked darkly again when the belt sprung free. "Good."

Her eyes lowered to the button of his jeans. With a flick and a tug of her wrists, his member sprung out eagerly to greet her. A moan of satisfaction curled her mouth as she let the jeans pool at his ankles, her eyes examining with approval the hardened flesh. When her fingers tenderly brushed the skin, Fallyn obliviously bucked at the touch.

"That bad, huh?" she asked, her fingers wrapping around the staff in a hungry stroke.

"Yes," Fallyn croaked.

Kathrin's fangs were full in her mouth. Her body already hummed with the arousal of her flesh. She eyed him hungrily with each tender stroke. Then, with a simple will of her fangs into suppression, she drew him into her mouth.

Fallyn's groan was noticeably loud as his hands that were once held at his sides wrapped around her head, petting and holding her mouth to his active member. Kathrin stroked him long and deep, Fallyn following the rhythm of her tongue and mouth with the small thrusts of his hips. He was in tune with her and could feel her own gratification as his own pleasure heightened. It was like she knew exactly what to do to drive him mad, and now that she held him at the hairline to insanity, she kept him there, seeing how long she could taunt him before his mind would escape him. He knew if she continued much more, he would surely lose the battle. And so, with a mindless panic, he yanked her off the floor and against his mouth.

She gasped with the sudden demand and wrapped her legs around him once again to hold her weight. And, as his hands braced her thighs and her arms enveloped his neck, Fallyn found entrance into her femininity.

"Oh, Kathrin," Fallyn hissed, claiming her lips again.

Kathrin couldn't prevent the moans of gratification as he pounded into her and couldn't stop the whimpers of regret when his lips would part from hers for even a second to trail kisses down her collarbone.

"Oh, please, Fallyn. Harder," she panted.

Fallyn acknowledged it by dropping them both to the bed, and with a swift move of his hips, he was nuzzled deep into her once more. Harder and harder, faster and faster, he took her. When her nails dug into his back in her climax, Fallyn joined in his own sexual release.

He rested above her while he regained his breath. Kathrin nestled her face against the side of his arm. With a smile, she placed a kiss to his cheekbone. Fallyn chuckled lightly as he turned to meet her lips.

"If I have not mistaken, that was much needed for the both of us."

"Oh yes," Kathrin nodded without hesitation. "It sure was."

With her quickness to reply, Fallyn laughed heartily and shifted next to her side. He drew her into his embrace. He was about to kiss her forehead once more when suddenly, a loud clunking knock echoed through all the rooms. Fallyn stilled.

"What was that?" Kathrin whispered as she watched Fallyn glance towards their doorway.

Without a word, Fallyn lifted from her and began to dress, his silence making her terribly nervous.

"Fallyn, answer me. What is that?" Kathrin asked, her voice raising slightly.

Fallyn didn't look at her as he continued, sliding on his shirt and buckling the belt of his pants before he finally replied. "Someone is in search of me."

"What?"

But as Kathrin rose to watch him leave the room, he told her over his shoulder, "Check to see if our young are still sleeping."

Then he was gone, and Kathrin's stomach clenched. He never kept that quiet anymore, not when they had shared so much. Now, he barely was able to look at her. Kathrin knew something was horribly wrong. Grabbing her housecoat, Kathrin listened to his request and checked on the infants, although she was pleased to see they were still sound asleep. So, she went in search of Fallyn. As she approached the entranceway of the cavern, Kathrin could hear the mutterings of conversations between two men.

Kathrin thought no one could find Fallyn's domain.

So, how was it possible for his man to find it so easily? When Kathrin got close enough to peek around the corner, she listened to the discussion.

"With us at our current disadvantage, I was directed, under the orders of Amun, to come for you." The man wasn't nearly as tall and broad as Fallyn. Fallyn brought his hand to his chin with contemplation.

"And what of the other entourages? How have they faired with their task?"

The man, a fair-haired youth whom Kathrin wouldn't figure older than eighteen, nodded, "All others have already returned successful, and, by our sources, Daimos is none the wiser."

Fallyn sighed as he announced what the other was thinking as well, "Obviously, no wiser of his diminishing strength because of his own nefarious deeds."

The youth didn't reply as Fallyn paced in his thoughts, unaware of Kathrin listening keenly in the hallway. It was moments that Kathrin worried about the direction their conversation was arriving to when Fallyn stated, "I will join your battle in a fortnight, giving me time to prepare my family for my departure."

Kathrin paled at the thought. Leave? The youth frowned at his answer, as well.

"You must have misunderstood me. I was not told to inform you; I was told to collect you. I cannot return without you before daybreak."

Fallyn glared toward the lad, no doubt shocked with the order that was so carelessly given for Fallyn's fate. Kathrin panicked but didn't dare to make herself known from her hideout. She gathered this was all about the current events with the destruction of Daimos' guardians. For Fallyn to leave now and fight the minions, Kathrin clenched that it may be the last time she would ever see him. Kathrin had already felt like the battle with Daimos' guardians had gone far too smoothly as it was. So now, she couldn't help but think that this final keeper would have a trap designed specifically for Fallyn's intervention. Please say no, Kathrin moaned to herself, please don't leave me.

Fallyn evidently didn't hear those pleas through her thoughts for, with a sigh of resignation, Fallyn answered, " Very well. Please wait in the fields of Taigana. I will arrive within the hour."

The man nodded and left the cavern, the sound of fizzled electricity dissipating with his departure. Fallyn lowered his head with another sigh and fanned his hand into his hair. How could he possibly make Kathrin understand without sounding so callous and cold? Mi joya preciosa, I enjoyed the bedding, but I must leave for an extended period, and I cannot say when I shall return. Or I know you are almost at wit's end with the infants, but I shall make it even more stressful by leaving for an extended period. Fallyn groaned aloud. He was about to go find Kathrin while he figured out exactly what to say when he looked up and saw her standing at the doorway.

Her eyes were filled with tears, her body quivering as she tried to hold her emotions in check. He knew, then, that she had heard everything. Fallyn lowered his head with a small level of shame before he announced what he was sure she already understood.

"It was my clan. They need my assistance."

Kathrin's arms coiled around her stomach as she shuddered. "Please don't go."

Fallyn groaned and closed the distance between them, drawing her into his arms so tightly it made the tears she was barely maintaining fall by the hundreds. "It is a task I have no choice in, mi joya preciosa. If I refused Amun's request, I would not only shame him, but we would lose all assistance in our battle for your protection."

Burying her face in his chest, she shook her head, "It doesn't feel right, Fallyn. Something bad is gonna happen, I just know it."

He rubbed her back in a comforting manner and rested his jaw on her head. " They spoke of no ill deeds with the task, Kathrin. They simply are outnumbered in the last threshold of Daimo's minion. Every other immortal that has empowered him has already fallen. Had you not felt the lightening of your burdens?"

Kathrin did. Since their return with the infants, she only had one attack within her mind, and even then, it was maintainable as if a simple migraine. Kathrin figured, though, that with all the mental shields that Fallyn had taught her to strengthen herself, they were the reason for her ease. But this comfort didn't lighten her overwhelming fear.

"I don't care! Fallyn, I'm scared I'm going to lose you."

Fallyn clenched her tighter, feeling her pain like a knife to his own heart. Fallyn didn't want to do it any more than she did. And he, too, felt the unease to the situation. "I will not leave you, mi joya preciosa, not when my heart has finally found you across the threads of time. Just relate this to as if my curse is upon me except it will be for a few nights longer. You will see, Kathrin."

"But you don't know for sure. This could go on for months; it has already been two months since they began their hunt and killed the ones they had. What if it's another two months? Or three? Or five? And the whole time I'm waiting for you with my heart lodged in my throat, you've been killed on the battlefield, and I never got to say goodbye."

Fallyn remained silent, for he truly couldn't reply to the 'what ifs' she was creating. Fallyn knew that his reason for life had returned with her and the wonderful sons she gave. If he was on his last breath he would find a way to come home. Not even death would keep them apart. Fallyn knew that because after nine hundred years, Kathrin had returned to him. With a kiss upon her forehead, Fallyn guided her to their room so he could prepare for his trip.

She sat at the foot of the bed as she tried to keep her tears from falling while she watched him pack a few personal belongings for his trip. And, when she became just too saddened to watch his departure, she explained she would retrieve all of his weaponry and left the room. She went to the items and began to cry all over again. Why was she so worried? He had shown her so many times how talented and exceptionally aware of things he was, things that she never even would've seen herself. So, why was she afraid for him when he was more than capable to take care of himself?

Because you love him, you idiot, she argued almost immediately in return. With a sigh meant to calm her, she reached for his belt, armed with his guns and his twin katanas, and began to wrap them up with binding so she could take them to Fallyn when his arms wrapped around her waist.

Kathrin stiffened only briefly before she relaxed into his solid frame, swallowing the lump in her throat.

"I know this feat is most difficult for you, Kathrin. This will be the first we have been apart. It is even more trying because, since our children's birth, I have hardly left your side. But I will return. I vow to you, with the breath I draw, that I will see you again."

Kathrin sighed and agreed, although her mind doubted it would be quite as quickly as he tried to assure her.

"I would battle the entire abyss if it meant I would save my family. I never fathomed I would be gifted with you three in my life. I know if you walked my path, you would do the same." Fallyn merely whispered in her ear.

"Yes," she shuddered, knowing he was right even though she didn't like it. "Just please don't do any reckless moves."

Fallyn chuckled, "My years of irrational acts have long since passed, I assure you."

Kathrin smiled in a sincere manner as she twisted around to face him. He gave a reassuring nod before he then spoke in her mind.

And, with our bond as strong as it has grown, you will be able to speak with me wherever I go. No distance will part us.

Kathrin had forgotten about that, and the sudden realization bought a calming to her. I love you, Fallyn. Don't you forget to come back, or I will personally kick your ass.

"Then, I wait for just a task with my return," he

grinned and then pressed his lips against hers, and I love you, Kathrin Rae Hanelon.

As she watched Fallyn leave, she felt her tears stream down her face once more. But she continued to wave to him with a weary smile. When she truly felt alone, she rubbed her hands against her arms to ease the chill on her skin. Then, she heard a faint wail of Zayden in his crib.

Rushing to his side, she picked him up and embraced him in her arms. As she tried to remain strong, humming a little lullaby tune, she reassured more for herself than for him, "Don't worry, honey. Daddy will be home before we know it."

Chapter Twenty-Seven

Taking care of Zayden and Roland was, indeed, a challenge on its own. Kathrin was almost thankful for it, as it kept the time passing by quickly. But, in some way, being forced to take care of the two of them without Fallyn's assistance also taught Kathrin some of her own tricks to calm them down. Zayden, she discovered, had a keen interest in Kathrin's ability to turn her eyes silver upon command, while Roland had an extremely hearty giggle when it came to tickling his feet. And every night, once she tucked them into their beds, Fallyn would speak to her for a fair portion of the night. Only once or twice were their conversations short, him explaining that they were currently hunting some of the squadrons of demons that protected the keeper. But each time, no matter what, he asked how she and the babies were fairing and what had they learned that day. Fallyn chuckled quite loudly when she told him of Zayden's fascination and Roland's ticklish feet. He admitted, much to Kathrin's surprise, that Roland must have received that unfortunate fault from him. With that little tidbit of info, Kathrin grinned with the idea of tickling Fallyn's feet the second he returned.

Before she knew it, two weeks had come and gone, and Kathrin finally felt like she could actually handle being a parent. One of the days when the infants were down for a nap, the familiar clunking knock that haunted them the night of Fallyn's departure echoed in the rooms once more, and Kathrin knew exactly what it meant. Pausing, she hesitated at the kitchen sink, where she was washing a few dishes. She swallowed hard and went to the cavern entrance. Much to her surprise, the moment Kathrin became alarmed, Fallyn questioned her in her mind.

Something is not right, mi joya preciosa; I felt it from our bond. What is amiss?

Kathrin calmed in the comfort of his voice as she continued to the opening, replying, Nothing yet… There is just a knock at the door…

There was no reply as she approached. When she looked to the passage with a question, she spoke to Fallyn what she wondered, Should I be concerned?

Kathrin could almost see Fallyn shake his head 'no' as he answered, only my most trusted comrades are able to reach my haven. They will hurt you none.

Good. Then, how do I open this contraption to let them in?

After a brief explanation, Kathrin opened the gateway, and another youth, who looked quite like the first, entered.

Tell me what they seek once you are done, was Fallyn's last request before he fell silent, having Kathrin agree before she drew her attention back to the young lad.

"I'm sorry, but Fallyn hasn't returned yet," was Kathrin's first reply. "He was directed by Amun to assist with the final guardian of Daimos."

The lad nodded, "I already know this. But their task is near its end. They are, as we speak, attacking the haven of the demon."

"They are fighting right now?" Kathrin asked, rather puzzled, shocked that Fallyn seemed so calm as he spoke to her in his mind.

The man nodded again as he continued, "I'm here to inform you to make arrangements to strike Daimos by tomorrow's eve."

Kathrin blanched, "But... What if Fallyn isn't done by then?"

The man frowned at the question before he answered, "This matter is for you to tend to, not Fallyn."

Kathrin paused. Was that what they agreed to? That Kathrin would take out Daimos by herself while Fallyn and the others took out the guardians? Kathrin didn't seem to recall that. But, as she thought about it, Daimos would be the toughest creature yet, and if Fallyn was tired of his own mission from the past couple of weeks, it would make sense that she should strike Daimos instead of him.

"If you do not strike Daimos by tomorrow's eve, the

opportunity will pass and may never return again."

Kathrin tingled with the idea of this being done all by herself. "I... I understand."

With her acceptance, he added, "Our investigations have depicted that Daimos is in the Hallways of Thesius. You will find him there."

Kathrin only nodded as she took in everything he said. With a bow of his head, he turned and left, the crackling of his departure announced as she exhaled an anxious breath. Tomorrow. She had to fight Daimos tomorrow without Fallyn's help. Never did Kathrin think that the day would come where she would face Daimos without his support and in only a few short hours. Who would take care of the babies? What if she couldn't do it?

Kathrin shoved the idea out of her mind. She had to do it. If she didn't, everything that Fallyn and his entire clan faced would all be in vain. As Kathrin tried to keep herself collected and consider all the facts, she found herself reasoning that this choice was, indeed, the better one. Fallyn was so much more knowledgeable and wiser of the abyss. If Kathrin died, who better than to have the more well-informed parent at the aid of their offspring? Also, she knew he would provide for them much better than she ever could. And, what good would it be if Fallyn did come and help her and they both died? Her babies would, then, be without either of them and, undoubtedly, become the very things she feared from the start.

What did they wish?

Kathrin jumped, startled by the voice. Oh, Fallyn, you scared me!

When you did not contact me, I was concerned.

You also didn't tell me you were currently in battle. Kathrin huffed as she crossed her arms.

It is of no alarm.

Like hell, it's not! You're talking to me and could very well be stabbed in the back because of it!

I find that quite doubtful. She heard a faint level of humor in his voice.

Well, still, you know what I mean!

Kathrin sighed as she found a seat in the living room, contemplating what she should say. After a moment of it, Fallyn asked again.

You still did not tell me what they sought.

Kathrin tried to sound upbeat as she retorted, Oh, nothing, really. Kinda' giving the rundown of what's going on.

Is that so?

Yeah. He came here looking for you, and when I said you weren't here, he said he would come back. But before he left I asked how was the progress with the task.

That is odd, Kathrin heard, Fallyn's voice sounding quite doubtful of her answer. My tribe usually does not seek me at my abode if they know I am out hunting with them.

Smart ass, she thought to herself. Well, I guess he figured you guys were done and thought it would be easier to find you here than out there.

Hmmmm was Fallyn's only reply.

Kathrin found herself readying her clothing, keeping it hidden in a cubby in her closet in case Fallyn did return before then. After that, she went to the entranceway and made sure her weaponry was all together and prepared before Roland and Zayden both woke up from their sleep. Sighing, she went to their room and started the morning routine all over again.

The next night, Kathrin tried to forget the mission she had to do to enjoy the last few moments she would have with her children. They were beautiful, she realized and enjoyed having the 'tummy time' with them both as they tried to strengthen their necks. Giggling aloud as they squawked and wailed their frustration, Kathrin was about to praise them for the hundredth time when she heard the drop of a sack across the room. Looking up, she saw Fallyn, and her heart missed a beat.

"Hello, alhaja," he grinned, not even noticing the infants on the floor as he took in her wondrous form.

Kathrin lunged to her feet and ran into his open arms

as she held on for dear life. "Oh, Fallyn!"

He held her just as tight as he buried his face in her hair, his tension escaping as he sighed, "Oh, my dear Kathrin."

Overjoyed tears streamed down her face as he claimed her lips.

"The keeper's dead? It's over so soon?"

Fallyn continued to hold her closely. "I took his head with my hands; as for the battle, it still goes on as we speak."

Kathrin's eyes widened as she drew back to look at Fallyn, "You left early? Won't that be bad?"

Fallyn shook his head, "My duty was to get the Keeper, the members of my clan can deal with the rest. If I was not mistaken, there were more pressing matters to tend to here, as it was."

Roland interrupted their conversation with a squawk of frustration, drawing both parents' attention towards the infants on the floor. Fallyn's grin was quite obvious as he gave Kathrin one last squeeze before he crouched down beside Roland and Zayden. With a light coo, Fallyn lifted Zayden into his arms.

"Forgive my dawdling, poco unos. I am sure your eagerness to greet me was quite frazzling," he chuckled.

Kathrin picked up Roland and handed him, as well, into Fallyn's free arm where he snuggled them both.

Within minutes of his affection, Zayden cried out in anger, and Kathrin responded before Fallyn had the chance too. She drew him into her arms and patted his back, and within seconds, her intuitiveness paying off with a small burp. Then, Zayden attempted to look up at his mother. With a faint smile, Kathrin dilated her eyes to silver. She was oblivious to the fact that Fallyn watched her interaction with Zayden. Zayden cooed his surprise as his arm flailed in desperate attempts to reach for the objects of interest.

"Perhaps my departure was much needed," Fallyn spoke up after studying the enjoyment Zayden was having, "It has strengthened your bond with our offspring in a manner I am sure would never have been if I was around all of the time."

Kathrin blushed before she argued, "I will never agree to that... although I am happy, I understand them a little better."

Fallyn smirked cockily and nodded before he returned his attention to Roland. The few hours left before the infant's bedtime, Fallyn, Kathrin, and the sons played as any family would. They taught the infants the wonders of simple things while Fallyn and Kathrin stole glances from each other from across the way.

With a notice of Fallyn's adorable dimple, Kathrin began to become saddened with her thoughts. This may be the last time she would have this. She may never see her sons grow up or enjoy a long life together with Fallyn that he had always promised her. Tonight may be the last for everything. The more she thought about it, Kathrin could feel her emotions a hairline away from pouring down her face. She would lose so much if she failed. But she knew they would have a wonderful father to take care of them.

"What troubles you?" Fallyn frowned, seeing the depression in her eyes while they readied the babies for bed.

Kathrin tried to put on a brighter face, smiling, "Nothing, just thinking."

He eyed her for some time until he returned his focus back to the preparation of the twins. Kathrin knew she needed to prepare for the night. She needed to head to the Hallways of Thesius. With that remembrance, she frowned. Kathrin didn't have a clue where that would be. Wouldn't that be crowded with other vampires if it was a hangout for someone like Daimos? Whatever the case, she needed to get there, find him, and kill him before she could even think about giving in to death.

"Where is the Hallways of Thesius," Kathrin found herself asking before she knew it.

Fallyn paused as his eyes narrowed on her. "What have you asking such a question?"

Blundering, Kathrin responded, "I think that was a place the messenger mentioned while he was here, that's all. I remember you referring to the runes on my hand as the text of Thesius. I just wondered if it was related and where it would be."

Kathrin was so sure by Fallyn's stern face that he didn't believe her story in the least and was about to speak up again when he answered. "The Hallways of Thesius is, indeed, related to the reference I made to your hand. It is the same vampire who obstructed that monument that created the text, Thesius. He designed it to be a meeting place for the 'holy bloods,' as he so keenly described, refusing entrance to any vampire that was of five generations down from his own. It is claimed to be not only be a sanctuary but a political government for the chaotic demons. It is well hidden to avoid mortal intervention."

Kathrin contemplated his words for some time until he added, almost drawly, "Because of the vampire who fathered you, you are welcomed in their gates without dispute."

Kathrin, startled, stared at Fallyn who seemed almost perturbed with the thought while he fitted Zayden in his sleeper before feeding him his evening bottle.

"Why do you say that?"

"Daimos is a grandson to Theisus, which makes you

a third generation to your vampire brethren."

"Third generation?" Kathrin gasped, "But… what generation would that make all of the other modern-day vampires then?"

"One 'generation' of a vampire could signify four lifetimes to mortals. But if a vampire was careless in his turnings… if is quite possible to have a lineage in the late twenties."

"Modern-day vampires are near their twentieth generation, and I'm a third," Kathrin questioned, but when the little infant that was almost asleep in her arms began to squirm, she lowered her voice to a whisper, "That can't be!"

"Nonetheless, it is, and because you are the only child sired by Daimos, that is why he has such a fascination to collect you."

Zayden had already fallen asleep with the bottle to his lips. Fallyn removed the drink and put it aside before he lifted his son high onto his shoulder to pat his back.

Even though Kathrin still was no wiser about where the Hallways of Thesius were, she was more enthralled with the news he gave. "Could the generation be the reason for our miracle of conception?"

Fallyn seemed perplexed as he glanced back at her, reasoning, "It is quite doubtful of its ability to convert your physical DNA, but it could have been the reason that your thoughts remained intact. Much younger vampires tend to be feral and carefree of concerns for what is right and wrong."

Kathrin began to pat Roland's back in the same manner as she gazed towards the floor. He avoided the question about the Hallways and quite smoothly, which she found he was so very good at. Frowning, once Roland expelled the little air in his tummy, she tucked him into bed and departed the nursery to pick up toys in the living room.

"Is this Hallway the only thing this messenger spoke of?"

Kathrin jumped, unaware that Fallyn had followed her to the adjoining room. Turning to meet his gaze, she found him leaning against the door frame, his arms crossed, with a face of intense scrutiny. She knew he was a hairline from doubting her as it was. It would be almost impossible to pass anything by him now- if at all.

"No. He made mention of that domain for Daimos or something like that, then said he'd return to discuss more with you."

Kathrin felt Fallyn's eyes bore into her, peeling away all the shields she erected to obstruct him from learning her intentions of leaving. He approached her. The nearer he got, the more nervous she became. She almost wanted to bet her life that he knew it, too. As soon as he was but a breath away, Fallyn drew the back of his fingertips gently to her cheek and stroked her with a soothing caress.

"I cannot understand why you feel the need to deceive me with your lies, Kathrin."

Kathrin blushed profusely, stuttering, "I'm not lying."

Fallyn smiled weakly as he continued to search her eyes, "I am sure we have had this conversation before of how your face gives you away. I know you are hiding things from me. It has kept you reclusive ever since my return."

"I have?"

Fallyn nodded, brushing a lock of her chestnut hair from her face. Kathrin swallowed. God, she wanted to tell him everything. But she knew if she did, even though she would explain that it was for her to do alone, that he would argue to the nines to fight alongside her.

"Did the messenger insult you? Are you trying to make light of your hurt?"

"No," Kathrin moaned, for once blurting the truth when she added, "I was told it doesn't concern you."

Fallyn's brow arched slightly before he pulled her firmly against his chest. "Everything that involves you or the welfare of my young concerns me."

"Fallyn-," she moaned finally, hating that he was pressing the matter so persistently.

"I will not let you harbor this quest yourself. The Hallway of Thesius, what was mentioned about it? Is that where we must go?"

Kathrin closed her eyes. Fallyn, with her silence, grew stern.

"Do not do this, Kathrin. I ask what news did my brethren bring? If I must, I will request such news myself."

"Daimos," Kathrin whispered barely, her heart hurting because of his anger toward her.

"Daimos," Fallyn repeated before he connected the relation. "That is where we will find Daimos. Were there any methods they suggested to accomplish such a feat?"

Kathrin shook her head, "Just to find him there."

Fallyn sighed and hugged her close. "You had planned to target Daimos by yourself, did you not?"

Kathrin remained quiet, which gave Fallyn all the answers he needed.

"I mean to protect you at any cost. If you took on such a task without my aid, everything we have accomplished together would be in vain."

Kathrin couldn't look him in the eyes because of her shame. But, in her gut, she felt like she had failed Fallyn's brethren as well.

"Upon the 'morrow, we shall leave on our journey to Greenland. I will arrange for Hakeem to care for our sons, then we shall tend with Daimos together."

Tomorrow? It had to be done tonight....

"But, I have plans I am sure you would enjoy to assist

in," Fallyn smiled darkly.

When Kathrin raised a brow in question, he drew her lips to his mouth, and Kathrin understood the plans clearly.

Fallyn brought her to their bedroom and made love to her long and slow, showing Kathrin, once again, how much she meant to him. But, in her heart, she knew she had to leave. So, she enjoyed his affection, relished in the tenderness he so freely gave, and remembered the feel of his flesh against hers. Then, when he fell asleep, she snuck out of the bed.

Fallyn stirred with her movement like he always did, but with the reassurance that she was going to check on the infants, he fell back asleep. With a saddened last glance, Kathrin readied herself and left. She hoped her family would continue to have a wonderful life if she didn't return.

Fallyn stirred to Roland's cry and frowned slightly. He was sure Kathrin said she was going to tend to them. But, if so, why was he crying so heartily? Fallyn pulled on his pants, went to the nursery, and, confusedly, picked up Roland while searching the surrounding in hopes of seeing Kathrin asleep. But she wasn't and, for once in a very long time, Fallyn used his inner sense to locate her in his domain to only return with nothing.

Fallyn cursed aloud as now Zayden's cry filled the cavern. She had left them, and Fallyn knew she didn't plan to return.

Chapter Twenty-Eight

Kathrin scanned the forest as she sped through the damp, moss grown floor to locate the vampire sanctum. She was amazed with how familiar it all seemed, even though she never traveled to this land before. Kathrin figured, after some time, that it must have been her connection with Daimos. But, no matter what the cause, Kathrin knew where she needed to go.

Kathrin regretted how she had left. She would have much preferred Fallyn was there helping her instead of her doing this all on her own, but she had to end it now, tonight. If she stayed with him till tomorrow, there may not be even a shimmer of success. Of course, Kathrin didn't think she was going to succeed, anyhow. Her body was weak. She should have been fed from Fallyn. Now, her stomach writhed in hunger. Nevertheless, now it was too late for second-guessing and debates about what should have happened. She was here, and she wasn't about to backtrack and have Fallyn discover she had left in the first place.

Coming to a cliff, Kathrin was awed by the large mansion that reminded her of the Parliament State Building, nestled in the valley below. So near to civilization but distant from mankind too. Kathrin sighed. How was she ever going to get into a place like that? Something of that size would, undoubtedly, be heavily guarded. So, how would she ever be able to get past one vampire, let alone hundreds, to get to Daimos? And, if she did, somehow, how could she ever fair against Daimos when his awakened power was far greater than her own?

Kathrin couldn't answer any of it. She didn't have a clue in the least. Talk about preparing for the onslaught, she moaned. Taking her first step to lunge down the cliffside, Kathrin was suddenly grabbed in mid-air and ripped back from the ledge.

"What - let go-"

"You utter fool!" Fallyn snarled in her ear, pinning her against his chest, "Do you wish for death to greet you so easily?!"

Kathrin sagged against him, relieved by the sound she never thought she would hear again.

"Why could you not wait for me?!? Why were you lunging into this task so carelessly?!"

Kathrin's wept at the tension that escaped her body. Yes, she knew she had no good way to do this, but how could she have prepared with the little ones and Fallyn's return?

With a bulge of realization, Kathrin panicked, "Where's Zayden and Roland?"

Fallyn growled as he spun her around to face him, squeezing her arms with frustration, "Yes! Where are they?! Do you not concern yourself with their welfare?! Were you so willing to leave us without concern for their needs or my own?!"

Kathrin shook her head towards the guilt that rose in her chest. She looked away.

"Why could you not wait?! I want to hear it," Fallyn shook.

Please.... please stop yelling, she shuddered and, even though it was to herself, Fallyn heard it.

Fallyn groaned and wrapped his arms around her. He could have lost her; he was so close to losing her if he didn't wake when he did. And now, he couldn't control the shudders of fear that vibrated his body as he held her tight. He wasn't mad at her; he was more upset with the scenario no... he was scared.

"The messenger said I had to destroy Daimos tonight," she swallowed in remorse, "Me and me alone. That's why I tried to hide it and why I left without telling you."

"So, even though I ran from a battle that still pended to be with you, you would hurry into another just as quick to be away?"

"No! I wasn't running from you!"

"Then why did my opinion have no say to what you insisted?"

"I," she stuttered. "I didn't want to shame your clan

by going against their orders."

Fallyn hissed, "I would not worry about shame in the eyes of a clan who holds less morals than even I."

After a moment of searching her, he leaned his head back and exhaled an exasperated sigh toward the sky before he restored his gaze, the level Kathrin personally knew he was common for returning as he announced, "With all my years of existence, I have lost things I could not control. Family, friends, companions. These are simply a few. But I will not lose you the same way I have lost everything else. I will not have you run to your doom and leave our young with the greatest loss fathomable."

"Fallyn...."

With another look, Fallyn frowned, "You are pale. You need nourishment."

"Yes, well, that was a little neglect on my part."

"A little!" Fallyn gasped, then growled aloud as he avoided the hundreds of other complaints he could spew. What mattered was she was safe and now he was here to help her.

"Zayden and Roland are with Hakeem, an elemental demon I have known for all my life."

"Thank you," Kathrin snuggled in. "Thank you for coming for me."

"You think I would not?"

"No," she grinned, "I'm just grateful you did."

Fallyn nodded. "Come. You will feed, and once you are done, we shall discuss how to invade such a monument."

The sheer words had Kathrin's stomach grumbling and her fangs enlarged, her eyes dilating without control. Fallyn leaned down to kiss her shoulder, leaving his throat opened perfectly to her view. Kathrin didn't hesitate to wrap her arms around him or pause to bury her teeth into his neck. With Fallyn by her side, Kathrin was sure they could face anything.

Chapter Twenty-Nine

Daimos eyes widened the moment he felt Kathrin's presence and grinned. Why ever would such a mere mouse find herself in such dangerous territory? Daimos swung out of bed with that consideration and exited his chamber. Perhaps it was her innate understanding of the holy day that began in only a few short hours, or perhaps her confusion as to what she didn't understand. Whatever it was, she was nearby.

Just as he headed to the entranceway to meet her, an announcement echoed down the halls.

"Lady Kathrin, child to Daimos of Raultenold."

Daimos smirked darkly. He liked the sound of that. When he reached the staircase and began his descent, Kathrin came into view, having Daimos pause.

She was much more beautiful than he remembered, although she was head-to-toe attired for war. She wore black jeans that hardly hid the curvaceous bottom and toned legs beneath, her shirt a snug, deep blue halter that was covered with a black pleated leather coat. Her belt was laced with ammo clips and handguns, and Daimos didn't doubt that there was probably more hidden elsewhere in her perky form. Her hair was loosely tied at the base of her neck, which, unlike the last time he faced her, was a hint longer, although now her silver tendril that defined her as an awakened vampire hung over the front of her shoulder. Daimos found himself pondering how easily she would come to his chamber if he demanded it.

Kathrin found him on the stairs as he began his descent once more. Two guards that followed near behind becoming visible to Daimos as he entered the mouth of the hallway.

"For you to come here…well, I couldn't be more surprised," Daimos chuckled as he closed the distance.

Kathrin smiled just as sweetly. With a point towards the weaponry on her hips, Daimos arched his brow, "And you felt the need for those?"

Kathrin shrugged lightly, unshaken by the question, as she crossed her arms under her chest. This, unknowingly, brought Daimo's glance to the perfect little mounds. "Well, after such a friendly reunion previously, I didn't know how welcomed I would be."

"All vampires are welcome here, friend or foe. And besides, it is against our brethren's law to destroy each other."

Kathrin arched her own brow then frowned, doubtful, "Yeah, right. So that 'join me or die' crap was just an idle threat?"

Daimos cringed as he looked at the faces of the vampire guards, each of them staring back in curiosity. With a groan, Daimos moved a hand to the small of her back and forcefully escorted her toward the gardens.

"Come," he emphasized so she would see his demand, "I'm sure we have much to discuss."

Though she fought for a minute, she eventually gave in, letting him direct her outdoors. Once the door was closed and it was visible that they were alone, he flung around with a hiss.

"What? Are you trying to have me killed?"

Kathrin stared at him for some time before she burst out laughing. Daimos glowered even further at the sound that beat his pride.

"Shut up."

"The look you're giving me. You're seriously want me to believe you're so concerned over your well-being? You're such a liar," she chortled.

Daimos gritted, the fact that he was on the property of Thesius being the only reason why he wasn't ringing her neck. "I'm not lying, you little bitch. If you knew our laws, you'd understand that."

Kathrin's expression narrowed as her arms crossed again, drawing his attention once more to her chest, to Daimo's frustration. Damn her for being so hot! "Well, I don't recall having the shithead that sired me be so kind as to inform me of them. So, I guess we're even."

Daimos growled as he looked away. His existence had become so dark that he did ignore many traditions and requirements that were designed for such a reason. But her creation was so unexpected. Because of his inability to sire prior, he didn't even consider the possibility of turning her that evening in her apartment. The fact that Fallyn didn't kill her also was unexpected. With the mention of Fallyn, he recalled everything else.

She carried Fallyn's child. How far along would she be now? Shouldn't she be at least five months pregnant? With her small frame, she should undoubtedly be showing, wouldn't she? Daimos turned his keener sense towards her but, unfortunately, only heard her one heartbeat.

"Tell me," he asked finally, "How is the little devil you carry doing?"

Kathrin's eyes enlarged, confused before she quickly collected her composure. "I'm surprised you didn't already know because of how often you've, so kindly, been invading my thoughts."

Daimos clenched his teeth: "Enlighten me."

Kathrin narrowed her gaze again before she turned her head to look across the garden to the rising moonlight. "I miscarried."

Daimos paused. That, he didn't plan on being a possibility. Daimos figured beings that every other sense and ability was tuned to its perfection and that the capability to conceive would be the same. As he explained the reasoning of it to himself, he also spoke it aloud.

"It must have been because of the disagreement of demon DNA."

Kathrin didn't answer as she kept looking towards the moon. Daimos, taking in her physique, stepped closer.

"Well, if I was a kind and caring person, I'm sure, right about now, I would give my condolences. But I'm quite pleased with the news that my child does not carry the seed of our enemy."

Kathrin turned her head to glare at him. "That enemy you so like to hate is the only person who gave a damn about me for almost a year. Now that I'm special is the only reason you care now."

"If I am not mistaken, you fought me when I came to collect you."

Kathrin, seeing his slow approach, stepped back, "You pinned me down and threatened to kill me!"

Daimos hissed for her to shut up once again before he growled, "I'd never have done it. I was trying to scare you."

"Bull shit," she spat back, "I've seen the horror you've done, disemboweling men. I can only imagine what you are capable of when you are in a fit of rage. I know you didn't care either way if I died or not!"

Daimos clenched. If he didn't want to fuck her as bad

as he did, he'd probably have killed her now, even considering the land he was on. "Well, you've had your own fair share. After all, you are still alive and not in chaos for blood. I'm sure you've slipped once or twice. So, how many have you killed? Ten? Twenty? Do you even know?"

Kathrin scoffed, "Well, unlike you, who can't control your vices, I've never preyed on mortals."

Daimos stopped his slow pursuit, his eyes narrowing, "You've had to have. How do you feed if you don't?"

The answer slapped him across the face as he asked, wide-eyed. "You've fed from Fallyn?! That heathen?!!?"

Kathrin backed away from him, feeling the heat of his anger. "So, what if I did?"

Daimos shot at her like lightning and grabbed her by her throat. "You've forfeited your life for such an act! It is a taint that Thesius, himself, deemed unclean and a punishment of death!"

Kathrin gritted to the suppression of her throat as she tried to remain cool and collective, "Gee, something else I wasn't informed of because of my father."

She was right. If the council discovered her acts and found out that it was because he didn't inform her of their laws, they would kill him, too. What a fine mess she put him in!

"Why are you here," Daimos gritted finally, done

with the kindness he was trying to give.

" Some important business," she croaked as she continued to sneer at him.

Man, she had a fire, he thought, and it was something he would be willing to test every second of the day. He was about to lean in and steal a kiss, too, when he heard a cocking of a gun and froze.

" That would be most unwise of you, Daimos," Fallyn growled a few yards away from them, his Glock keenly on Daimos.

Daimos turned towards Fallyn without a movement before he returned to Kathrin with knowing fury.

"You're here to kill me?"

Kathrin grinned devilishly, "Well, I've broken so many rules anyhow; why not another?"

Daimos snarled and tossed her away. With a bellow in Lucian's tongue, Daimos called a slew of vampires to his side. Before they arrived, Fallyn tried to take aim at Daimos, but he whisked out of sight before it landed, calling to them prior to his disappearance, "Challenge me if you dare."

The wave of vampires intercepted both Fallyn and Kathrin before they could give chase. So, with the unsheathing of Fallyn's blades and the building of Kathrin's awakened powers, they readied for combat. Like a pulse of lightning before the crackling of thunder, they connected in battle, Kathrin and Fallyn back-to-back to cover the other's weakest point as they spun and phased, swiped, and clashed in their quest for a championship. Kathrin discovered, quite quickly, that her brethren were not intending to kill her; they simply were subduing her while they tried to slay Fallyn. This was her advantage, for they assumed she would adhere to a rule she had only heard minutes before.

As positive as their progression was, for every five that would fall, it seemed like five more would replace them. They battled for what seemed like an eternity before Fallyn roared toward Kathrin, "Go! Give chase to Daimos!"

Impaling a vampire with her elongated claws, she kicked him aside before dueling with another. "Not without you!"

With a heave of his Katana, Fallyn barked, "Now is no time for debates! Go!"

With a disposal of another, Kathrin hesitated for only a second before she obeyed and fled into the night, following the scent of her father that she could never forget. None of her brethren followed, which made her a little uneased over Fallyn's safety with the odds of them all to himself. It was when she was a few hundred yards away that Kathrin heard an explosion from where she came and screeched to a halt.

"Fallyn!!" she cried out, panicked at the idea.

Run, alhaja! I am behind you!

The sound of this voice was like balm to a burn, and she sighed in relief.

Thank God!

We must not rejoice yet, alhaja. We must find Daimos before dawn!

Kathrin swallowed and took off like lightning again into the woods. Slowly, Daimo's stench filled the air. It was then that Kathrin noticed Fallyn racing beside her only a short distance away. Somehow, this show of ability drew a smirk to her lips.

And here, you're never the first to reach the babies at night.

Kathrin heard a tension-easing chuckle in her mind as she focused ahead of herself once more. With another inhale of air, Kathrin knew Daimos was close.

He's around here somewhere, Fallyn. Stay sharp.

Fallyn nodded as his senses spread outwards, his eyes blazing yellow to his heightened sight.

Coming to a meadow, the forest dissipates like a curtain pulled open. Both of them slowed to a halt. Scouting the blackened land with their eyes of gold and silver.

"No more games, asshole! Come on out!!"

It wasn't long before Daimos responded, drawing

both Fallyn's and Kathrin's attention to him yards away.

"I would have never imagined that frail, panicked little mouse from that night over a year ago would become such a cocky little vampire."

Fallyn didn't move, seeming unbothered with the second-generation vampire before him, while Kathrin snorted.

"People change, Daimos. It's a fact of life."

Daimos nodded as he took in her shape once again in some twisted form of desire. "That they do, yet you still seem to think you will not become like me. You seem to think Fallyn, beside you, will not, one day, hunt you down and stake you for what you are."

Kathrin laughed sarcastically, "It'll take a lot more than that to have me afraid, Daimos."

Daimos grinned. "Yes, I suppose it would."

He stared at her for some time as each of them waited for the others to move until Daimos' smile widened.

"Do you know why Fallyn saved you that night so long ago?"

Kathrin frowned as she noticed, out of the corner of her eye, Fallyn stiffened. She had always wondered, and when she would try to ask Fallyn, he would simply walk away.

Seeing her pause and Fallyn's discomfort, he added,

"After all, you know that you are the first victim he's ever let survive past the bite."

Kathrin's eyes bulged. She glanced at Fallyn for answers, "What?"

Fallyn didn't return the gaze as his lips pressed into a thin line, explaining after a moment, "Generations such as you and him can pass your curse to others by a simple feeding. That is why The Infernals have laws against letting the victim live past that moment."

"Laws he broke because of you," Daimos added. "But yet, you were the only one he ever had for. Why would that be?"

Kathrin focused back onto Fallyn, confused, "Fallyn?"

Fallyn's brow furrowed, troubled with the position he was put into. After a long moment of debate, he finally announced, "You reminded me of a woman from my past."

Daimos cut in before Kathrin had a chance, "So, Gurath wasn't being a fool when he returned to me."

Kathrin remained fixed on Fallyn as she asked in a low whisper, "What woman?"

Somehow, even though she didn't know the answer, a piece of her mind was screaming that this was all too familiar. It was like this conversation had happened before. Fallyn looked at her for only a second, with pleading eyes for forgiveness, before they returned towards Daimos.

Daimos laughed at Fallyn's anxiety, piping in, "What? Too afraid to tell her the truth? Then let me do it for you."

Fallyn tensed, "You shall do no such thing!"

Daimos grinned as he looked over to Kathrin, "Do you know that your family line is connected to Fallyn's even before now?"

She heard Fallyn hiss, but she was far too curious to stop what Daimos was going to tell her. She needed to understand this for so long and now that it was being given to her, she just couldn't refuse the opportunity. Kathrin shook her head.

"I didn't think so. After Gurath returned injured from your meeting in the mountainside, I began a little investigation myself and discovered that your family was the very same one that resulted in Fallyn's curse."

Why did Kathrin suddenly feel guilty? Like even though she, herself, wasn't there, she was the very reason he was cursed.

Do not listen to him, Kathrin.

She wished she could, but it was like her mind was about to explode if she didn't.

"Almost a thousand years ago, there was a lineage that was completely obliterated. I didn't know at the time, but the youngest daughter had a child and gave it to cousins to save face, which is why you even exist. Fallyn was there because he was in love with the youngest daughter, and so nobly came to her rescue, only to become involved in the crossfire. Tell her, Fallyn. What was the woman's name?"

Fallyn swallowed, for he knew what would happen if he did. He may lose Kathrin forever. He watched her with all the love in the world. He didn't love her because of who she once was. He loved her for who she was now. Kathrin, the mother of his children, his soul mate. Her eyes were pleading for the answer, almost on the verge of tears. Fallyn sighed, dismayed.

With a lower of his head, he answered, "Tonia."

Kathrin's eyes widened to the unleash of her memories, such like they had before, and her knees gave way onto the earth. Daimos' chuckle of victory broke Fallyn's intention to go to Kathrin's side, drawing Fallyn's hateful glare back toward him.

"She really was Tonia all along, wasn't she," he asked, although he knew the answer already.

Fallyn drew his blades, wanting nothing more than to seek vengeance on the man who could have, very well, destroyed his future with his mate. Daimos grinned evilly at the act of defiance and nodded.

"That's right, Fallyn. It's now just you and me."

Fallyn wasn't a man to act impulsively or even take

the first strike in any battle. His strength was the dependence on finding the other's weakness. But, at that moment, he went against everything he learned. He lunged out first, irrationally swiping as the aggressor instead of being the defender. He struck towards Daimos with all the abhorrence he could imagine. Daimos simply toyed with it like a man playing with a mere child.

"Keep tiring yourself, Fallyn. I can wait till you're weak to strike," he chuckled, shifting out of each strike only seconds before contact.

Fallyn heard the threat and knew that was, very well, what would happen if he kept it up. But his need for retribution overwrote any clear thought. He'd never been so irrational, so full of emotion since the night he was turned. It was like he was reliving the sensation of loss, confusion, and anger all over again, but only now he had the means to inflict it. Even though he was powerful and fast, the cackle from Daimos as he toyed with Fallyn still ate apart his insides.

I'm sorry, Fallyn.... So sorry....

The calming voice was like a slap to reality, his narrowed rage clearing only enough to realize it was Kathrin who spoke.

I've never wanted.... I tried to come....

Fallyn slowed, girdling his rage that was obliviously swelling in his chest to reply.

I understand more than you know, Kathrin.

Fallyn was only able to look at her shuddering body for an instant before he dodged out of the first strike from Daimos. Fallyn growled again as his chest tightened. He wanted Daimos dead so very badly. The hairs on Fallyn's neck prickled with hatred; his own skin felt like it was restricting his body.

I've hurt you so much…. I'm sorry….

Fallyn shook his head. He had to focus, had to restrain his fury.

Never have you done such things, alhaja. Our fates were destined for this before we knew it.

Kathrin cringed at the praise. I'm not who you loved. I'm Tonia. I don't deserve such endearments.

You received that endearment after I was informed of our past. Tonia died eons ago. What you are is simply a woman who has been gifted with the knowledge of your previous life. It is not you, alhaja, and I love you for who you are now, not what you once were.

Daimo's voice cut into Fallyn's and Kathrin's private conversation with a sneer. "At no point have you even come to wonder how I knew all of this, Fallyn?"

Returning his attention onto his opponent, Fallyn readied his sword, "Your mindless dog returned to your heels with such knowledge."

"Well, there was that, but I think you're not quite

getting it."

Fallyn could feel the tether on his anger slipping to the insult of his intelligence and Fallyn knew that was what Daimos hoped for.

"You will see the hells no matter what reason, Daimos."

Daimos chuckled, "Well, think of your comment a little, will you? ... That is if you're able to. If Gurath was such a mindless dog, then who gave him the orders to destroy her lineage?"

Fallyn clenched as soon as the answer came. "You...."

Daimos grinned with devilish delight as he readied again. "Smart man, after all."

The girdle loosened from Fallyn's wrath, but it no longer mattered. He was so enraged at his loss, at the information, at the opponent that destroyed so many lives that any reason Fallyn had to hold back his fury was washed away. Fallyn tossed aside his katanas in a mindless act as his skin tightened to the point of bursting.

Fallyn's clothes stretched and tore as he suddenly found himself growing to a stature beyond probability. Coarse hairs bristled down his palms, then his torso to his feet. Daimos stared in awe at the transformation of Fallyn to his curse. Hands to claws, mouth to snout, skin to fur, Fallyn became a massive monster of destruction. Half man, half wolf.

His eyes were golden saucers, his height looming over Daimos now petite form. Feral and primitive, Fallyn's new guise was broad and defined with black regal fur. Never had he had such strength as he did now. His voice was almost incoherent with its unearthly roar as he bore down toward Daimos. Daimos backed away.

Though there was a noise of hesitation in his voice, Daimos snarled in return, "Do you think, if she ever comes out of this, that she will love you now that she sees you for what you really are?!"

He didn't believe any of it mattered now, but hearing that possibility almost diffused his anger completely. He finally accepted himself to be the werewolf he was, using it as a means to inflict justice, but at what cost? Would she really run from him now that she knew the monster that was supposed to be her demonic enemy for centuries, let alone the man who was meant to kill her that night?

He was afraid to glimpse over at Kathrin for fear of the horrid look that would be returned. If she hated him now... he didn't know what he would do. But, before his eyes even found her, Kathrin's voice spoke up for both men to hear.

"You know... I was wondering when you would do that," she smiled, astonishing them both.

"Blasphemous," Daimos spat, confused, "You knew

what he was but yet remained with him?! How could you fuck such a monster?!"

Kathrin rose from the ground, finally at terms with everything now that she understood that it was Daimos that started this all to begin with. She walked over to the eight-foot-tall werewolf who watched her every move, looking like a mere child in his presence and grabbed his massive paw between her two hands.

"He loved me before he knew I would be a vampire; I fell in love with him before I knew he was a werewolf. Demonic blood doesn't stop who you love."

Fallyn looked down at Kathrin with admiration, his head bowing with relief to his mate as the tip of his fingers rubbed the side of her face.

Alhaja....

Never doubt we are in this together, no matter what. Got it?

A smile contorted his monstrous face as he nodded, and Kathrin turned her attention to Daimos. Her own revenge for finishing this millennial-long torment billowing within her as she stood by her mate. She finally understood how very awful the man before her was and that it was time for him to come to an end.

"No more games, Daimos. You will fall tonight," she promised, calling to her own powers that turned her eyes to silver beams.

"How do you think you'll accomplish that? A half-wit werewolf and an adolescent vampire? Surely, you must know that I'm more powerful than the two of you combined."

Kathrin grinned knowingly, "You're right. That's why I'll be the brain; he'll be the brawn."

Daimos' brow furrowed for only a second before Fallyn lunged towards Daimos. Daimos lost track of Kathrin in a second, barely able to dodge out of the hulky attacks of a beast weighted like an anvil. When Daimos would have a second to collect his thoughts and attempt to find Kathrin, Fallyn was upon him again. Frantically, Daimos lunged out of the werewolf's path yet again when a violent scream shrilled through his head.

Clenching his skull, Daimos doubled over to the temple pounding noise. He couldn't register functions, he couldn't think past the white-hot pain, and when he looked up, he barely comprehended enough to move out of the beast's path.

"What's wrong, father," Kathrin sneered sarcastically, her voice echoing within the air all around yet nowhere to be found. "Something on your mind?"

Daimos gritted out to the taunt while Fallyn paused to watch him collapse to his knees. His visions were hazy and unfocused, but within seconds, he saw Kathrin's face meld into his skull like hot lava.

"Get... out of... my head!"

Kathrin's chuckle was so audibly evil it made even Fallyn's hair prickle anxiously. "Not this time. It's time you see everything you've done."

Kathrin's form shifted only slightly within his thoughts. No, it was Tonia, Daimos realized after an instant in his trembling paralysis. Then, the world around him morphed into the eve of their slaughter in the eyes of Tonia as she witnessed her family die one by one. Each of them disemboweled before her as she ran, each of their screams gurgling to silence as she tried to flee the insanity. Then, as her only thought to find her love came into volition, to find herself stilled by death in his very arms. But though her heart froze in her body, he saw the happenings thereafter. The sorrow by Fallyn, the confusion then, as the claw of Gurath impaled his mortal form, the understanding that Daimos was the reason the vampires had the enemy, to begin with.

And, like the vision was repeating itself, Daimos heard the squishing crunch of his torso as Fallyn's claw entered his chest, an agony that paralleled his own from almost a millennia before. It was then Kathrin lightened her influence on his mind, easing her torturous invasion to a dull sooth as she showed Daimos the truth about her pregnancy. He saw her birth; he saw her twin sons and how they were nurtured by both Fallyn and Kathrin and how they were currently under the protection of Hakeem.

"Does the fate I received feel desirable, Daimos? Do you see the errors of your selfish hunger," Fallyn snarled, his voice thunderous.

Daimos gagged as everything became clear, Kathrin finally appearing before him as he dangled above just like Fallyn had before. The steps of Kathrin's approach were like a drumbeat of the earth. Daimo's eyes grew heavy to his death as it approached.

"Your victory... is only brief, Kathrin, for there is more... in play here than you can even... imagine. Who you think are friends... are truly foes in disguise. And what your children will become... it will quake the earth in corruption."

His final words of promise did not slow her stride as Fallyn lowered Daimos for Kathrin to stare him squarely in the face. She smiled devilishly, her fangs protruding out the corners of her lips as she announced. "I may be oblivious to many things, Daimos, but I do know enough to know that if I feed from you now... I shall gain your strengths and your generation."

Daimos would have fought if he was able to resist another deed that would hinder his brethren even more, because of his short sight. And, as Kathrin nestled her fangs into his neck, his own force oozing into the child he sired, he grinned. Kathrin was young and naive, but

Daimos was there at one point, too. Kathrin will see his past soon enough and then, perhaps, she would become clear to the life their kind were destined for. But his time had come, and he was glad he had sired such a daughter before his demise.

As the last breath escaped Daimos' lips, Kathrin lifted and wiped her mouth, her veins humming with new-found energy. Kathrin thought she was strong before but now she felt ethereal. Fallyn flung him aside like the garbage he was, and he glanced down at her with caution.

Her appearance transformed even further than it had when she first awoke. Her silver tendril was now practically to her waist while the rest had grown to her mid-back. Her eyes, instead of being turquoise with silver pearls, were now a dull powder blue with turquoise speckles. Her complexion had bronzed, and her body filled out even more than it had before. Her beauty was remarkable. With an inhale of pure completion, Kathrin looked towards the horizon where the sun was planning to crest. She sighed before she turned to Fallyn.

Even now, in his monstrous form, she wasn't scared of him. He reached a paw out to her, and she, without any hesitation, leaned into it, nuzzling the massive hand with her cheek. Slowly, he reverted to his human form.

"I do not comprehend how you can be so at ease with what I became," Fallyn frowned as his face returned to its handsome physique.

Kathrin shook her head, "I didn't see you sign up for this, did you?"

Fallyn pressed his lips together before he argued, "But, it is a beast you witnessed create such horrors... With your memories returned, you have seen the monster I have become."

"And a demon that never injured anyone in such violent manners as they did. You are different, Fallyn."

"I am more similar than you believe."

"And you are ashamed of it. You've told me to embrace what I became; I think it's about time you did, too. After all, you've been a werewolf for nearly a thousand years, and you've remained as human as you could have. Seeing you maintain your humanity has given me courage that I'll be able to keep my own."

So understanding, Fallyn thought. So forgiving. He drew her into his arms in relief.

"I will never stop loving you, mi joya preciosa. You have given me much and asked for so little. And now, we have rid our family of the torment Daimos could have inflicted," he cooed in her ear.

Kathrin hesitated. "What about what Daimos said? What about our children?"

Fallyn held her close. Fallyn couldn't predict what would come. All he could do was enjoy the moments he had now. "Whatever fate hands us, as long you remain by my side, we will withstand it."

Kathrin sighed and buried her head in his chest. "I suppose so."

As Fallyn lifted Kathrin into his arms, Kathrin clenched his shoulders tightly. They did it... They took out Daimos. Their children were safe.

"Come, let us return home. I will collect the twins once you are nestled safely in my haven."

Kathrin nodded as they took off into the woods. Together, they fought their greatest evil, and together, they found each other across the fabrics of time.

"Fallyn. I love you. And, if you didn't have a clue before, you're stuck with me for good...."

And as they escaped into the night, Fallyn's laughter could be heard echoing into the sky.

www.ingramcontent.com/pod-product-compliance
Lightning Source LLC
Chambersburg PA
CBHW060426310726
48977CB00001B/65